THE BOMB WAS ABOUT TO EXPLODE...

A voice stopped him, "Comrade Major."

He turned to see a lieutenant and a sergeant holding machine guns in his direction. "We would like to see your papers again." The lieutenant came toward him, holding out his hand.

"Of course," he answered, his hand moving to his pocket. He was smiling, and he knew he couldn't erase it. His fingers flipped his holster open, and his pistol swung up with a crashing sound. The sergeant, eyes wide open, grunted and twirled as the bullet smashed into him. The lieutenant's mouth was open to shout, but before he had enough air in his lungs the second bullet ripped into his throat and the black package hidden in the satellite station control center blew walls and bodies into the heavens with the first powerful explosion...

Other Avon Books by
Charles C. Vance

THE DRAGON ROBE

A GRAVE FOR A
RUSSIAN

CHARLES C. VANCE

 AVON
PUBLISHERS OF BARD, CAMELOT, DISCUS AND FLARE BOOKS

A GRAVE FOR A RUSSIAN is an original publication of Avon Books. This work has never before appeared in book form. This work is a novel. Any similarity to actual persons or events is purely coincidental.

AVON BOOKS
A division of
The Hearst Corporation
1790 Broadway
New York, New York 10019

First Avon Printing, November 1985

Printed in the U. S. A.

WFH   10   9   8   7   6   5   4   3   2   1

To Mary Ellen, whose endearing patience as my wife and whose remarkable expertise at producing final manuscripts helped immensely in making this novel possible.

And to the courageous members of the Ukrayins'ka Povtancha Armiya, the Ukrainian underground, who earned our deep respect and admiration.

CHAPTER ONE

The Turkish Coast

Mikhail Karlov, eyes adjusted to the dark expanse of the Black Sea, saw the conning tower of the submarine silhouetted against the faint moon glow that spread across the wind-whipped water.

He wore a Turkish seaman's parka, its hood pulled over his head against the night chill, protection against the spray that shot up from the waves as the motor launch neared the submarine. In minutes the launch was alongside the submersible, its crewmen reaching for the line thrown to them. He timed his move, reaching for the boarding ladder lowered from the sea deck, hearing the Turkish voices above him.

At the top, hands reached to pull him up and guide him into the tower. He went easily down the steel steps, blinking in the shaded light. At the bottom, he faced a small man in a uniform without insignia.

"Mikhail, welcome aboard!" Captain Pell said, extending a hand. "So now it starts?"

Overhead, they heard the sounds of the Turk crewmen coming down and the hatch closing.

Mikhail unzippered the parka and flipped the hood back. He looked past the officer to the other Americans and to the Turk crewmen stationed at their controls. They all eyed him with intense curiosity. The four Americans wore no insignia. He recognized none of them.

Pell led him down the narrow passageway to the captain's room. Inside, with the door closed, he said, "Obviously the flight went well, Mikhail, and the ground transport. You're here on time." The unwavering eyes studied him carefully. "You still want to go in?"

"Yes."

Pell nodded. "I asked out of courtesy. I knew nothing would keep you from going in." He smiled. "Now, we'll have a drink and some food and go over the entire plan."

Mikhail could not return the smile. "I'm going in and get my father out, and then I'm going to kill the son of a bitch who put him there."

Pell's face sobered. "I know you will."

They felt the pull of the sub's engines.

It was headed for the Ukrainian coast of the USSR.

The Prison

The hawk soared over the old Dombosky Prison, searching for one of the roving rats that burrowed under the sagging buildings covered with rust-stained sheet-metal roofs. It saw none in the early-morning August sun and flew toward the fields of the Ukrainian collectives in the distance.

A door opened in one of the decrepit buildings, and a guard stepped out carrying a rifle. A line of prisoners came through the door. They formed a circle in the exercise yard near the main gate. The guard swung his rifle lazily at the silver-haired man. "Move along!" The man stumbled, righted himself painfully, and hurried to join the moving circle of men, all spaced well apart, heads tilted down, wearing shapeless gray uniforms.

A young guard in the watchtower near the gate shouted, "Ho! The one with the fruit comes!" At the signal several guards ran down from the nearby towers to join the barracks guards and the machinery-center guards at the chain-link gate.

The peddler trudged heavily in the rising morning heat, moving slowly along the dusty, rutted road leading to the old Bolshevik prison, pulling the dirty, weathered handcart behind him, creaking noisily. Sweat trickled from his broad, expressionless Ukrainian face, and more stained his floppy peasant clothes.

He slowed as he neared the gate. Two long lines of metal-and-wire fences, topped with rolling layers of barbed wire, five meters high and five meters apart, ran around the entire prison, encircling an area the size of two city blocks. He stopped at the gate, as he had done every morning for a week, and bowed to the waiting guards, his mouth opening in a toothless grin. From the edges of his eyes he saw the circle of shuffling prisoners, as shabby and hot as he. Beyond the exercise area were the confinement barracks and the work buildings. He heard the high whine of metal-working machines from the nearest building where other prisoners labored.

"Buy from me fresh fruits?" he said. He watched the guards take what fruit they wanted, accepting the kopecks they dropped into his damp, outstretched hand. Then he was on his way, pulling the cart, careful to avoid looking at the crest of the small wooded hill overlooking the prison to his right. There was no alarm behind him, and he sighed in relief. His simple, well-timed diversion had worked.

The one concealed in the brush atop the hill with the long-range telephoto lens had the time to take pictures of one man who moved in silent loneliness in the circle of prisoners.

The man with the silvery hair matted wetly down across his once handsome face.

Pictures that would be important to the one who came.

The one who was going to kill Colonel Gregorski.

The Odessa Military Supply Center

Stripped to his waist, his torso glistening in the oppressive heat of the immense supply warehouse, the senior sergeant made his fifth full count of the materials delivered by rail hours earlier. He scratched his close-cropped hair in irritation. Then he began cursing, drawing the mild attention of the other shirtless Russian soldiers working the detail. He went to the bay door that led to the railroad spur from which the supplies had been unloaded. He prowled through the empty boxcars, searching for the carton.

The mugginess of the air so near the Black Sea was insufferable. He looked around the center, at its two-story-high cement buildings, housing a thousand or more military personnel, thirty warehouses exactly like the one in which he worked, and barracks for the troops. He cursed again in muttered tones. The sun glinted from the metal roofs of the buildings where tanks, weapon carriers, self-propelled field artillery pieces, armored fighting vehicles, other weapons, and ammunition were stored. There was an almost lazy movement of men and vehicles around the place.

He was disturbed. "What have I done to get marks like these on my record?" he said aloud, harshly. "Those damned Ukrainians have got it in for me!" Clipboard in hand, he stomped in his army-issue boots toward the small office at one end of the sprawling high-roofed concrete building crammed with crates and dusty military vehicles. He was met at the door by the junior lieutenant in charge.

"Comrade Lieutenant," he said, scowling, "another damned short!"

The officer was unimpressed. "Now what's missing?"

"A carton of officers' uniforms, summer issue."

The officer shook his head in resignation. "Check again. It's got to be here somewhere."

"Five times. It's not here."

They looked at each other silently, thinking of the long list of shipment foul-ups and how they would have to explain to the commanding officer of the Odessa Military District supply depot that now a carton of uniforms was missing. "What do you think?" the officer said.

"Like the others. The explosives, the petrol, the flares, all of those damned shorts! The UPA got them off the train somehow."

The senior sergeant wiped the drop of sweat from the end of his nose. "Those dirty fuckers!"

The Odessa Military Testing Compound

The six T-72 main battle tanks, fresh from final fittings at the Nizhniy Tagil tank plant, sat handsomely on the railroad flatbeds waiting to be unloaded at the massive military testing compound north of Odessa. Only dried raindrops marred their stark attractiveness.

Beyond the railway entry area the compound spread into the distance. It featured a large oval testing track on which military vehicles and weapons were tested. Its stuccoed buildings housed a vast array of testing equipment, computerized and linked to other Soviet testing sites, security personnel, and quarters for soldiers and officers.

The military inspectors stood in the hot midday sun, admiring the sleek monsters on the flatbeds. They watched as the soldier-drivers climbed up to open the hatches, eager to start the turbocharged diesel engines.

The first driver opened the hatch, started in, then whipped his head back. "This one smells!" He coughed loudly. "Something wrong!"

The nearest inspector leapt aboard and bent to look down into the interior. He drew back and waved his arm frantically. "Acid!" he shouted. "Move back!"

He and the driver jumped to the flatbed, the driver leaning for support against the tank's slightly winged hip, gagging.

The inspector looked blankly at the others. "They poured sulfuric acid down the gun!" He pointed at the long barrel. "It's eaten into the automatic loader!" He turned to see the driver fall to the ground, wriggling in pain.

The inspectors stared fascinated at the soldier before one of them had sense enough to reach for his radio and sound the alert. Quickly the other T-72s were unhatched. Vapors poured from the open turrets.

In moments the military compound was alive with movement.

The Village

Bissa stood outside the small shop, his bulbous nose pressed against the dirty glass, peering inside, his pale brown eyes fastened on the unfeathered poultry hanging by their pinkish legs from iron hooks.

He waited until the line of grandmotherly babushkas finished their purchases and left the shop strangely empty of customers for a moment. He moved his short, dumpy figure through the open doorway, standing patiently on thick stubby legs until the shopkeeper came to confront him from behind the counter.

"Wood-carver!" the Ukrainian said with distaste. "What do you want?"

Bissa pointed a fat finger at a plump goose hanging a few feet from the shopkeeper's head.

"Rubles you got, fat one?"

Bissa nodded exuberantly. "Three horses and two cows I am selling," he said in his hesitant, uncertain way.

"On the counter put them."

Bissa fished inside his spacious, worn pants and poured the coins on the tired wooden counter. The shopkeeper flicked a finger through them, counting. "Enough you have, wood-carver. Well you do fleecing the tourists with your wood statues." He reached up and unhooked the goose, plopping it on the counter. "Take it."

Delight spread across Bissa's face, and he hopped in eagerness.

"For that young truck driver it is?" the shopkeeper said harshly, wrapping the goose in a sheet of newspaper.

Bissa nodded happily, his thick black curly hair shaking with the movement.

"That woman wild is," the shopkeeper said. "In the ass a pain she is."

Bissa's face turned angry. He reached for the goose with one hand, holding it to one side of his wide belly. He straightened from his habitual slouch in a warning gesture. Then his free hand smashed down flat on the counter, jarring everything on it.

Startled, the shopkeeper shrugged in blinking apology. "You and that skinny electrician take good care of her, you do." He forced a weak smile, not unaware that the village idiot who faced him was by far the strongest man for many kilometers. "Eat well, wood-carver!"

On the sidewalk again, Bissa trotted with the goose held in his massive arms, trying to keep the sheet of newspaper from coming loose. A joyous expression on his potatolike face, he made his way along the tree-lined main street of the village toward the municipal buildings and past them to the small cabin far from the village's outskirts.

Raysta straightened from his work.

He wiped his long thin hands with an oily rag and looked with satisfaction at the motor he had repaired. He plugged it into the test console, nudged the switch, and listened to the sound. He turned it off, leaning tiredly on the work-bench.

The roar of military trucks on the dirt street outside the small Quonset-type building that served as the village electrical maintenance shop drew him to the door. He watched ten trucks—some loaded with troops, some carrying a few—go down the street, spewing dust into the hot late-afternoon air.

A man stood in the doorway of the House of the Soviet, the village center. Their eyes met across the distance, and Raysta saw the familiar secret hand signal. He knew. Trouble again at the Odessa testing compound, a few kilometers to the southwest. And he knew what the trouble was.

He allowed no expression on his face, gave no return signal, for none was needed. He leaned against the doorway, his triangular face blank. Sweat gleamed from his narrow forehead and his grayish facial skin. He shrugged his narrow shoulders unconsciously and ran the rag across his shiny black hair, which hung in clumpy strands in the back and bristled in thinness at the front.

He moved from the door and dug the vodka bottle from underneath a pile of empty corrugated cartons that had held electrical supplies. The other man had disappeared and Raysta knew that he, too, was drinking a toast. He raised the bottle and let the milky vodka trickle down his throat.

A short, broad form materialized in the doorway, and he turned. Bissa stood, silhouetted against the bright sunlight, hugging the goose. Its long head and neck hung from the paper wrapping.

Raysta hid the half-filled bottle and went to Bissa. "You fat sack of cow turds," he said. "Where'd you steal the goose?"

Bissa did a happy little dance through the door. "Pay for it, I did! Wood-carvings I sold!"

Raysta looked at the goose. "You dumb little bastard! What a nice present! She'll be very happy."

"Yes, happy!" Bissa swung the goose in his cradled arms like a baby.

Raysta put his long skinny arms around the wide muscular shoulders in a fatherly hug. "Come on, it's time to go home. My crew is out working on that damned collective power station." They went outside, and Raysta locked the door. He gave Bissa another hug. "Almost thirty-five you are, you pile of sheep manure." He hugged tighter, the goose pressing against his flat belly.

"You dimwit! What would Shirn and I do without you?"

Arms around each other, they made their way along the street, attracting the curious stares of the villagers and tourists in the shops and on the street.

The Kollektiv

Shirn stepped down from the cab of her truck, the last in a long line stalled by still another foul-up at the collective's grain storage center.

She wiped her hands on the seat of her faded blue jeans, more to refresh her boyish rump than to clean her hands. She'd been driving back and forth all day between the agricultural warehouses at Odessa and the collective, and the cab seat was a thick hard board.

Her green eyes took in the activities around her. Three young boys galloped by on *kolkhozphyk* horses, pretending to be cossacks. One of them waved happily at her and she raised a hand in turn. They raced away. She turned to look moodily at the line of trucks ahead of her waiting to be unloaded, heard the high whine of noises in the repair barn where old tractors were undergoing refitting by machinists. Clouds of dust rose in the distance as other machines worked the Ukrainian fields spreading flat in the hazy space.

A knot of truck drivers, all of them women wearing boots and cotton dresses, broke into a loud argument with two of them pushing and shoving in anger. Someone shushed them, and they stalked away from each other.

She removed her bright red head scarf and let her long, unruly black hair fall down past her shoulders. She stood, hands on slender, attractively rounded hips, legs braced apart, staring at the cloudless blue sky to the south. A few kilometers away was her cabin; beyond that the village with Bissa and Raysta, her protectors; and farther south, Odessa and the Black Sea, from which the one who was coming would emerge.

The lowering sun told her the workday would soon be over. She was lonesome for Bissa and Raysta, thinking of them now in the underground code names rather than their Ukrainian names. She wondered if they would have a surprise for her on this day. Her twenty-first birthday.

A dusty Moskvich sedan came up the main road leading into the collective. It came to a stop near her, its old engine chugging noisily. She caught her breath. The Russian who stepped from the rear seat was the object of her intense dislike. The Muscovite had tried repeatedly to get her into his bed, in the *kolkhoz* building set aside for guests of the State. He was an unattractive man in his forties, dressed in a lightweight business suit that was too large for him, who paraded his importance each time he arrived to examine the collective's records.

"What's the difficulty?" he said in Russian.

She shrugged and spit at the ground.

He acted offended. "Perhaps you don't like to work here?" he said, his eyes half-lidded. "The daughter of convicted anti-State parents should be more cautious."

She resisted the temptation to spit in his face. Her eyes flashed in anger. "My father was the best manager that damned engine plant ever had! My mother was guilty only of protesting his unfair arrest!"

The Muscovite slapped a hand against his hip. "You don't seem aware of the serious situation you are in. You are questionable. You have a bad record here. Your temper has gotten you into trouble." He tried a smile and it came off poorly. "There is considerable resentment against you for living with those villagers who are not your relatives." He waited. She kept her gaze on the line of trucks.

"So that's it again?" he said harshly. "I offer to make your life easy. I need companionship when I come to this collective. I have influence. Why are you so stubborn?" He turned on his heels. Over his shoulder he said, "Think of it. Your case is under review. You will end up in a camp like your anti-State parents!" He got back in the sedan, spoke curtly to its driver, and it chugged past the trucks toward the administration building.

Shirn pulled her blouse from the blue jeans to let the late-afternoon breeze, very slight but welcome, blow up onto her perspiring body. Her firm breasts pushed against the damp fabric. She felt the heavy fear the Muscovite had triggered within her. He was a revengeful Russian bastard. She knew he was capable of trying to overturn the arrangement that Raysta had made through the underground leaders who worked in the oblast, the State, headquarters, and the *silrada* officials at the county level, who had allowed her to remain in the cabin instead of a collective dormitory. It was a tentative, questioned arrangement that could be upset by the Russian accountant if she continued to refuse his advances, or by an informer, the review panel, or by the KGB or the GRU. She breathed deeply with the unsettled feelings within her, thinking of Raysta's years in the underground and how she had helped him, along with Bissa, and how the whole thing might come crashing down at any moment, sending them to their deaths or to a work camp. Death would be better, she thought.

The trucks ahead of her started up again, and she climbed into the cab, grateful that things were moving. They would unload her truck, a pitiful-looking vehicle that had an enclosed cabin, a rear door, and a wooden step protruding from the back. The cabin was filled with large cans of oil and cartons of spark plugs, tools, and replacement parts for the tractors and other field equipment.

She started the truck, thinking again of her mother and father and the six years since their deaths in the work camp near Karaganda. She thought of the Ukrainian family that had taken her in, protecting her as long as they could until they were forced to let her go under pressure from the State authorities and a GRU officer.

Her father, manager of a Ukrainian plant making military engines, had been accused by the same authorities, charged with not meeting production schedules set at an unreasonably high level by bureaucrats in Moscow, a guilt held by the Russian supervisors and not by her father. He'd been sentenced to the camp, and her mother, protesting, had been charged with provoking the State and had been sent to the same camp, where they had died in a typhus epidemic.

She drove the truck slowly, remembering her parents, remembering the happiness and comfort of being with them, remembering the loneliness without them. She fought back tears and stared at the *kolkhoz* activities as if she were in an alien land.

She was unaware that she was speaking aloud, barely audible over the sound of the engine: "I was fifteen. That man came and made the family put me out in the street. He went to arrange for me to be picked up as a parasite of the State. I didn't know it then, but the Lavchenkos who had taken me in were in the UPA. They had friends who smuggled me from Kirovograd to Nikolayev and from there to the village."

The trucks stopped again. "I wandered through the village looking for two men the UPAs said were waiting for me. I was hungry, afraid, carrying a little suitcase with what clothes I could manage. Bissa and Raysta came running toward me, drunk, throwing their arms around me, giving me their *kootir*."

Tears rolled down her cheek: "They are my family. They'll help me repay that damned Colonel Gregorski for what he did to my mother and father, and to me!"

She thought of the problems Raysta had solved after the authorities had discovered where she was. By that time the colonel had left the Ukraine, money had changed hands, UPA pressure had been applied, and the situation remained in limbo for the moment. She saw the Muscovite leave one building and enter another, and the fear returned. But she still had her family, Raysta and Bissa, and she served as their leader and lookout when they went in the night to do their work for the UPA. The Ukrayins'ka Povtancha Armiya were everywhere. She was accepted by them. Her cheeks were wet and she wiped them with the red scarf.

Her truck was unloaded by two young men who cast friendly, appreciative eyes at her, though they said nothing. They were confederates of Raysta and would be among those who would help the one who was coming. She parked the empty truck, her temper returning, and she cursed Colonel Gregorski, whom the underground had learned was returning to Odessa to hunt the UPA again.

She wanted that man dead!

In the gathering darkness she began the long walk across the silent fields, the machinery all driven in for the night, taking the paths that led to the little cabin near the village.

She wondered if her two protectors had a gift for her on her birthday.

Her steps quickened, and she was almost trotting in anticipation.

The Black Sea Defense Center

Built five stories deep into the gravelly soil southwest of Odessa, the Black Sea Defense Center was an anthill of movement as the shift change took place.

Men and women in their greenish khaki military uniforms filled the labyrinth of concrete rooms, carefully air-conditioned to protect the sensitive equipment.

The chief of operations, coming on duty for the night, strutted importantly through the lower level, making certain the duty posts were filled. He arrived at the main control room and went into his glass-enclosed office from where he could see the entire display panel. He received reports from his juniors: a storm was coming from Moldavia; some equipment had malfunctioned and was being repaired; three duty officers had come in ill, been replaced, and sent to the infirmary; and all was quiet in the Black Sea. The aerial surveillance, sonobuoys, and ship sonar had found nothing unusual despite the heavy sea traffic.

He studied the display, which filled an entire wall of the large room. Thirty-one operators sat at computer stations receiving a constant flow of electronic information. This was fed into sections of the display panel. On the panel were locations, directions, and identifications of all ships in the Black Sea, all aircraft, all weather conditions, and the alertness condition of all military, naval, air, and support-equipment personnel and equipment.

He peered at the Russian numerals on the panel, nodding in recognition. There were nearly six hundred units in the Black Sea fleet and the Caspian flotilla. Twenty new MiG-21/Fishbed N all-weather interceptors had been added to the air control that day. A Liev-class guided-missile aircraft carrier was now in the Black Sea, along with two Echo-class nuclear-powered attack submarines. The air defense forces interceptors were all marked at ready.

He glanced at the headsetted operators, at the blinking lights and rapidly working video display units. Satisfied, he sat at his desk reviewing the computer printouts. The Radio-Electronic Combat System was working smoothly, combining all types of intelligence from the center's sea-based platforms and the ground and air systems. He became absorbed in the details of the night watch.

In a small room at the far end of the lower level, two men worked feverishly to wire a small intercept-timing device into the electronic control unit into which came the signals from those platforms, leaving the computer stations in the main control room flashing their last reports until the timer clicked off on schedule after dawn. It would be removed minutes later.

Finished, they quickly replaced the unit's panel, gathered their tools in canvas bags, and left the room. They wore uniform patches identifying them as senior electronics repairmen.

They made their way to their regular stations and received a dressing-down for reporting late. Their faces revealed nothing of their hidden pleasure.

The Kootir

There had been a birthday surprise.

Shirn looked at the remains of the goose on the table and rose from her bench to hug Raysta and Bissa. "You cooked it to perfection," she said to Bissa. "And the ribbons are beautiful!" she said to Raysta.

In the light of the single overhead electric light Raysta had managed to wire into the small cabin, Bissa's face glowed with a broad smile. "For you another present I have!" He bounced like a rubber ball to a corner, fished something out of the wood box, and returned with the object held behind his back. "A guess you get!" He jiggled up and down in happiness.

"Something you made for me?" she said, feeling her own happiness.

He handed it to her, still wrapped in the smeared newspaper that had covered the goose. She removed the paper and stared at the two figurines, holding hands, standing on a solid wooden base. The entire statuary had been carved from a single wood block.

Bissa couldn't wait. "Your mother and father!" he shouted. "With you now you have them!"

Raysta put down his glass of vodka. "He made that from the description you gave us. Do they look like them?"

Tears came to her eyes and she nodded, holding the statuary tightly to her. Raysta rose and got another package from the wood box. He handed it to her gently, then realizing that she didn't want to put down the little figurines, he unwrapped the gift.

Bissa couldn't wait, again. "Boots for you he bought!"

"Had them made in the village," Raysta said roughly, trying to hide his own enjoyment.

Her green eyes flashed her love for them. She wore the brightly colored ribbons Raysta had given her. Her black hair sprayed in two high-tied masses down her back. The simple cotton dress she'd made fitted her smoothly rounded body, emphasizing her narrow waist and taut breasts.

"You've been so good to me," she said in a tight voice. She blinked, looking again at the figurines. "Yes, it's them. My mother and father!"

Raysta picked up the vodka glass. "We're a family!" He drank a toast. Bissa, standing, swayed from side to side in happiness.

She wiped her eyes with the back of a hand and placed the figurines on the table. "The birthday present I want is Gregorski!"

"Here, don't do that," Raysta said. "You know what's going on."

"I want to kill him myself!" Her voice rose.

"It's your birthday. Don't lose your temper." Raysta was conciliatory. "Look. We're all working to get him. The UPA commanders made a deal and we stick with it."

Her voice came down. "I want to kill him myself, I told you that."

"You'd die," Raysta said evenly. "That bastard colonel's a big man. Important. The GRU'll pack him in with guards day and night. He's coming here to work on us. We can't risk our network trying to get him ourselves."

She flashed a sharp look at him. "I'll kill half the stinking Russians in the Ukraine to get at him!"

"Let you we won't," Bissa said quietly. "Family we are!"

She resisted the temptation to pick up her plate and throw it at a wall. "Gregorski! Why do we play these secret games? Why don't we go kill him!"

Raysta gulped more vodka. "The Americans are sending this man. Our commanders worked out a plan. If the *Amerikanski* carries his part out, Gregorski will be dead and the UPA won't be rounded up and slaughtered. Now hold your temper!"

She slapped the table in disgust. "Hundreds of you, thousands, all those machine guns and grenades, all the infiltration, all the wrecking and destroying, and you beg the Americans for help!"

"Take it easy!" Raysta sighed in sympathy, knowing how she felt.

"I saw Gregorski when he came to get my father. I saw him at the trial when he accused my mother of anti-State agitation." Her eyes misted again. "I've never forgotten his face or what he did. I want him dead!"

Bissa came and put his loglike arms around her, sympathetic tears in his own eyes. "Dead he will be," he said.

Outside a sudden gust of wind struck the tall trees around the old cabin, echoing through the cabin and the small addition they had added on to it for her room. A branch struck heavily on the old shack in the rear where Bissa slept, a place where the former tenant, a tanner, had dried his hides.

"Dead he will be!" Bissa repeated over and over.

The Odessa Waterfront

The courier, a frail youth of twenty, was trapped, seconds away from arrest or death.

He swore silently in Ukrainian, listening to the booted clumping of three militiamen approaching him along the poorly lighted quay, sweat drenching him in the damp coolness of the night. His eyes darted, searching for an escape, his heart beating wildly as he crouched behind the huge crates stacked along the shoreside of the massive concrete quay. In the distance he heard the nighttime noises of the giant cranes at the shipyard warehouses unloading the berthed cargo carriers under the arc lights.

He flinched as a loud voice shouted, "You, there, stop!" The boots of the civil police made running sounds. Cautiously he peered around the edge of the wooden crate. Relief flooded through him. The patrol had flushed out a vagrant who was running in the other direction along the quay, the militia in pursuit. He watched, wide-eyed, as they caught up to the screaming man and began pummeling him heavily.

The courier pulled back behind the crate and moved slowly, bent over, keeping the large boxes between him and the noisy protests the vagrant was putting up. In minutes he made it to the unlighted small-craft area at the end of the quay, a mass of fishing boats tied up for the night. Far enough away, seeing no other patrols, he straightened and walked quickly along the narrow jetty to the last boat. He heard sounds on some of the boats but saw no one.

He boarded the boat and in the darkness opened the heavy wooden door to the cabin, his breath still coming in gulps. A tiny pencil flashlight snapped on. A man sat behind the cabin table, a pistol pointing at him. He blew air through his pursed lips. The pistol was laid on the table, and the dark figure stepped from behind the table.

"Commander," the courier said, "they found him!"

The commander's heavy voice was low as he used the pencil light to indicate a bottle. "Where?"

The courier brought out the thin packet from under his jacket and placed it on the table. He reached for the bottle eagerly. The light moved to the packet. The commander opened it and studied the photographs in its glow. The cabin curtains were pulled tight against the night and prying eyes. He held up one of the enlargements. The prison was obvious, the exercise area apparent, the man's face was clear.

"So this is Karl Stepanovich Karlov?"

"At the Dombosky Prison," the courier said in hushed tones. "They match the pictures of him when he was at the Dneiper power station." A long swig at the bottle. "The one we've sought in all the prisons and work camps these weeks!

Compare the Dneiper picture, fifteen years ago!"

The commander shook his head. "Look what they've done to Karl Stepanovich! They've aged him well beyond his years. The man's only fifty-three." He jerked an arm upward in anger. "Damned Russians!" He took the bottle the courier handed him. "Now comes his son. Soon we'll see what price those crazy bastards will pay for what they did to this man and his wife, what they've done to us."

The courier nodded. "Also, this news. The device is in place for the underwater ears. Tomorrow morning it will work." The courier left, scuttling up the jetty to the quay, alert for patrols, and was lost in the night.

The commander sat brooding about the plan. What had been missed, overlooked? Was everyone in place? Would it work? He went over the information he'd been given that night by a small string of couriers from the underground about the man who was to arrive. He thought of what he'd have to do to help that man, of the many attacks on the Russian security system designed to fit into the plan. The UPA network was alive, working steadily at his bidding and that of the other commanders spread around the southern Ukraine along the Black Sea coast.

Fatigue closed in on him. He swigged again from the bottle of Ukrainian vodka, stretched out on the rough wooden bench, put the pistol within reach, pulled a woolen blanket over him, and was asleep in an instant.

The Black Sea

Mikhail Karlovich Karlov jerked the zipper of the frogman's suit toward his throat.

He studied the face of the smallish intelligence officer seated cross-legged on the bunk of the submarine's tiny officers' compartment. The metallic noises around there were soft, muted. He knew the submarine was rising to the depth where it would release him into the restless waters of the Black Sea, unusually close to the shore.

"The one question I haven't asked you," he said, "is how you guys got Turkey to go along with this." He grinned quickly. "And I don't want to know."

Captain Pell rose from the bunk and began handing him the weights, knife, depth gauge, wristwatch, and special gear to put on. "No, you don't. You've got too much secret information in your head as it is."

Mikhail looked into the captain's eyes, brown with flecks of copper. A jungle animal's eyes, shaded, shielded. Hidden danger in a darkly tanned oval face. A small face compatible with a small lithe body that moved slowly and deliberately, with gray coming to the faded brown hair.

Captain Pell moved to the cabin door, his hand on the latch. "Mikhail, you've had one hell of a training stint for this job. We've put men in there and we've got them out. You're the only one I haven't worried about."

Quick memories of the training flashed through Mikhail's mind: the underwater training by the navy; the weapons and explosives training by the CIA; the long, hard training by the Ukrainian elders in Canada; the Russian military training by G-2 and the group from the Pentagon. He straightened and spread his legs against a gentle roll of the submarine.

"Any last questions?" Pell said.

"This woman, Shirn? This Raysta and Bissa? I still don't know very much about them."

"You know all I know. Code names. We had to protect them as well as you. They're simple people, peasants, unsophisticated. They're not under direct surveillance, which is what made their commanders choose them. They've been damned active in the UPA underground, and they're extremely important to this operation. They're hell on Gregorski, just as you are. Remember, Raysta's the skinny one, Bissa's the fat one. She lives with them."

"They know I'm Russian?"

"They know you're an American. You'll have to handle the Russian part when you get to them. They'll help you, but the nationalists don't want one of their own getting caught trying to take Gregorski apart."

"Bloodbath?" Mikhail arched his back and felt his muscles press against the rubber suit. "If I'm in and out on schedule, they'll get what they want and I'll get what you and I want, and the Russians won't have anything to hang on the UPAs."

"You know we had to horse-trade. They want Colonel

Rakoski and the Nikolayev base." The captain paused. "When Rakoski was with State security, he executed a gang of UPAs in a public square. Three men have been caught trying to get at him in the year he's been building the new satellite station." He opened the door. "Anyone with a strong Ukrainian accent and appearance isn't going to get within spitting distance of the base. You speak Russian and Ukrainian, so you can get along on both sides."

Mikhail put on the hood, the dry rubber pulling at his Russian-style blond hair. His blue eyes were serious. He tucked the mask and flippers under an arm. "Let's go."

They made their way down the narrow passage. A group of four Americans in unmarked uniforms waited for them by the underwater escape hatch. Pell turned to Mikhail, his face close to the hood. "The UPA, remember, has penetrated the Soviet Army and everything else. Their information has been priceless. They have one of the best clandestine radio and courier hookups I've ever seen. We'll know every move you make."

Mikhail glanced at the sub's crewmen preparing the discharge tube. "The plane at Odessa? It'll be there?"

"You want a signed receipt?" Pell said easily. "The tunnel plane will be there. Just bring out the electronics stuff."

Mikhail grunted. "You know what I'll bring out." He felt Pell's hand grip his arm with a strangely ironlike caution. "Don't give in to your death instinct," Pell said. "Don't blow it by going animal. Stick to the plan." The hand fell away. The Americans and crewmen were watching them curiously, waiting. Mikhail felt a sense of weightlessness; hate into frenzy, frenzy into despair, despair into fear, fear into sudden resolve.

"I won't."

The captain motioned to the men. "Let's get him out. The timing's perfect."

The Americans surrounded Mikhail, checking his equipment, helping him to don the double air tank, made of fiberglass to lower sonar detection. After he put on his mask and flippers they fastened two black packages, each the size of a book, to his chest. He worked his air regulator and nodded.

He heard Pell's voice in his ear. "Remember what we

told you about the underwater sled. It'll be tricky by the time you get to shore. Watch the currents and watch the time." He whispered one more sentence.

Mikhail saw the sub commander with a headset talking to the control room, as casually as if it were an everyday affair to set free a muscular frogman astride a long-range fiberglass underwater propulsion unit in the Black Sea as close as the sub could safely come to the Russian limits from the southern Ukrainian coast. The officer looked at the clock, pointed to him, and the hatch was opened. He moved toward it and climbed in.

The underwater sled was waiting for him at the end of the tube. He crawled to it. The hatch closed behind him with a small metallic sound. In the blackness he felt for the familiar holding straps into which he slid his arms. He felt for the control levers and lay facedown on the sled. The tube filled with cold seawater and he shuddered. He waited for the sea hatch to blow open and send him out into the Black Sea, long before dawn, toward the heavily guarded coast.

A coast crusted with rocks and shielded with craggy hills, guarded by the Russians with one of the largest naval and military concentrations in the world.

The outer hatch opened and he shot through the tube. In his ears were the last words from Captain Pell.

"I hope you find your father," Pell had whispered.

CHAPTER TWO

The two-hour rainstorm that swept across Odessa in the hours before midnight had been torrential, leaving the area sodden with a dense fog covering much of it.

The convoy of dark green trucks jammed with Russian soldiers rolled noisily through the deserted streets. It went snakelike, waved past intersections by white-jacketed militiamen and convoy patrols, to the vast military compound to the west. Inside its gates, it wound through the murky, lit streets toward the barracks area, blocking the path of a Chiaka army sedan coming from the army airport within the installation.

The rear windows of the sedan, despite the night, were shielded partway by curtains. When the convoy ended, the sedan sped from the halting point to a sliding stop on the rain-soaked pavement in front of the general's headquarters building, garishly lighted from without and with most of its windows streaming light into the mist.

The driver emerged and opened the passenger door. "Comrade Colonel," Sergeant Timkin said, "we're here."

Colonel Rykan Gregorski got out and stood looking with disdain at the long, four-story steel-and-cement building. His face was set in bitterness. A stringlike scar ran in a senseless pattern up his right cheek almost to his eye. His jutting jaw was topped by a thin mouth with an upper lip that curled at the corner. The back of his summer uniform was sweat-stained, his blue-green eyes uneasy. "That damned rain delayed my arrival by two hours," he said with words that were like slivers of ice.

Sergeant Timkin remained at attention. "Comrade Colonel, the landing lane was filled with water, and then the fog came. Nothing landed until your aircraft was permitted."

A low rumbling made the colonel turn. He recognized three new T-80 tanks moving slowly along a nearby street, led by a jeep. The sound and the moving lights in the haze made an eerie picture in the distance. Behind the tanks he saw the shapes of four 122-mm self-propelled howitzers. Further in the distance he saw the fitting hangars, wide open and brilliantly lit, as ground crews worked on MiG-25, high-altitude supersonic interceptors and MiG-23 Flogger B all-weather counterair fighters. Their high tail assemblies were visible in the fog-misted light.

The colonel was impressed by the nighttime activity. *This is what I like*, he thought. Power, strength, force. I'd like to command it all. He slapped his gloved hands together. "Mother," he said aloud, falling abruptly into an old fantasy, "I'd use it all against you!"

Sergeant Timkin was surprised. "Did you say something, Comrade Colonel?" The blue eyes in the round peasant face were innocent.

"And against you too!" The colonel snarled at the shocked man. Timkin's brown-green flat-topped garrison cap was set properly, the shininess of its small peak set directly over his broad forehead. Despite the cleanliness of his khaki uniform, it looked as if Timkin had slept in it for a week. Damp from the rain, it was oversize and sagged loosely on his spare frame.

The colonel moved away in disgust. The assignment of this man to him after his landing at the military airport following the long delay of his flight from Moscow because of rain was another affront to his station. He strode to the entrance, seeing the waiting guards within and without. Timkin had reminded him of the strange events that had been piling up at his feet. He scowled at the comedown he'd had since his days of training at the Military Diplomatic Academy at Moscow in his youth, when all things held promise for a hardworking officer dedicated to espionage, counterespionage, and counterrevolutionary work.

He'd gone from Novgorod, his birthplace, to Moscow and been smitten by its power. He'd been too young for the Great Patriotic War in which Hitler and the Nazis were defeated. He'd been only a boy at war's end, but he'd made junior lieutenant in the fifties, worked hard in the GRU and had been raised to senior lieutenant, then captain in the sixties, been sent on worldwide assignments for eighteen years, making major and then lieutenant colonel, coming back for internal assignments from time to time as ordered.

Despite his promotion to full colonel five years past, and his five citations, when he'd returned to Moscow a month before, he'd found the climate ominously changed. Forces were at work against him, forces that instead of moving him into command in the GRU had shunted him to the Ukraine once again to ferret out the demented UPA nationalists who wanted Ukrainia free of the USSR.

He bounced up the concrete steps into the building, showed his folder of papers to the guards with their submachine guns strapped across their chests, and strode quickly on bandy legs down the empty hall, his boots making loud sounds.

He stopped at the door with the metal plate that announced Minister of State Security, Odessa Military District, Glavnoye Razvedavatelnoye Upravlenie. His name was underneath, on the wooden door, freshly lettered. He touched the paint. It was tacky. His lips twitched. The GRU, the Soviet Army's intelligence and espionage apparatus, was under another vicious attack by the KGB, whom he regarded as bumbling idiots in their internal security work in Moscow.

And Colonel Rykan Gregorski was under attack again. The soft-bellied fools in Moscow had been able to transfer him to this miserable task in Odessa. A scapegoat. He'd been told he was being given one last chance to redeem himself. The reason: His personal life might compromise him and the Soviet.

Redeem himself, indeed! He slapped his hands together in quick impatience as he moved down the long corridor. He stopped before the two armed guards, pulling his credentials from his tunic again. Before a guard could reach for them, the door was thrown open.

"Enough of that!" Colonel-General Petr Zagorsky said roughly, his bulk seeming to fill the door. The clear blue eyes behind the gold-rimmed glasses were smoldering with ill-concealed anger. Across his chest he wore the Red Star, Order of Lenin, Defense of Moscow, First Degree Glory

and Hero of the Soviet Union atop five more rows of medals.
His shoulder boards were gold, trimmed with blue piping
and with three stars on each. His white-frosted hair was
long and combed neatly back. The skin of his face and
hands was pink, marred by the dark spots of advancing age.
He looked exactly what he was, Chief of Operations Directorate of the Odessa Military District. He turned from
the door.

The colonel entered and heard the door close firmly behind him. He stood straight and saluted when the general
was behind the large desk set in the middle of the room.

The general ignored the salute. He removed his tunic,
loosened his tie, and pulled the heavy chair back, letting
his bulk sink into its padded comfort. "This damned Ukrainian heat and now the rain and fog," he grumbled. He looked
acidly at the colonel. "Sit and relax. It is now a quarter to
the third hour. Relax because you'll have no time for it
when you leave here." He let his head sink and appeared
lost in thought.

The colonel sat stiffly erect in his tailored but damp and
sticky uniform. His small rounded belly was almost hidden,
but it felt hard and restless to him. He removed the case
from his pocket, slid the pince-nez glasses out, and placed
them on his nose. He replaced the case, patting his pocket.
His eyes, staring coldly from behind the glasses, held a faint
yellowish interior glow. He brushed an impatient hand along
his thinning black hair, which he wore straight back against
his head. He waited.

"Your orders from Moscow are clear," the general said.
He raised his eyes and met the colonel's. "Your office is in
order. You have an apartment. Your daughter is here. She
was able to arrive by air many hours before you, Comrade
Colonel."

The colonel nodded. That was characteristic of Vera.
Punctual. Obedient. His transfer to Odessa had come just
as she was starting her vacation from Intourist, the Directorate for Foreign Tourists. He'd insisted that she join him,
a small move to help compensate for the bitterness he felt
for his demotion of duty and exile from Moscow. After
eighteen years of world assignment he'd had less than a
year of duty in Moscow. Now this!

The general shifted through the pile of papers on the desk, found what he sought, and leaned back in the chair. "Perhaps this assignment is more than you can handle?" he said coldly.

The colonel adjusted the pince-nez, meeting the older man's hard stare, carefully avoiding any visible reaction to the insult. It was clear what the paper was about. Well, there were advantages to being held over the fire. A successful ending to the hunt for the UPAs could springboard him back to Moscow, restored to full favor. Moscow appreciated success.

The general studied the paper. "You've quite a history. So many successes in capturing enemies of the State, in espionage in other countries, five citations. On paper, you're one of the best espionage and counterrevolutionary officers." He raised his eyes. "Off paper, you have enemies."

"Marshal Stalin once said that few good military officers go through their careers without making enemies." The colonel scratched his long nose with a gloved hand.

"You've made more than most."

The colonel shrugged and was silent.

"You have weaknesses, Comrade Colonel. Now that you are in my district, you will control those weaknesses." A pause. "That Karlov affair in the Washington embassy should have gotten you a prison term. At that time you had friends in high places who smoothed things out for you, since you were in sensitive espionage work over there. You do not have those friends now. Your record has many complaints from women who say you mistreated them." The general cleared his throat. "You were in this district nineteen years ago and you brought in scores of the UPA. You returned six years ago and did a creditable job." He placed the paper on the desk. "No protest about the record, Comrade Colonel?"

"None. I'm here to destroy the enemies of the State, not to worry about my enemies or women who have complained against me."

"Yes, enemies of the State." The general's voice hardened. "This is why I waited for you at this beastly hour. The nationalists have started another campaign. Yesterday, six of our T-72s were severely damaged by acid poured down their guns. Rail and truck shipments have been broken into. Uniforms, explosives, ammunition, petrol, and electronic communications equipment have been stolen." A deep breath. "Something big is going on with these damned Ukrainian *khakols*. You're to get right on it. In the morning you'll meet early with your staff. Captain Prokov will be your aide."

The colonel started. Prokov in Odessa? He'd long suspected the man of being a KGB plant in the GRU. Then he relaxed. Well, he *was* in charge of the GRU counterrevolutionary network. Its men were posted everywhere in South Ukrainia. The locals called it Tavria, such as the Americans called their southland Dixie. "I believe I know Captain Prokov."

The general handed him his official district orders. "Study these tonight. In the morning you'll have to move quickly. They're back to changing road signs to misdirect our troop movements. They've slashed tires on our vehicles, they've fouled gas tanks. You are to put a stop to this nationalist nonsense!"

The colonel glanced at the orders. "Along with that, my specific assignment is to protect the microminiature computers under development at this base?"

The general leaned back, showing his weariness on his face. "They're essential for our new system of destroying enemy satellites in orbit. Read on. You are also to protect the new tracking station at Nikolayev. It's a backup system to the Crimea tracking stations at Simferopol and Feodosiya. The *banderivtsi* fleas may have them in mind. They've gotten into our army and navy apparatus again. We don't know where they are, but we know they must have infiltrated again. You are to dig them out."

The colonel finished reading his orders. The Odessa and Nikolayev bases were superbly protected, he knew. Impenetrable. The UPA destructionists were idiots. The massive GRU network would finger the nationalists. One out of fifteen persons in the Soviet Union served as an informer. He would make it more attractive to the Ukrainians who knew something about the nationalists to turn them in. It had worked before and it would work again. He would gather in the UPA like a net full of fish and end their stupid attempts to reverse the annexation of the Ukraine by Russia in 1922.

"Why are you smiling, Comrade Colonel?" he heard the general say.

He blinked, suddenly embarrassed and unaware that he'd been smiling. "I'm a hunter. I've hunted the Ukrayins'ka Povtancha Armiya before. I'm eager to get at them. These UPAs are the children of the Ukrainian cossacks who do these things against the State out of ignorance. Their damned anti-State agitation! Look how they show their appreciation of Communism and what we've had to do to protect it!"

The general's face darkened, and the sight of it worried him. "These UPAs aren't stupid," the general said. "You're replacing a good officer who couldn't handle them."

The leather gloves tightened on the orders booklet. What had happened to the "good officer?" He hadn't been told in Moscow.

The general went on. "They're clever. They've infiltrated our armed forces, our schools, many sensitive areas. They're still structured in small cells, interlinked by only one person. Sweep in one cell and it's almost impossible to find the link to the others. The ones we've nabbed mostly have been very young, those who act as couriers." The heavy voice rumbled on. "They appear to be led by older, more experienced hands, those who remember the *kulaks* and the campaign for collectivism. They're playing hell with our military installations along the Black Sea. We caught three of them in the last year trying to kill Comrade Colonel Rakoski at Nikolayev."

"I want nothing more than to bring these *banderivtsi* gangsters to justice!"

The general stood, reaching for his tunic. "They will know you are here. They're resourceful and dangerous. No public agitation for them. They have a damned good underground working against us; I'll give them credit for that! You've been assigned here twice before. They know your record of being hard-fisted, even brutish. I warn you to be careful."

Colonel Gregorski was puzzled. "Careful?"

"That *you* don't become the hunted!"

*   *   *

Raysta roused himself to wakefulness.

He didn't have to dress. He still wore the same clothes he had on when he'd passed out from the vodka. He stoked the embers of the fire, added wood, watched it grow, bringing the water to a boil for the morning tea. It was dark outside the cabin. He saw the empty bottle and winced at the pain that had been growing in his belly, a recurrent torture he'd had since the time he'd been a boy-soldier in the Great Patriotic War, hardly able to lift and aim the old rifle they'd given him. A pain coming and going, weeks or months in between, wiggling in him now like a strand of barbed wire.

He sat down, waiting for Shirn. She'd tidied up the simple, sparsely furnished cabin before going to bed. Bissa, he knew, was gone from the old tanner's shed, a place that still smelled raw and unwholesome long after the old tanner's death. Bissa had trotted away in the dark to get their day's instructions.

He thought of the network, how the ones up north at Kirovograd had sent this lovely young girl to the village to be under his protection, how the *silrada* agent, protective of his township, had been against Raysta sharing his miserable *kootir* with the fifteen-year-old girl, even after he and Bissa had built onto it the small room in which she slept. But UPA money had exchanged hands, influence had been exerted, and an uneasy truce had been in effect for six years. It was once again under attack.

He sighed, listening to the bubbling water. How safe were they? His UPA friends, embedded secretly at the raion, the county level, and the oblast, the regional level, had so far been able to keep them together. Shirn had been assigned to drive a truck for the collective. Bissa, considered under the devil's control, had been left alone to make his wood carvings for the tourists.

He shuddered from the pain again, knowing what he and Bissa had to do to help the one who was coming and what it might do to their family. Love for Shirn and Bissa flooded through him, nullifying the pain. He looked around as Shirn came into the cabin, wearing her new boots. He rose and turned on the single light bulb, looking at her with appreciation in its light. "Hey," he said, "you remember when I tried to teach you the *hopak* and I fell on my ass?"

She laughed with him. She made the tea and put sausage and cheese, with dark bread, on the table. Her green eyes were serious. She sipped the steaming brew. "For six years we've done what the commanders asked," she said, sitting on her narrow bench at the table. "They've given us code names. Now we use them all the time when we're together, as if they were real. I'm Shirn, you're Raysta, he's Bissa. Crazy names that mean nothing. Sometimes I don't think we're real."

"Just cover names with a Russian flavor. I'm still Volodimir Kirichenko, a damned good name around here. He's still Andrey Hrushevsky. He was turned out of that school for the dumb. They tried to get him through a vocational school and that didn't work. I took the poor bastard in to be my helper and he damned near electrocuted himself the first day! I found he could whittle, and look what he's done with his wood-carving knives." He knew her parents' statues were in her room, on the little table under the icon.

"Look," he said, "everyone has a code name, so if one of us gets caught, the names don't lead the GRU anywhere." His voice was defensive. "You want Gregorski dead. So do others. The man's a butcher. We made a deal. The *Amerikanski* is coming. He'll be in and out in days, and no one can lay it at our doors. We're all building alibis. We get what we want and they get what they want."

She studied him. "The others will be in crowds of witnesses, except you and Bissa. You'll be with this American. What if this man doesn't make it? So he's an American Superman. One of their assassins, but what if he blows it?"

Raysta shrugged. "A lot of us will die."

"We've done their dirty work at night," she said loudly. "I think this plan you've been talking about stinks. If we're going to die, let's take Gregorski with us!"

"Now, hold your temper down, damn it! They'll hear you shouting in the village and think I'm beating you."

She settled down and ate, her mind wandering to the village, a small cluster of clay houses with some wooden *dachas* thrown in, clay houses with walls nearly a meter thick and roofed with straw or swamp reeds, *ocheret*. The wives would be cooking breakfast in their *piches*, ovenlike stoves, burning birch and what other wood they had, and huge piles of straw, *skytra*. The same wives who'd made her stay so unpleasant, who'd make her an outcast because she lived with two unmarried men, one of whom was an idiot. She'd never been invited into the village to share their few parties and celebrations. Her day was like theirs, chained to the collective. The Russians had artificially created the collectives scores of years before, and the villagers were farmers, *kolkhozpnyk*, who labored at the immense farm from sunrise to sunset. The *seliankas* of the village had turned their wrath against her, warning their young sons against her. There would be no matchmaker to come calling to arrange a wedding. She'd been left alone at night to read to her two men, for they were both eager for stories. She read them Yevtushenko, the poet; Pushkin, Turgenev, Gogol, Chekov, and Dostoevsky. She traded secretly for English-language literature to improve her reading her mother had started her on.

Reading, embroidering a new blouse or two, *bluzkas*, or helping Raysta and Bissa with their UPA assignments made up her life. She finished her meal. She made the best borscht in the area. She was the best truck driver, better than the dumpy, stocky women who also drove. She received the same payments in cash as they did, and in grain and potatoes. She was twenty-one, ripe for marriage, but there were no men available to her in the *silrada*. Those who'd shown interest in her had been chased away by the wagging tongues of the broad-beamed, fat-legged *seliankas* of the village and the collective.

There was a soft sound at the door. She and Raysta stiffened. He went quickly to the door. He moved the latch gently and it was touched from the outside in a similar manner. He opened the door to the faint morning light, and the short, stocky figure bounced into the cabin.

"Bissa, you pee sack!" Raysta said, pleased. "What took you so damned long?" He swatted at his shortlegged friend, missing Bissa's potato-shaped head by inches.

"Is come the message from the American!" Bissa said in his blunted voice. His curly black hair was sweat-soaked from trudging rapidly along the back hill paths to the cabin. He wiped his thick lips with the back of a plump hand. His soft brown eyes were aglow.

"What message?" Shirn said, going to him and putting her hands on his damp face.

"The one who comes will be here by the fifth hour."

"Here?" Shirn pulled her hands away in surprise.

"By the beach." Bissa pointed with a stubby finger. "Down there the old beach."

Raysta grabbed Bissa by his fat shoulders and shook him soundly. "You little bag of horse gas! They can't mean that! The beach is the worst place for them to put him! Get your mind straight!" He shook him again. "Start at the first and tell us what the courier said."

"Don't jiggle his brain loose any more than it is," Shirn said, moving between them. "Bissa, tell us what the man told you."

Bissa straightened importantly. His fat fingers kept tapping against each other in front of his belly. His Ukrainian pullover shirt, the *vyshyvanka*, hung below his jacket, worn and wispy with tired, hanging threads. His soiled pants clung wetly to his thick, stubby legs. His eyes were shiny with obvious urgency. In his uncertain way he said, "Someone will bring the one who comes close to the shore. He'll have whatever it is that under the water makes him swim."

"A frogman?" Shirn's eyes blinked.

Bissa smiled brightly. "That's it, Shirn. Frogman. I forgot."

"You'd forget your ass if it weren't so damned big!" Raysta growled.

"Raysta and me, down we're supposed to go by the beach with clothes, for him here to bring to wait, a tourist swimming he is, and then a boat there'll be."

"Get your breath," she ordered. "Don't talk so fast."

Raysta bent toward him. "What boat?"

"A fishing boat."

"What's the boat got to do with the American?"

"On it they hid all sorts of things." Bissa's eyes shone brightly. "Did it someone out at sea."

"What sort of things?"

"Explosives, supplies, and uniform."

Shirn slapped her hands together flatly. "He's going to blow up Gregorski? Raysta, is that how he's going to kill him?" She twirled in excitement. "This assassin will do it that way!"

Raysta looked at her sharply. "He's no assassin."

She drew in a quick breath. "That's why he's coming, isn't it? Just to kill Gregorski?"

"He has other things to do. I haven't told you everything, for a damned good reason." He turned to Bissa. "How does this one get to the boat?"

Bissa nodded eagerly. "That I remember. Here we keep him for the night, and before sun tomorrow the boat we meet at the Ochakov fisherman's pier."

Shirn exploded in irritation. "That's stupid! The pier is right in the middle of the vacation resort. The place is crawling with Russian tourists, all those damned militiamen!" Ochakov was nine kilometers to the east of their village. A large agricultural and fishery center, it drew tourists from everywhere to its beaches and pleasures and to the excavation of Olvia, twenty-two kilometers away where a Greek colony had been established twenty-five hundred years before.

"How will we know the boat?" Raysta urged.

Bissa screwed up his forehead in concentration.

"Go ahead, you remember," Shirn prompted.

His eyebrows raised and he nodded. "Now I remember. The mast a leather belt will have nailed to it."

Raysta and Shirn digested the information. "Oh, sweet St. Cyril!" Raysta said at last.

"Are you sure, a belt?" Shirn prompted again.

Bissa's head bobbed up and down.

"All right," she said, "so the boat is marked and we find it. Then what happens?"

"The American we help get his things from the boat." Bissa smiled happily. "The courier, that's all he said."

It was silent in the cabin with only the hissing sound of the teapot to match their heavy breathing.

"My windup clock isn't working again," Shirn said. "We don't even know what time it is."

Bissa held up a thick arm. He pulled back the wrinkled

sleeve of his jacket and pointed to the cheap wristwatch. "I the time have!"

Raysta reached for the arm and studied the watch. "The courier gave you this?"

Bissa looked around, a guilty expression moving to his pudgy face. "Too much vodka one of the tourists had yesterday. From him I took it when he shook my hand after buying a carving!"

Raysta guffawed, and his large, stained teeth shone. "You sow's snout! You remember what I taught you after all!" He looked closely at the dial face. "It's almost a half to the fifth hour."

"We'd better go!" Shirn moved toward her room to get her jacket.

Raysta's voice stopped her. "You'll stay here. We'll go. Who knows what we'll find down at the beach?"

"This is my free day," she said defiantly. "I asked for it and got it. I want to come."

"It could be a trap. We know what to do. We'll look it over. If it gets messy, we can get away."

Bissa hitched his pants. "A man's job it is."

She looked at him, his powerful frame larded with a layer of fat. She looked at Raysta's scarecrow shape and said nothing. She watched them leave, a sack of peasant's clothes and an old towel in Raysta's arms, then savagely bolted the cabin door. She turned and leaned against it.

"I want to see Gregorski dead!" she said to the silent room. "I went with the UPA to help wake up my Ukrainia and to get help in killing Gregorski. What do they give me but Raysta, Bissa, and a damned American!" She went to the shabby table and picked up the teacup. She hurled it at the far wall and it made an angry, crashing sound.

"Ha!" she cried, feeling the terrible poison of hate bursting through her.

She reached for more things to throw.

CHAPTER THREE

Mother Russia was coming.

She was on time and on course, bursting through the Black Sea toward him in obscene arrogance, her fat belly filled with military cargo for Cuba, her red flag with its gold hammer and sickle whipping sharply in the predawn breeze.

Mikhail waited, listening to the approaching freighter, moving slowly in his frogman gear. The *Ustyug* had left Kherson hours before, coming down the wide Dneprovskiy Liman, bound along the shore lane for Odessa as a first stop to pick up more military cargo, then to Istanbul and the Mediterranean. He adjusted the sensitivity dial of the tiny underwater sound receiver built into his rubber hood. He looked again at the depth meter and watch strapped to his left wrist. He was at the correct depth and directly in her path. A ship the crew called *Mother Russia*.

A kilometer away, the fiberglass underwater-propulsion unit that had ferried him the long distance from the Turkish submarine to a position near the freighter's path was buried deep in the thick layer of black hydrogen-sulfide silt of the sea floor. It would be difficult to detect. Its final strength when he nosed it over had forced it almost completely into the silt.

He began his last-minute drill. He switched on the small underwater broadcasting unit attached to the bottom of his air tanks. It emitted the familiar sound of a school of Black Sea fish. *Mother Russia* would be listening on its sound unit. He untied a packet of aluminum foil strips from his side and shook them loose into the water. They floated freely and began to spread in the current. *Mother Russia* would hear the fish and pick up the strips on its scope, a reflection that would look like a cluster of fish. If it went well, he'd be obscured behind his shield of metallic decoys. The overhead watch of helicopters would find it difficult to pick him up visibly; he blended into the blackness of the sea's bottom, a bit darker than usual where he lay off the Ukrainian coast a short distance from the beach village of Ochakov.

Her noise grew louder until it became a thunder. He unhooked one of the two black packages from his chest and held it before his mask. The radium-marked timer was set for two hours. With one rubber-gloved hand he held the package, the size of a large dictionary, and with the other he activated the timed detonator switch, the big nonmetallic magnets and the propulsion-rise unit. He pushed the package upward and watched it rise swiftly. Looking up from his depth, he saw the massive shadow of the freighter's bow bearing down on his position. He dove, using powerful strokes of his arms and flippered legs to move him shoreward. The water twisted and beat around him, sending him rolling. The metallic thunder passed on, and the waters became quiet.

The package was fastened to *Mother Russia*'s belly. His timing had been perfect and he felt grateful to the underground for their precise information about the freighter. He thought of the underwater training he'd had, exercises such as this, where he'd placed magnetic-hold units on ships' bottoms to make their position and identity by American patrols more thorough. Trawlers off the coast of the United States, trawlers manned by Russian data-gathering specialists. It had been simple to convert that training to this mission. The package was superplastic explosive. Unless it was somehow dislodged or discovered, it would rip a hole in the *Ustyug*'s belly long before she arrived at the Odessa port.

His sound receiver picked up another set of screws. Captain Pell and his Ukrainian informants had been right. A submarine was escorting the freighter to Odessa where it was to pick up surface companions for its voyage to Cuba. The sub was to the protective seaward flank of the ship's path. Farther away he heard the terrier sounds of SO-1 and P-4 surface patrol boats.

The air from his tanks tasted rubbery, and he dragged at
the regulator. It purred softly, and the bubbles from it twirled
upward in an expanding cone. The water had long since
crept in between his rubber suit and his body, and he was
warm. He checked his compass and began to swim toward
the shore. He was too elated to feel tired, but he knew he
had less than half an hour left on the tanks. He pressed the
face mask to his nostrils and blew gently, equalizing the
pressure of rising from the lower depth. His ears cleared
with a hiss and a soft pop. He swam evenly, pacing himself.

His respect for Captain Pell had grown. The little intelligence officer was a professional. The plan had been worked
out meticulously. With the arrival of Gregorski in Odessa
there had to be a starting point to turn the first shovelful of
dirt for the colonel's grave. *Mother Russia* was carrying
new missiles and new long-range jet bombers to Cuba.
Stopping it would create a vast and immediate problem for
the new GRU commander. The GRU and KGB would, in
time, begin to understand what had happened. The trick
was to have them relate it to Gregorski. A dangerous trick.

As he swam he reviewed the danger that Mikhail Karlov
was in. At any moment he could be discovered. Had the
Ustyug really failed to spot him? Had the sub not missed
him? Had one of the helicopter spotters become suspicious?
What would be waiting for him when he reached the shore?

With ten minutes showing on his tank he pulled the
reserve valve and surfaced, allowing only the top of his
hooded head and his masked eyes to come out of the water.
The shore was two, perhaps three kilometers away. Ochakov
was in the distance to the west. He looked back at the trader
route. Another freighter was coming. He could see its white
trail on the horizon. Seabirds circled noisily overhead. Far
out to sea he heard an airplane moving at a low altitude
over the waves. From its sound he knew it was an old
Ilyushin-18 turboprop. He breathed easier when it bore south
on a new course, away from him, and disappeared. He
turned and studied the shoreline. His target was straight
north, between a tall cluster of trees to the northeast and a
rocky prominence to the northwest.

He began swimming landward. The water was lighter
but somehow colder in the fast current. He found the rock

shelf where Captain Pell had said it would be and was grateful it wasn't as deep as it was thought to be. He dived and his hands groped for a rocky pipe standing up from the sea floor, one of hundreds in the area, an upward finger of one of the rocky spines extending under water from the rock-littered beach out to sea. He dragged slowly at the regulator, making the remaining air last as long as possible. He hit the quick-release buckles for the weight belt and the harness for the tanks. He stripped the suit and fastened it to the scuba tanks. He gathered the watch, compass, depth gauge, the nonmetallic leg knife, the weights and fins, and tied them all together. He bound the cluster to the rock shaft, using a nylon cord he unreeled from a spool at the side of a tank. The black package was the last, and he tied it in such a way that it would have to be moved first. He set its triggering device. It was simply a booby trap but a well-concealed one.

He was naked except for his Russian-style swim trunks and so was shocked by the cold water. Satisfied that the entire unit was tied securely, he took a last breath from the tank, disengaged himself from it, and began the climb to the top, rising leisurely. His head broke water, and he blinked away the seawater, gulping in air. He set out for shore and a drowsiness overtook him. His arms began to feel like tree branches. Had he been in the water too long? He aimed at the cut in the high sandy cliff and locked his mind on the determination to get there.

But he heard voices.

Why was his mother screaming behind that door? Why was he alone and helpless? Why couldn't he get through that door and save his mother?

He fought to keep from thinking of what he found when he got through that door after his mother's screaming stopped.

"Is he dead?"

"I don't know."

Mikhail felt hands turning him. His face left the gritty sand, and he knew he'd been rolled onto his back. He fought for consciousness.

"Him you're sure the right one is, Raysta?" a hesitant, dullish voice said near him.

"Listen, you fat sack of goat dung!" the other voice answered sharply in a high, wheezy tone, "who else would be on this damned beach at this time except *him?*"

"If dead he is, Raysta, I'm sick going to be."

"He's not dead. He swam in from a damned submarine. He's out cold, that's all." Raysta was irritated. "Stop shaking like a rabbit. And don't puke! We're not supposed to leave any trace on the beach."

"I'm afraid of him," Bissa's voice said defensively. "Afraid you're not?"

"Hell, no, I'm not afraid."

"Military training you've had, that's why."

Mikhail managed to open one eye. The lid felt as if an old rusty hinge held it on. He shook his head slowly and the other eye opened. A short, lumpy villager who looked a good two hundred pounds of flab knelt next to him, his fat hands clasped prayerfully. His stare was returned by pale brown eyes set into a flushed, potato-shaped head. The beach was in the glow of the coming sunrise.

"You," Mikhail said in Ukrainian, "you're Bissa?"

Bissa nodded timidly, his eyes worried and unsure, his curly black hair hugging his plump forehead in damp desperation.

"You're the American?" the other voice said, and Mikhail turned his head, pain shooting into his neck, to see the other villager. This would be Raysta. The taller one was regarding him with dark suspicion. Tall and skinny, about six feet two or three. His words were rapid, his voice high and crisp. His triangular face was unhappy, and his stringy hair flapped loosely around his head in a grayish swirl in the gathering morning breezes. His peasant clothes, hanging loosely on his thin frame, were whipped by the harassing air. His shoulders seemed pulled together in an air of perpetual defiance. He carried an old tattered beach towel.

"I'm Mikhail Karlov," Mikhail said, rolling onto one side and lifting himself on an elbow. "You're to take me to Shirn."

"An American I thought you were," Bissa said in amazement. "A Russian name you have and Ukrainian you speak!" He blew out his cheeks and his eyes bulged.

"Bissa, you pile of cow manure," Raysta said unpleasantly, "help me get him up." He extended an arm to Mikhail, and Mikhail took the skinny hand in a tight grip. Bissa, hurrying, sniffed in loud complaint as he helped pull Mikhail to his feet. Upright, Mikhail leaned heavily on the short villager. Raysta wrapped the large towel around him.

Mikhail saw Bissa pull his short arms around his fat belly, hugging his shabby jacket against him. His soiled pants flapped noisily against his thick, stubby legs. He glanced past Bissa to the ugly beach, covered almost entirely with sharp-edged rocks and with only a few clear patches of sand. He looked at the high cliff. Small wonder the beach wasn't used much by the hordes of vacationers.

"For a saint's sake, let's get out of here," Raysta said, peering nervously at the sea. "My boots are gettin' wet."

Mikhail heard the seabirds wheeling in noisy alarm in the growing light over the sharply rising coastline. His strength was returning slowly to him. The warmth of the towel was making itself felt, but his naked feet were icy cold. He studied the villagers for a brief moment. Captain Pell had told him about them, simple men who'd taken in the woman, Shirn, and protected her, who would do anything she commanded. He hadn't expected a scarecrow and a tub of lard. The sight of them was so ridiculous, he nearly smiled. After all the training, after the voyage from the submarine, after giving *Mother Russia* a surprise gift, the turn of events on the beach was a letdown.

It's damned close to being comic opera, he thought. *How can these two peasants help me in what I have to do at Nikolayev? At Odessa?* They were the least likely grave diggers he could imagine. These were *cossacks?*

The Black Sea rolled in its restlessly probing waves in upward swaths across the rock-studded sand. Mikhail felt Raysta's sharp shoulder jam under his right arm, and he was moved toward the cliff, Bissa's surprising great strength on the other side. He noticed that Raysta's rumpled jacket was missing half its buttons. The food-smeared *vyshyvanka* pullover was unbuttoned at the throat, and a small patch of gray hair thrust out of the opening. The tall villager's trousers, sizes too big, were drawn tight at the waist by an old leather belt, reddish brown with rot in places. His *tchoboty*, knee-high boots, were scuffed and sand-caked. He smelled of body stench.

At the top of the cliff Mikhail stiffened. He pushed Raysta and Bissa away from him. "Down!" he commanded. "Get under cover!" He dove for a bush and pushed himself underneath it, pulling the towel around him. Bissa following on his heels, came bouncing after him.

"What's the matter?" Bissa said in a choked voice.

"Shut up!" Raysta growled from a clump of tall grass.

The helicopter was skirting the beach, flying low but fast. The sound grew until it filled their ears. The machine seemed to pause at the beach and then moved on.

Mikhail stood up, searching the skies. "That was close. No time for me to dress. Raysta, get back to the beach and wipe out our tracks. Bissa, you show me where the *khootir* is." Bissa seemed struck deaf. "Move!" he commanded sharply. "We've work to do tonight!" Bissa turned and started down a narrow path along the edge of the cliff. Raysta, he saw, went long-legged over the edge of the cliff, a branch of bush in his hand to sweep the sand and rocks. Bissa's path led to another and to others. They were soon in the forest, a thick, cloistering, wide spread of trees veined with narrow trails.

Mikhail, following the dumpy villager, was impressed. Captain Pell had said the Underground respected these two. No one knew the back trails as well as they did, trails of the hills near the coast.

"Late we are," Bissa said. "Angry Shirn'll be."

"How long have you known her?"

"Shirn? Six years."

Six years? Shirn was supposed to be a tough fighter in the nationalist Underground, a woman who could throw grenades at army convoys, cut fences, burn military buildings.

"To the village she came then," Bissa said over his sloping shoulder. "A little girl, fifteen. From Kirovograd. Dead was her family. Our *khootir* we gave her. It we inherited from the old tanner."

"Where do you stay?"

"In the back a stable. The tanner his hides cured there."

Mikhail grunted. The stink of the old tanning was still on Bissa. "Is that what you do, tan leather?"

Bissa pushed some branches out of the way. "A wood carver I am." There was a note of pride in the blunted voice. "I sell to vacationers my own wood carvings."

"How long have you known Raysta?"

Bissa cast another look over his shoulder, but Mikhail couldn't see his face in the forest gloom. "Him I've known since I a boy am. He was in the Great Patriotic War. A hero he was, a great soldier! In he took me and gave me a home."

"Why?"

Bissa was puffing loudly with the effort of walking fast and talking over his shoulder. "Died my family when the factory in which they worked exploded. Many died. They died."

Mikhail nodded in sympathy, holding the towel tight around him, keeping his eyes on the shuffling man in front of him. The UPA Underground, through Captain Pell, had said Bissa was thought to be about thirty-five, a ward of Raysta who was either fifty-four or fifty-five. Even the Underground wasn't certain. If what Bissa said was true, Shirn had to be twenty-one. That was too damn young for a job as important as this! Trailing in the heavy body odor of Bissa, he became irritated.

"What does Raysta do?" he asked, trying to stem his annoyance. He recalled what Pell had said about the scarecrow; Raysta's family had been killed by the Germans in an air bombing.

"He an electrician is," Bissa said proudly. "Education he's had. The electrician trade after the war he was taught. In the war a great soldier, the best rifle shooter!"

"Does he live with you?"

"Room we have. In the village he works, a *selianya*."

"Tell me about Shirn," Mikhail persisted. "What does she do?"

Bissa stumbled and caught himself, hopping quickly to ease the pain of the hurt toe. "A truck she drives," he said. "For the collective."

"You know about Gregorski?"

Bissa stopped suddenly, and Mikhail slammed against him, nearly knocking the villager to his knees. In the dim light he saw Bissa's fat face, worried, one fat cheek twitching. "Him a cruel man is!" Bissa said in a shaking voice. "Shirn's mother and father he sent away, far away, and died they did."

Bissa shook his head in simple bewilderment. "Her father a factory is managing, army engines is making. That's all I know. Fast enough no one made them. The GRU sent them away to a far place. And died they did."

"Gregorski, he's the one who sent them away?"

Bissa nodded rapidly, his fat head pumping up and down vehemently. He turned and pointed down the trail. "The *khootir,* it's there."

Mikhail saw the dark silhouette of the cabin ahead, almost hidden in the thick grove of trees. Bissa began to lope down the trail, and Mikhail followed. At the door Bissa moved its latch timidly and it was thrown open. A feminine voice, vibrant and exciting but vastly irritated, burst into the clearing.

"Where've you been?" Shirn shouted accusingly. "You're late! Where's Raysta? Where is *he?*"

Mikhail moved from behind Bissa and into the light streaming out of the door. He stared at her, unbelieving. "You can't be the one," he said in confusion.

She motioned to the cabin. "Come in, quickly!" There was a sound down the trail, and Mikhail turned. Raysta, wheezing and panting heavily, joined them, lugging the sack of clothes.

"I thought I'd never get up that pissy cliff again," he said between squeaky breaths. "I'm too old for running in the hills." He fished out the extra bottle of vodka hidden in the wood box under the birch logs and began drinking thirstily from it. He avoided looking at Shirn as he did.

Mikhail followed Bissa into the cabin, padding on his bare feet, and heard the door shut and bar latch slam into place. He turned to meet the green eyes probing him.

"What do you mean, I can't be the one?"

He shook his head. "They didn't tell me how young you'd be. I thought you'd be older." He paused, searching for words to dispel his disorientation. How could anyone in their right minds put a beautiful young girl like *this* into the plan!

She raised her face to the ceiling and let out a shriek. "Who the hell did you expect? Catherine the Great?"

He looked around at them, knowing his face must be mirroring his astonishment. It was too ridiculous to be a trap. The one thing that convinced him of what the truth was in the mean little *khootir* was the fire in the girl's eyes. Honest fire. Honest hatred. Honest distrust. She was four years younger than he, despite the fact that she'd earned her spurs in the Underground. He recovered and made his move to adjust to the bizarre situation. He removed one hand from the towel and held it out to her, American-style, not quite able to give the traditional Russian bearhug greeting to a fiery Ukrainian nationalist girl.

"Shim," he said gently, smiling suddenly at the outrage stamped on her thoroughly attractive face, "I'm Mikhail Karlovich Karlov."

She refused to accept his hand. "The commanders said you were an American." She withdrew a few feet and studied him cautiously. "You've a Russian name and you speak Ukrainian."

"I'm all of these things."

"They said you'd have code words to identify yourself."

He nodded and felt his smile fade. Captain Pell had been right. The girl was a tough one. A good fighter.

"A grave for Gregorski," he said.

For a long moment their eyes were locked, and then she seemed to relax. "Raysta," she said with authority, "stop your drinking and go get him clothes that fit. He's bigger than what we have in that sack. Bissa, build up the fire and go with him. You must report to the commanders that he's here." She turned to the *piche*. "I'll make you something to eat."

Mikhail watched her, admiring the sweep of her hips and the curves of her legs. Pell, again, had been right.

They *would* make a great pair.

He wrote down his sizes on a scrap of paper and handed it to Raysta. The two villagers were arguing, pleasantly, about the best way to rekindle the fire. The tall, thin one drank a lot. That was obvious. The fat one was retarded but not dangerously. There was an air of brotherly affection between the two despite their sharp words and needling banter.

Bissa came to him, holding an object. "I this made," he said, "and welcome to you I give." It was a wooden carving of a horse and a Ukrainian cossack, and it was beautifully done. Mikhail turned it slowly, marveling at the fine knife-carving work. The expression of the cossack was intense, determined. It was faintly similar to Raysta, a long, triangular face. The Cossack had an arm raised, and in his hand he held a curving sword. His head was shaved except for a single lock of long hair in the middle of the head.

"This *poostoholovyi* does good with the knife?" Raysta said, motioning to the carving.

"Who's a numskull?" Bissa objected, glaring unhappily around him. "I a cossack am!"

"Oh, sweet saint," Raysta said. He took Bissa by the arm and they left, going noisily through the *khootir* door on their way to contact the UPA commanders secretly in the village, to get the clothes and to report that the big American had arrived. Mikhail studied the carving again. Something bothered him. What was it?

The way they talked. A mixture of Ukrainian and Russian. That was it. Mikhail experienced a strange sensation. He was able to translate the Ukrainian and Russian of Shirn and Raysta into English, easily and naturally, because they spoke at the normal pace. But Bissa's halting, uneducated style interrupted this process, and what came to him was the literal order of words. If Shirn were to say, "We don't have enough food" in Ukrainian, he would understand it in those words in English. But if Bissa said the same thing, it would remain literal, "To us there is not enough food."

Mikhail shook his head, wondering to himself what else there was about the fat little villager that jarred the translation process he'd so patiently learned at the Ukrainian village in Canada. Bissa had a strange, totally personal way of fracturing even the Ukrainian idioms. The fat one was not purely a *patiakalo,* a talker without any sense, but he good-naturedly came close to it.

He looked at Shirn, bending over at the fireplace, and felt a quick reaction again to her smoothly rounded hips.

Uneasy, he forced his gaze to the wooden carving he held in his hand. It was one of the best he'd ever seen. Bissa might be retarded and difficult to understand, but he was full of expression with his carvings. Bissa and Raysta, what a pair! Then he smiled.

He was in the Land of the Ukrainian cossacks!

Vera Gregorovich listened at the door of her father's bedroom and heard his rasping sounds of sleep.

Satisfied, she went through the compact living room of the army apartment and entered her own small, plain bedroom. The light was off, and she carefully closed the door behind her. She went to the window and pulled the drapes shut against the Odessa morning. She turned on the light and studied the room. She'd finished her unpacking, and most of the things were put away neatly. She sat at the tiny desk and looked at her Intourist folder. Printed on it was the title Directorate for Foreign Tourists with the Council of Ministers of the USSR.

She ran a small hand over the folder. Yesterday she'd been in Moscow, packing for a vacation and debating whether to dress up and go to the Labyrinth Club in the cellar of the Arbat restaurant that evening before her plane left for Sochi. Yesterday she'd completed the tour with the English group, flying back from the Samarkand archaeological center near Tashkent.

The disappointment had been bitter, but the two GRU officers made it perfectly clear. Colonel Gregorski wanted her to join him in Odessa. Odessa! Her vacation had gone flying. A GRU matron, fat and unsmiling, escorted her on the military transport, herded her and her baggage into the apartment, and remained with her until her father returned from his meeting with General Zagorsky.

She patted the folder and placed it in a drawer. There was still the report on the English group. She'd been rushed from Moscow so quickly, she hadn't finished it, and only a frantic call from the airport to Intourist had gained her the time to finish it in Odessa. Well, a GRU colonel's daughter had *some* privileges.

The sight of Odessa had depressed her. It had none of the flair and beauty of the vacation resorts near Sochi along the eastern shore of the Black Sea. Odessa with its population of one million was the most highly Russianized city in Tavria. Vacationers came, but they were party members, thick headed, stolid Russians. It was a great seaport, but the concentration of grain elevators destroyed its appearance as far as she was concerned. Still, it had beautiful beaches and sun, and it had some possibilities for her, scant as they may be with her father at hand.

She turned to the bureau and studied herself in the mirror. Her face, framed by her braided blond hair, was sober, squarish, set off with incredibly blue eyes that held a touch of sadness. She began to dress, watching herself in the faded, streaked mirror. Sadness, yes. She'd hoped to meet someone in Sochi, perhaps someone she could love. A man to marry, a man to have as her own.

A man to take her away from her father.

She put on a dress and slipped into shoes. A small transitor radio lay on the table next to her and she flicked its switch. She would leave the radio on to ward off the loneliness of the strange apartment. It smelled damp, musty from the sea air.

The countless army migrants who'd lived in it probably had suffered its same loneliness. She curled her small body, waiting for her father to awake. They would breakfast together. She sat for a long time listening to the radio, not really hearing it, thinking the same bleak thoughts that had worn grooves in her mind.

She had to find some way to free herself from her father. How many times had she prayed for his death? Prayed for the joy of hearing he'd been killed? That one of his women had found the courage to thrust a knife into his heart?

She closed her eyes and thought of her mother, remembering the warmth of her arms, the tenderness of her voice. She reached out involuntarily to touch her mother's face and felt only the moist air of the room.

For a long time she sat rigid, fighting tears, fighting the need to sob it all out.

Then she surrendered to her tears.

The warm, friendly odor of the teapot filled the cabin. Sipping a cup, Mikhail studied the *khootir*. Everything was in the one room, the worn furniture, the single bed, the darkened fireplace where Shirn did the cooking, the water bucket from the outside well, old frayed rugs on the floor. Cheaply framed lithographs of the Ukrainian steppes and the coastal hills of the Crimea hung on the walls. A wardrobe was built into one corner. The two small windows were shut, latched, and covered with heavy curtains. The businesslike fireplace competed with the smell of the tea. The single light bulb hanging from the ceiling was still on.

The borscht she'd made had been excellent. He'd watched her curiously as she put in the stewing chicken; red beets; stewed tomatoes; potatoes; cabbage; parsley; parsnip roots for flavor, taken out later; and a large handful of dill. The kasha, a thick serving of cooked pearled barley, and the *kovbasa*, homemade pork sausage, had appealed to him. He'd gone heavy on the *varenyky*, which resembled stuffed dumplings filled with farmer's cheese, mashed potatoes, cabbage, mushrooms, and meat. Shirn had boiled the *varenyky* in water and served it with sour cream and fried onions. With all that there'd been sweet-smelling white bread. Looking at her, he wondered how with such food she'd been able to keep her figure as trim and as desirable as it was.

He'd wanted a cup of coffee, a habit he'd picked up in the States, but the tea was pleasant. He knew that in the Ukraine, coffee, as Americans knew it, was almost nonexistent. Barley sometimes was scorched and used like coffee, but it wasn't popular. He was drinking *tchajz vareniam*, tea with cherry preserves. Watching Shirn move around the cabin, he thought of their code names. *Idy do bissa* meant "go to the devil." Bissa? Touched by the devil? Raysta meant a gray horse of Arabian stock, one with white round spots. Raysta a wild horse? Shirn had no Ukrainian meaning he knew of. He wondered what her real name was. Iksana, Marika, Hanna, Natalka, Lesia, what? And she spoke passable English.

"How long will it take them?" he asked.

Shirn, cleaning up from his meal, glanced at him. "Who knows? Those two! When they're out together, they're like traveling circus clowns." She poured herself tea and sat down across the table from him. "Are you warm enough?"

"I'll feel better when they get back with clothes. This towel doesn't exactly do the job."

"Why did you leave your underwater suit tied to the bottom? Why didn't you bring it with you?"

"We want it found."

She was surprised. "Why?"

"The GRU and the KGB will know a saboteur was put ashore. We want them to worry about it."

"That's stupid. Why do you want them to know you're here?"

"It takes the play away from you Ukrainians. The Russians will believe there's some sort of international plot under way. They won't blame you at the outset."

Understanding flooded to her face. She put her fingers around her cup. "Now I see."

"There's something else. One of their ships will blow up in about a half hour."

"How do you know that?"

"Just believe it."

"Your submarine will sink it?"

"A frogman put an explosive on its bottom."

Her eyebrows rose, but she said nothing.

"We've got to get to Ochakov very early in the evening and get my things off the fishing boat," he said. "The crew will take me out with them. I'll transfer everything to a rubber raft and bring it back to the beach. Bissa and Raysta can help me bring it here."

"Ochakov! That's risky. Why pick that place?"

"The old theory. You're least noticed in a busy place. No one will notice me going on board. The touchy part will be getting back to the beach. That's why we want to do it just before the evening meal when everyone is inside."

"Why did they send only one man?"

"Because it's harder to track down a single. There's the element of surprise of there being just one man. They'll have a hell of a time figuring out *why*."

"Our people helped you with the fishing boat?"

"It was part of the plan. I can't do much good here if I don't have the things I need. I couldn't bring them ashore. The boat was the easiest way."

"Wasn't it dangerous to bring a submarine so close to shore?"

He thought of the underwater propulsion unit but allowed nothing to show on his face. The sub hadn't been that close. The one-man propulsion unit had made the difference, and it was buried in the silt.

"Damned dangerous. They've been doing it deliberately every night for two weeks. This fitted into it."

"But the Russians, won't they know you got out of it?"

"Every evening at the same spot the Turks dumped their sacks of food wastes. Today they dumped me instead."

He poured tea into their cups, holding the towel with his free hand. He studied her from the corners of his eyes. "I'm curious about you. Why are you willing to work with me?"

Anger replaced concentration on her face, and it surprised him. "That's a stupid thing to ask! Why else are you here?" Her voice rose. "To work with *me!*"

He wouldn't allow his astonishment to show. He forced a smile to his face. "We'd better get this straight. This is my mission. Your commanders said you, Bissa, and Raysta were assigned to me."

She rose so quickly, she knocked her chair backward. *"Who* assigned us to *you?* The hell anyone did that! I didn't ask for any damned American to come here. I asked our own men to do this and they were frightened, like mice!" She smashed her teacup to the floor.

He kept the smile on his face. "That doesn't match what I was told." He sipped casually at the tea. "The picture was that Gregorski is in Odessa and that you and the Underground want him killed. Your commanders want to avoid mass imprisonment and retribution deaths. They worked it out with the Americans to send me in."

Shirn's anger faded slowly. "You will kill Gregorski?" she asked suspiciously.

"The colonel will die."

She nodded and looked at the floor. "All right, but we don't belong to you. You can't run around here giving us orders."

"Then forget about it."

The soft way he spoke shocked her. "Forget about it!"

she shouted. "I'll be damned if I'll forget about it!"

"Gregorski is going to get it, but I'll need help. It's too big a job for one man. The Americans worked this out with your Underground. It was understood."

"It wasn't Shirn who understood it."

"If you and your men don't help, I'll go it alone." He paused. "But you can wait for the bloodbath because I won't be able to keep my out-tunnel clear."

"You damn Americans," she exploded. "You act like you own the world. Who the hell are you to tell me what to do?"

"American? Who's an American?"

"You are!"

"Because I came from a Turkish submarine with Americans on board?" He laughed and pulled the towel over his bare legs. "Didn't your people tell you anything?"

"Only that a man would be sent in to kill Gregorski."

"Shirn," he said evenly, "I'm a Russian. I was born Mikhail Karlovich Karlov in Kalinin. You know where that is?"

She bit the words. "North of Moscow."

"My father was an electrical engineer. One of the best. He helped rebuild the Dneiper Dam transmission-and-distribution system after the war. My mother was a cryptographer, a code clerk in Moscow."

"If you're a Russian, how'd you end up with the Americans?" Her eyes were dark with suspicion. "And how do you speak Ukrainian like"—she searched for a word—"like one of us?"

"They assigned my mother to the code room at the embassy in Washington. She worked there for a year and then told them that if I wasn't sent to her, she wanted to go home. She was lonely for me and my father."

"They sent you?"

"I was nine years old. My father visited me at Kalinin as often as he could, flying in when he could from the Dneiper project. He couldn't keep me there. He was an important engineer. He had friends then in Moscow who helped get the approval to send me to America."

"But now you're working with the Americans. What kind of a Russian are you?"

"That's hard for you to understand?" He leaned back in the old chair, and it protested against his weight. "My mother was killled in the embassy." His eyes were half-lidded, and his chin was on his chest. His voice seemed to come from a distance.

For a moment Shirn thought she saw him shiver under the thin towel. She found herself unable to move.

"She was killed by an army intelligence captain."

Stunned, Shirn made a move toward him, but he stood up suddenly, his head cocked. She heard the same sounds. The latch moved gently. She went to the door and opened it. Bissa and Raysta stumbled in, laden with heavy newspaper-wrapped packages. They both breathed in short gasps from their exertion. Sweat poured down their faces. Raysta leaned wearily against the table with one trembling hand and fished an envelope from a pocket with the other. He handed it to Mikhail.

"Before we left," he said between gasps, "the courier told Bissa to tell you a ship went down thirty kilometers out of Odessa. I don't understand, but they said to tell you that."

Mikhail moved to the packages and began untying them. "The timer was accurate," he said thoughtfully.

"The fishermen were caught by a patrol," Raysta went on. He held his stomach with both hands pressed to it. "This damned gut!" He winced with pain. "It's not at Ochakov."

Mikhail was stunned. "Where is it?"

"The courier told Bissa the patrol took it to Parutino."

Mikhail leaned on the old table. "How far is that from here?"

"A hell of a good walk, I'll tell you that."

"Where is Shirn's truck?"

"In the collective. Locked up with the others."

"Did the patrol tear the boat apart?"

Raysta shook his head and sweat flew from it. "The courier told pee sack here it was brought into the harbor this morning. The navy bastards looked it over but didn't do anything to it. It's sitting there, tied to the dock."

"The crew?" Mikhail straightened. "Were they arrested?"

"The navy talked to them and let them go. They sold

their catch and disappeared." He sniffed. "The patrol went back to sea."

Mikhail looked at them in turn. That was part of the plan. If anything happened outside of the plan, the crew was to leave the ketch and go into hiding. He made the decision. "Then we'll have to get my stuff off of it as fast as we can. We won't wait until evening. We'll go to Parutino now." It would be dangerous to take the truck and travel by the roads. They'd have to go cross-country, sticking to the back trails.

"Oh, sweet saint!" Raysta moaned. "We're only cossacks, not supermen!"

"Give me a hand with this," Mikhail said to Shirn.

Silently they undid the rest of the packages and in minutes he was dressed in Ukrainian clothes, old and used, with long *tchoboty* boots. The embroidered thread of the collar and foot-long button slit of his pullover shirt was the only fresh item. It was blood-red. He opened the envelope and read the message, then handed it to Shirn.

"These are orders from your people. You're to be my team. Bissa's to be the only contact between us and the cell. From this point on all messages are verbal."

Shirn read the message, then took it to the fireplace and watched it turn to black ashes.

"This captain?" she said to Mikhail.

He adjusted his belt, pulled on a cap, and began stuffing his pockets with forged identification papers, a pipe, tobacco, rubles and kopecks, and the small items Ukrainian men carried. The forgeries were excellent, done on regular Russian forms.

"Rykan Gregorski," he answered tonelessly. "The same man who shipped your mother and father away. The same man who hunted UPAs here nineteen years ago and again six years ago. The same man who's having a grave dug for him right now."

Shirn held her hands tight together in front of her. "You knew? When you were talking to me, you knew?"

"We had to get it established who's in charge," he said. "It either had to be your hate or mine."

He turned to the villagers. "As soon as you get your breath, we'll go to where the boat is. We haven't any time to waste."

Raysta was appalled. "Sweet Cyril," he complained. "Can't we have some vodka first?"

"You've had enough vodka here," Shirn said slowly. She seemed lost in thought. She began putting on her boots, jacket, and a head scarf.

"For God's sake, then some tea at least!" Raysta held a hand to his throat in a plea.

"In what would we drink it?" Bissa's hesitant voice said. "In the cabin only one cup is left."

Mikhail emptied the last sack and held up a small bottle. "They had you in mind," he said, and grinned as he saw Raysta's eyes beam at the cloudy pale yellow vodka. Raysta moved toward it, and Mikhail slid the bottle into his jacket pocket. "First eat, and then the boat. I'll give you a drink along the way." He waited until they finished eating and then looked at Shirn. "We've a long walk. Let's get going."

Outside, he halted them as they formed a single line on the path. He listened for a long time to the noises in the wooded area. They were near the village, but the cabin was set in the deep forest and the way to it was tricky. He heard nothing unusual and started off behind Bissa and Raysta on the long trek that would take them to Parutino, a village of fishermen on the Black Sea. Where the small boat waited.

He felt a tug on his sleeve from Shirn, who walked closely behind him.

"He had no reason to deport my parents. You know that?"

"Yes."

"He wanted another mark on his record. He beat my father with a blackjack, but my father wouldn't sign a confession."

Mikhail walked in silence. She tugged at his sleeve again.

"Why did he kill your mother?"

Without turning he said, "She wouldn't become one of his conquests. She fell from a window trying to escape him." They walked in silence, hearing only the boots of Bissa and Raysta ahead of them.

"I stood outside her bedroom and heard her screaming. I beat on the door with my fists until they were bloody. She stopped, the screams stopped, and he came out of the door and walked right by me. He didn't see me. His eyes were like a madman's. I ran into the room. The window was open. I looked down and saw my mother on the courtyard below. I ran down to her and tried to lift her. She'd been whipped and her clothes were torn. She was dead. . . ." His voice trailed off.

"Oh, Mikhail!" Shirn found his hand and held on to it.

"There was blood coming from her mouth and her nose," he said.

They spoke no more for long hours until they crested a small hill and saw the village of Parutino ahead of them. He pulled the bottle from his pocket and handed it to Raysta.

Then he sat down, brought his knees up, and buried his head in his arms.

Shirn sat near him, waiting.

CHAPTER FOUR

The colonel was the first to respond to the rough pounding on the apartment door. Pulling on a robe, he opened the door. Sergeant Timkin's pale blue eyes, set high in his round pink face, were excited. He saluted quickly. "You are to come at once, Comrade Colonel," he announced importantly. "The Comrade General's orders."

"Come in. I've got to get dressed." He shut the door and saw Vera peering from the edge of her bedroom door. "Some sort of emergency," he said to her.

Her blond head disappeared. He dressed rapidly and followed the sergeant to the sedan waiting on the street outside the apartment building. The air was cooler, fresher. The first rays of the sun were striking the harbor.

"You know nothing?"

"No, Comrade Colonel. They woke me and told me to bring you without delay. That's all I know." The sergeant drove quickly through the streets. Only a few people were out, some wearing the red armbands of the citizen watch-guard. The drab streets and unopened shops had a depressing effect.

"You're a fool, Timkin," the colonel said, buttoning his tunic. "You've obviously never learned to keep your ears open and hear things. The GRU is plagued by idiots like you."

He watched sourly through the sedan's window as Timkin turned the sedan into the vast compound, stopped at the gate, waited for the guards to check and clear them, then spurted the sedan to the general's headquarters building. He heard the loud sigh with relief as he dog-trotted up the steps. Over his shoulder he saw Timkin pull out a rag and begin wiping off the dead insects the windshield had collected.

General Zagorsky was red-faced. "They sent a nice welcome to you, Comrade Colonel. The freighter *Ustyug* blew up thirty kilometers from here."

He took his cap off and laid it carefully on a chair. "Where was the *Ustyug* bound?"

"Cuba. It was carrying our newest shore-to-sea missiles." He growled. "Sunk! Half of the crew went down with it!"

"What caused the explosion?"

The general folded his arms in disgust. "Don't ask a childish question! How do we know? We'll have to send divers down to find out. There was no radio message, nothing. Our helicopters and the submarine escort reported a tremendous series of explosions. The freighter rolled and sank almost immediately." He slapped the desk with a thick hand. "It's for *you* to find out what happened!"

The colonel saw the ill-concealed look of dislike in the general's eyes. "What do the intelligence reports say?"

He watched as the general picked up sheets of computer reports. "It could have been the Turkish submarine. One was reported in the general area of the freighter's route only four hours before it reached that area. It's the same sub that's been laying just off the international line every night at the same time. It jettisoned its trash, and our divers are looking for it."

"That's all? Just a submarine report?"

"No, that's not all. One of our helicopters reported what appeared to be tracks leading from the water to the top of a hill at this beach." The general strode to the area map and marked an *X* on it. "Here. Near Ochakov. It was still dark, and they saw no one on the beach."

"That's a vacation spot. It could have been anyone."

"This doesn't sound like a hunter to me." The words were salted with sarcasm.

"When will the Navy have its divers down for the *Ustyug?*"

"They're moving in now."

The door opened and a young officer entered.

"I believe you said you know Captain Prokov," the general said, a faint trace of a smile on his face. "He'll get you all of the men you need and work as liaison between the ground, naval, and air forces."

The colonel nodded a curt greeting to Captain Prokov, who stood at ease near the general. He studied the man carefully. So that's the way it's to be, he thought. Prokov was cookie-cut from the state security apparatus. Young, muscular, broad-shouldered, tightly contained in body and action. The blue Russian eyes revealed nothing. The face was unlined with care stresses. It looked pink and healthy in the bright light of the office. His uniform fit perfectly, and he looked GRU. So Prokov, whom he'd known briefly in Moscow, was to keep him in sight at all times? A watchdog for the general? And, if his suspicions were right, a double agent for the KGB. The Komitet Gosudarstvennoi Bezopasnosi ranked far more importantly in Moscow than did the Army's GRU. It was part of their game to infiltrate the GRU with agents. He felt himself swallow. The KGB had more than a hundred thousand trained operators. It could spare quite a few infiltrators to keep an eye on its competitor, the GRU.

"I would like copies of all of the reports," he said to the general, avoiding Captain Prokov's eyes. "I read the material you gave me earlier, and I have a list"—he took it from his tunic pocket—"of the men I request be assigned to me." He smiled bleakly. "In addition to Captain Prokov, of course."

The general studied the paper and said nothing. Captain Prokov spoke. "Comrade Colonel, the communications room is in full operation. The code room is well staffed. The entire network is functioning. We have planes in the air. The navy has put more of our observers aboard to work with theirs. Every military installation is on full alert." He paused. "There was nothing from the sonobuoys this morning. That puzzles me."

He nodded. The captain *was* efficient. Young and ambitious. He would find a way to discover if this young genius *was* a KGB man. If Prokov was, he could not easily be eliminated. But he could be neutralized. There were ways. "I request to be excused, General, with the captain, so that we can get our hunt under way at once."

"There's one item that's not fully emphasized in those reports," the captain said as they entered the colonel's office.

"What's that?"

"A fishing boat. It was seen tied up alongside a Turkish supply ship yesterday. The crew was taken in custody as soon as they returned to shore. They said the Turks helped them fix their engine."

"Had it been worked on?"

"That's the strange thing. It had new Turkish spark plugs and two new gaskets of Turkish make. It had been repaired, no doubt about it."

"Nothing else on board?"

The captain grimaced. "Fish, nothing but fish and three Ukrainian fishermen."

"I'll have a look at it." He pointed to the map. "This beach. What do you know about it?"

"Not a very good one. Few vacationers use it because it's a bit isolated from the others. That cliff is a mean one to get down and up."

"The *Ustyug*. Will you get me more details on its cargo and crew? I want to know everything about her. What was her route?"

"She was fitted and loaded at Kherson. She left there late yesterday." The captain looked at his wristwatch. "She carried missiles, you knew that?"

"The general mentioned it."

"The hottest ones. Cuba's been begging for them."

"What stops?"

"Odessa was the only one. She was to pick up new radar equipment for the Cuban air force. She had eight helicopters, three long-range jet bombers, six torpedo boats, aviation fuel, and a great deal of small ammunition aboard."

"Small wonder she blew. With the evidence we have now, what would your guess be as to what caused it?"

Prokov's smooth face was unworried, but his eyes betrayed his concern. "The Turkish submarine was involved somehow. I feel certain of that. But its closest inshore position was fairly far from the beach. It was south by southwest of Ochakov, well out in international waters. Too far out for a frogman to make it on his own. Very suspicious. I don't know why they'd come that close. They didn't surface. Approach and return. It doesn't make sense. Still, there were those footprints the helicopter reported."

The colonel remembered that he'd left his cap in the

general's office. He decided he would send Timkin in for it. He sat down at his desk and motioned the captain to be seated.

"Now, let's go over all of the reports once more. Then we'll check all sources of information and continue through the day. I want you to get my staff assembled as rapidly as you can. We're going to set up the biggest hunt this district has ever seen." He looked squarely at the young officer. "I agree with you about the footprints at the beach. Our trail may start there." The captain, however, was staring at something on his desk.

He looked down and saw that the fingers of his gloved hands were caressing each other.

Mikhail studied the village spreading below them. Far on its other side was the seacoast, rugged and impressive under its sunlit mantle. Rutted into the land were two spiny canals, begun centuries ago to bring fishing boats into the small manmade harbor, one for passage in and the other for exit. The church steeples and the antennas of the police station were the tallest fingers with which the tired village reached into its sky.

Parutino was a fisherman's village, tied with the surrounding agricultural enterprises. A market, granaries, a slaughterhouse, a school, a bus depot, a children's playground, a wide central square, and even an Automat for sweet Russian soft drinks. Magnolia trees were everywhere.

The houses were made of coral stone and some of clay. Most of them had straw roofs. Many of the houses were surrounded with white coral stone fences. Cherry and poplar trees stood silent in the late-afternoon heat. Every house had its well. In the center of the village was the *silbood,* the communal house. It held the central radio transmission unit. The State radio propaganda transmissions were received and broadcast by loudspeakers both inside and outside the *silbood.* When the loudspeakers were on, everyone in the village was forced to listen to them. There were only a handful of TV antennas visible, owned by the most influential persons in the village, the party leaders.

The harbor had nearly a hundred boats of all sizes and shapes. The larger ones were tied to the docks and wharfs.

The smaller ones rode at anchor. The harbor was graced by more magnolia and eucalyptus trees and tended beds of sunflowers, lilacs, and tiny rosebushes.

"Too many of the boats look alike," he said. "I'll have to get closer to see which one is ours." He stopped, peering at the harbor. "Do they always have a guard on the dock?"

Raysta crawled near to his shoulder. "Guard? What kind?"

"Army. With submachine gun."

"Only ones I've seen there are the crappy militia louts."

"That one looks like a soldier to me." He took the small telescope tube from a pocket, pulled it to its length, and studied the area carefully. He handed it to Raysta. "Take a look. A soldier. Something's up."

"What's up?" Bissa asked nervously.

"Shut up, you bucket of lard," Raysta said, the spyglass to his eye. "And stay down out of sight."

"If there's soldiers there, going down I'm not."

"Well, there's one." Raysta handed the spyglass to Mikhail. "I'm not going down, either."

"Heroes," Shirn said. "Cossack heroes!"

"They know all about the boat," Raysta said. "They're just waitin' for us to walk up to it. They'll shoot us without mercy."

"You're wrong," Mikhail said. "If they knew about the boat, they'd hide and wait for us to come. I think the reason they're guarding it is because they're expecting some big shot to come and inspect it." He grunted. "They've probably been trying to find out what happened to their freighter."

"Mikhail's right," Shirn said. She knelt under a bush, her face barely discernible in the shade of the surrounding trees. "If they knew, they'd let us walk into a trap. Why warn us with an armed guard?"

Bissa made a noise. "What are you doing?" Raysta asked in irritation.

"I well don't feel. Myself I'm relieving."

"The guard changes the situation," Mikhail said. "We must get the boat out of the harbor at once. I'll need time to get my equipment out of it. I can't do that under his nose."

"You'll never get it away from that harbor," Shirn said.

"If I can, where's the best place to meet you just before dark?"

"There's a small cove two or three kilometers east of the beach where we found you," Raysta said. "You could come ashore there." He described it carefully. A path skirted the cove, and a grove of small trees at the top of the butting hill would serve as a meeting place.

"Come here, all of you." Mikhail waited for them to squat near him. "We need a diversion. Raysta, take the bottle and pretend to be drunk. Go up to the guard and get him talking to you. Shirn, you and Bissa work your way down to the wall around the park. Pick up whatever you can along the way, things to throw, bottles, rocks, bricks. If Raysta can't get the guard diverted long enough, you start throwing things over the rooftops onto the streets. Make plenty of noise and then get the hell out of there. Meet me at the cove."

"What about me?" Raysta said, worried. "That bastard might shoot me!"

Mikhail put a hand on Raysta's trembling shoulder. "You've got the best excuse in the world. You're drunk. Just lie down and go to sleep."

"What are you going to do?" Shirn asked.

Mikhail moved off. "I'm going to get the ketch," he said simply.

Raysta, his guts in a knot, staggered from the side street.

"Who's there!" the guard said, pulling his machine pistol into a ready position. Another guard, asleep in the shadow of a large flowering bush nearby, rose and joined him.

Raysta clattered in a drunken prance around the cobblestone intersection at the entrance to the harbor.

"You're drunk, Granddad," the young guard said. "Go on home. The militiamen will catch you and put you in the dry-out tank."

"No goddam kid in a uniform tells me what to do," Raysta shouted. He swung a bony fist at the guard and missed.

The guard grinned and put the strap of his weapon over his shoulder. "Now, Granddad, calm down."

"I told you once, I'll tell you twice!" Raysta shouted,

glaring down the lengths of his cocked arms, "I'm a citizen of the Ukraine. I have rights. You can't push me around!"

The other soldier was disgusted. "Let him have one. See if that skinny belly of his will take your fist."

"The old man's drunk," the young guard said easily. "Look at him. He's drenched in sweat and his clothes look like a manure heap." He shook his head. "Go on and find a place to sleep it off, Granddad."

"Like hell I will," Raysta said, lowering his head and charging. The guard sidestepped and swung an uppercut that went into Raysta's chest, missing his face completely. Raysta grunted and went to the ground, falling to his knees and outstretched hands.

"You didn't have to do that," he said thickly, shaking his head sadly. "That hurt."

The guard helped him to his feet. "Are you ready to sleep now?"

He nodded. He brushed the street dirt from his clothes. He felt the bottle. It was still in one piece. He sighed in relief.

"Not much of a fight," the other soldier said.

"What did you expect from an old drunk? Keep an eye on the harbor. I'll find a place to put him down to sleep it off."

Raysta remembered to weave and slip as he walked with the soldier's support. "Don't leave me, son," he pleaded as they went along. "I want to tell you my story." He hiccuped. "I want to tell you how I became a lonely old drunk."

Mikhail saw the ketch.

The mark on its old painted foremast was visible in the fading light. An old leather belt was nailed to the wood. He removed his boots, shirt, cap, pants, jacket, bundled them, and tied them around his neck with a cord. He went into the inky sea. The water rose around him. He began a long, slow swim that took him away from the rocky beach at the edge of the village to the east canal leading into the harbor. Head out of the water, he hugged a rotting pile while he listened. Raysta was working up a storm. He could hear loud voices over by the street. He pushed into the canal, and holding his bundle out of the water, he moved slowly into the harbor. He swam noiselessly to the small ketch. He treaded, cautiously pressing his ear to the wooden hull. He heard no sounds except the waves slapping against it. No one was on the rutted deck, and he pulled himself up slowly. He rolled over the side and lay listening. Raysta's voice was fading. People moved down the street, but the harbor was quiet. The working fishing boats were still at sea. Was the top deck rigged with an alarm? He put the boots and his clothes down carefully, and with all of his senses alert, he moved inch by inch to the cabin hatch. Nothing brushed against him, no wires, no strings. And he hadn't been seen.

Carefully he opened the hatch, grateful that the hinges didn't squeak. He slid down the narrow stairway on his belly. The harsh wood grated against his wet body. He froze.

Someone was asleep in the bunk! The cabin deck was inches from his nose. There was no light, not the faintest, in the tiny cabin. Minutes straggled by as he listened. One man was sleeping.

He moved like a serpent, swaying his hard body down the stairway across the deck. He sent his fingers exploring the side of the bunk. He touched cloth. A uniform?

"What's that?" a Russian voice said thickly. "Who's there?" A trigger latch clicked off, an ominously loud sound in the miniature cabin. An armed soldier was in the bunk!

Mikhail rose swiftly and brought his fist crashing into the soldier's face. The swinging army pistol found his shoulder, near the neck, and sent a spray of pain through him. He staggered back, and his head hit the beam behind him. The soldier found him with the pistol again, a glancing blow against a palm he held up against the sound of the oncoming man. Then his arms went around the soldier, and they struggled in the cramped space, feeling each other, hearing each other, seeing each other only vaguely in the light from the hatch opening. The soldier flailed at him with the pistol until his seeking hand found it and wrenched it away. He flipped it to one side.

"Help!" the soldier called out in Russian as Mikhail closed his fingers around his throat. He held him as the man beat wildly with his fists and kicked and thrashed to free himself. Mikhail smelled the man's breath, foul with decayed teeth, smelled the man's body drenched in a terrifying sweat. He made no sound of his own as the man's feet ceased their frantic movements and the fingers fell away loosely from his own rock-hard hands. Boots scraped softly on the wooden deck, and an outraged sound gurgled somewhere in the man's chest.

Mikhail let the body sink back to the bunk. He lifted the legs and straightened them out. He was having difficulty getting his own breath and he felt dizzy. He braced himself against the beam over the bunk and waited for his control to return. He was covered with sweat, and his hands felt as if they'd been cast in iron. He tried to straighten out his fingers and they responded slowly. He'd felt a terrible desire, like the urge to swing a two-bladed sword in a crowd of people.

He bent to explore, running his hands along the body. Russian, tough, well muscled. A knife was still in his tunic-belt scabbard. He forgot it, Mikhail thought. He could have shot and seen me in the flash. He could have used the knife. He didn't and he's dead. A stubby machine gun rested next to the pillow, leaning upright against the corner of the bunk.

Mikhail went slowly up the narrow stairway. They'd put a guard on board, but there obviously hadn't been much concern over the fishing boat. The guard had felt he could get away with a little sleep. There were no detection devices aboard. Had the single outcry been heard? As he inched his head through the hatchway he saw a distant flare of a match as the shore guard lighted a cigarette. Security was wide-open. Guards sleeping and smoking on duty meant that the officers hadn't shown any undue interest in the little boat. Not yet. He felt the ketch rising and falling smoothly on the sheltered waves. The old breakway kept the waters nearly placid.

There were strange sounds up the street bordering the fisherman pier area. A bottle smashed. A rock crashed against the wall, and the guard stubbed out his fresh cigarette and moved away to investigate.

Mikhail came out of the hatch, bent over, on a run. He untied the bow rope and, with his foot, pushed the boat away from the dock, aiming its bow toward the east entrance canal. He ached where the pistol had struck him, but he had no time to nurse himself. Everything he needed—the items the UPA couldn't give him—were concealed on the boat. He had to get it out of the harbor.

He tied the smooth bow rope around his waist, grateful that it was an old, well-worn rope and wouldn't saw him in half. He went over the side into the harbor water, shocked again by its coldness but revived. His lungs took in deep breaths. If he couldn't move the little lightweight boat, the plan was in for a complete revision. Or an abort.

He started to swim on his back, using his arms and legs and wide, sweeping motions. The ketch shuddered gracefully and then obeyed him, riding high on the water. The wettened rope dug cruelly into his waist and hips but held. He shut his mind to everything except pulling the boat. Slowly, silently the obedient ketch followed him out of the harbor, through the narrow canal and into the sea. His arms and legs moved powerfully and without interruption until the force of the larger waves warned him that he was in deeper water. He swam to the ketch and crawled painfully over its side again. He struggled to get the rope from his waist. Shoreward, only the red beacon lights of the harbor entrance were visible.

He went below and started the motor. He would have preferred to sail silently, but he was alone and he had no choice. He set the course, tied the wheel, and went below to take his materials from the hiding place concealed on the boat the Americans on the Turkish ship had hurriedly built. A section of one of the beams overhead was false, and he pried it loose with a large fishing gaff. Packed inside was a regulation army briefcase containing his explosives. False wooden plates were nailed in the corners of the cabin, looking old and weather-beaten. They concealed his uniform, the various insignia he needed, more forged credentials, a small makeup kit, a transistor radio, a medicine kit, a Russian officer's pistol and holster, two cylinder explosives, and two cloth carrying cases, identical to those used by Russian officers when they moved from billet to billet. There was a compass, a watch, money, a sheathed knife, and cover items such as books of poems, official-looking documents that officers carry with them, pictures of a non-existent Russian family, letters to him from his nonexistent mother and father.

He dressed quickly, putting on the peasant clothes over his wet shorts and barely dry body. He carefully stuffed the items in the cloth carrying cases. He lugged it all to the deck, checking the course carefully and looking for a long moment at the sea around the boat. Nothing moved in the slight haze that hugged the water. He heard no sounds except the chugging of the engine. He ripped off the cover to the aft tool bin and removed an inflatable rubber lifeboat. He triggered the air capsule, and the small boat sprang into substance. He snapped the collapsible oars into usable lengths and fitted them into the side harnesses. He lowered the boat and put the briefcase and carrying cases in it, holding it to him by its nylon cord.

The hidden self-destruct system had been wired into the ketch to control six high-heat bursts that would blow out its bottom. The control switch was hidden at the top underside of the tool bin with a six-volt battery that would set off the individual bursts, each no larger than an aerial fireworks explosive but enough to destroy the old timbers of the ketch. He found the switch and pressed its lever.

He went over the side quickly into the rubber boat, pushing it away from the ketch. He rowed, and when the self-destruct system went off, he watched the ketch, fascinated. Streaks of sizzling vapor engulfed her. There were popping sounds in her ancient belly, and she went down, not bow-first as he somehow had expected but aft-first. She sank with a monstrous bubbling sound.

The Americans had known what they were doing. Captain Pell's original plan had been to have the crew take Mikhail aboard at Ochakov, go to sea, transfer the materials to him, and put him ashore in the rubber boat. They were then to scuttle the ketch and swim to shore, leaving the Russians with another mystery. Mikhail shook his head as he rowed. The ketch had been taken in by the navy patrol for a closer study, and that had changed the plan. Any good KGB or GRU investigator would have found the stuff. He'd had no choice but to get the boat out of the Parutino harbor and away from the investigators.

The rubber boat grated against the beach, and he jumped out, avoiding the wettest part. He pulled the boat after him, unloaded it, and deflated it. He found a pile of rocks and covered the mottled gray rubber with them the best he could. He kept looking cautiously around the deserted place, not quite certain it was the cove Raysta had in mind. From the sea it had been difficult to tell. Still, he was ashore and had more work to do. He took the cases and the briefcase and struggled up the hill, following the rocks to prevent outright footprints, stopping at the top to take leaves and wipe his boots. He cleaned his hands in the damp grass along the edge, his breath coming in gulps from the exertion.

He waited, standing with his back to a clump of tall bushes, until a shape materialized out of the bushes. He heard the boots, recognized their sounds, and said, "Shirn, I'm over here."

She came to him, holding her hands before her in the dark. She touched him and drew back. "Mikhail? Are you all right?" Her voice sounded tired. "Did you get your things from the boat?"

"Yes."

"We'd better leave here. This part is patrolled."

"I'll need help. It's heavy."

"I'll take some of it."

"No, we'll wait for the others."

There was a sound on the path, and they turned as a wheezy old voice struck them. "What are you doing here?" The old man approached them. "You are not supposed to be here at this time."

Mikhail moved forward, blinking as his mind worked. "And you, comrade, what are *you* doing here?" He made a motion with his hands.

"I'm Militia shore patrol," the man said. Mikhail studied the man with a short-cropped white beard. He had a holster strapped to his waist.

"When did they give you pistols to carry?" Mikhail asked.

"This is not a pistol," the policeman answered. "This is a rocket-flare gun. If I see anything suspicious, I'm to fire it into the sky." He made it sound important. "It makes a fine red explosion, and it comes down on a little parachute."

"There's nothing suspicious here."

"There's you and that girl."

Mikhail chuckled softly. "Now, don't tell me you were never young and had a girl?"

"Rules are rules. You're not supposed to be here this late in the day. Someone gave that order."

"All right, we'll go along."

"See that you do, comrade," the policeman said. "I should report you, but I've never liked doing that. I'll just warn you. They say I can do that when conditions warrant it." He turned and started down the path away from them. "But you should hurry. The next patrol might not be as concerned about lovers as I am."

They heard his footsteps fade down the path, and then it was quiet. Mikhail turned to Shirn, and a slight movement caught his eye. He froze.

"It's me," Bissa said, ambling close to them. "A good thing it is he left. Bop him with this I was going to." He held up a length of gnarled tree limb.

Far out at sea there was another sound. "Come on," Mikhail said, galvanized. "Give me a hand with this stuff. That's a navy patrol boat. They must have seen the explosion when the ketch went down." He hefted the briefcase and the larger bag, saw Bissa lift the other with incredible ease, and started quickly down the path behind Shirn. Bent over, he followed the sounds of her boots until they suddenly stopped.

He slowed and stiffened, and Bissa plowed into his back. The three of them remained motionless.

"Another patrol," Shirn whispered.

The colonel was elated.

He strode from the map on the wall to the desk where he reread the report. He went back to the map again.

"We'll have them here," he said, drawing a circle around the spot where the ketch had been stolen from the Parutino harbor. "They can't have gone far." He looked at Captain Prokov, who was standing with a telephone receiver in his hand. "The fishermen?"

"Forged papers, obviously. Whoever they were, they were part of this scheme."

The colonel felt completely at ease in the GRU communications control center. One entire wall was a map of the Southern Ukraine District. It was dotted with hundreds of small colored lights. A computer room at the far end, separated by a glass partition, funneled data into electronic readouts on the wall. His gaze swept across the wall as he listened to the earphoned operators responding to radioed dispatches while others moved magnetized symbols from position to position on the wall. Familiar with it, he saw with reassurance that the district was under full security. All the roads and streets were patrolled, airports secured, ports under surveillance. Communications were wide-open with the KGB, the local militia units in the district, and the navy.

"Why didn't the fools throw them in jail when they picked them up?"

The captain's face was moody. "There was nothing but fish on the boat. The only reason they took the boat into custody was because it was seen near the Turkish ship. The Turks fixed the motor. The patrol held the boat for experts to look it over."

"Why were the men allowed to leave?"

"Their identification papers seemed in order. The shore post checked on them by telephone. There are three fishermen who matched the description. They were at sea at that time in a similar ketch. But not the same. No, not the same ones. The real ones docked an hour ago, thirty kilometers to the east."

"Then there was something on that boat."

"We'll find it."

"And when you do, find how it was taken from the harbor under the noses of our guards."

"Remember, Comrade Colonel, there was a guard on board."

The colonel put on his cap, buttoned his tunic, and began slipping his hands into his gloves. "The helicopters are ready. We'll start at the fishing village at once." He stopped as Prokov reached for a ringing telephone. He saw the captain's face take on a strange look. "What's the matter?"

"The navy just reported a sighting from the area near Parutino, a cove not far away." Prokov held the phone carefully, listening.

"What is it?"

"A red flare. Two minutes ago. One of the shore patrols must have flushed our game."

The colonel was halfway out of the door with barely a

glance at his watch. Almost dark. Prokov would stay with
the GRU headquarters group, handling messages in the in-
terchange of information. He walked quickly down the hall.
Its mustiness made his long nose wrinkle. Each room was
filled with men, all assigned to the task of ferreting the truth
about the fishing boat and disaster that had struck the *Ustyug*. He grimaced. The crew had called her *Mother Russia!*
He heard computer machines rapping their messages, the
radio sergeants in communication with the action units, and
the sounds of a dozen men on field telephones.

Sergeant Timkin was waiting, lolling easily against the
sedan. He watched the sergeant scamper to open the door
for him. "The helicopter area and hurry!" He held on to the
seat as Timkin drove at a breathtaking pace through the
military complex. The lights were on at the heliport and
the night-flying units leaving and arriving filled the cold
damp air with a multitude of popping, fluttering sounds.
Holding on to his cap, he ran to the Kamov KA-26 helicopter
the ground exec pointed at. The downdraft buffeted him
and he nearly lost his footing. Halfway into the machine,
he turned to see where Timkin was. The sergeant was still
at the sedan. Angry, he motioned wildly to him and watched
the round face turn beet-red in surprise. The sergeant hadn't
understood that he was to come. He ran awkwardly and got
aboard. The machine lifted into the air, and the sergeant
was left with one leg out the door, holding on desperately
to the inner grips. The colonel ignored the pleading look
on Timkin's face. He fastened his seat strap and turned to
look out the small square window near him. The lights of
Odessa were passing out of sight, and the dark coastal land
was ahead when the sergeant finally inched his way to his
seat and pulled the door shut. He could hear the man breathing in sharp gasps and smell his body stench of fear.

"Comrade Sergeant," he said without turning his head,
"you'll get extra duty for that. Why do you forget that where
I go you go?"

"I won't forget again, Comrade Colonel," Timkin said
in a strained voice.

"We're going to Parutino, then the beach and the cove.
We'll be there in time to land on the beach before dark. Ha?
What?" He leaned forward to hear the pilot. "Ha? Yes!" He

picked up the radio handset on the wall near him and heard Captain Prokov's voice.

"The navy reports it's located a sunken vessel just outside the cove. By its underwater electronic gear. It believes it's big enough to be the fishing boat."

"Ha! Very good!"

"There's something else."

"I can't hear you. Speak louder."

"There's something at the bottom about one kilometer out from the beach where the helicopter reported the footprints."

"Do they have any idea of what it is?"

"None whatsoever. They just say something is there. The navy is ready to go down as soon as possible. Our men are with all of the naval units."

"I suggest you join us as soon as you can, Comrade Captain. I think we're drawing the noose on them." He gave orders to change their destination.

The helicopter started downward.

"Any word on the flare?" he said into the microphone.

"Yes. A shore patrol ran into a man on one of the trails at the top of the cliff."

"Who is he?"

"They don't know. They're still chasing him. Whoever he is, he's fast on his feet."

"Put more men onto it. We must capture him!"

There was a laugh from the other end. "They'll catch him, Comrade Colonel. The patrol reports he's just another drunk. He was waving a bottle of vodka over his head as he ran."

The colonel replaced the handset. He looked at Timkin, and the sergeant withdrew as much as he could, as if to avoid being spit upon.

"Where will he have gone?" Mikhail said.

"If catch him they don't, out near the cabbage seller's he'll hide," Bissa answered, his voice low and blunt. "Did you see how he ran?"

"Better that he bumped into the patrol than us," Shirn said. "He led them away from us."

"Can you find him?" Mikhail persisted.

Bissa nodded and looked at the sky. "Dark it'll be soon." He started off, his lumpy form sagging under the weight of the big cloth case. Shirn followed along the narrow path. Mikhail was last, his case balanced on his shoulder.

"Those flares are silly," Shirn said. "What good do they do?"

"It shows there's a shortage of walkie-talkies around here," Mikhail said. "I'll guess that every third or fourth patrol has a radio and the others have the flares."

It was light enough to see a hundred feet when Bissa finally halted and put his case down. He pointed with a fat finger and went ahead, tiptoeing in a grotesque mockery of a hunter sneaking up on a rabbit.

"You big bag of goose necks," Raysta growled from the dense thicket. "If I had my rifle, I'd have blown your head off two minutes ago."

Bissa's face was a delight. He pointed wildly to the thicket. "I knew there he was, I knew, I knew!"

"Oh, shut up," Raysta said, coming out of the hiding place. "I saw you with those bags before the patrol came. I wanted to pull them away from you." He almost smiled, but his face was too tired to make the muscular formation necessary. "I got this cart." He pulled it, creaking and protesting, from the thicket.

"Whose is it?" Shirn asked suspiciously as Mikhail piled the heavy cases in it.

"The cabbage seller's."

Bissa snickered. "Smells like it, it does."

The last rays of sun had long since tipped the tops of the trees surrounding Shirn's *khootir* when they finished unloading. "Hide this," Mikhail said, pointing to the handcart.

"I'll go push the damn thing into the sea," Raysta said morosely, sliding to the ground.

"Do that," Mikhail said easily. "You'll be able to push it through the soldiers down there."

Raysta's eyebrows shot up. "Soldiers?"

"With that flare and the patrol boat, you can bet Gregorski will be at the beach looking around." He glanced at his watch. "About right now."

"It isn't very far away," Shirn said nervously.

Mikhail was busy unpacking the carrying cases when

Raysta returned from hiding the cart. "I say we'll have an hour or more. Then we better be the hell and gone out of this cabin."

Raysta dropped to the floor and moaned. "I can't move another muscle. My gut's killin' me!" He glared. "From hard work a horse will die!"

Bissa sat down next to him and moaned mockingly. "Can't move a muscle!" he whimpered delightedly.

"You sack of chicken fertilizer!" Raysta growled. He raised a hand and whacked Bissa's head.

"Shirn, get some food ready," Mikhail ordered, busy with the cases. "Feed them and let them sleep a half hour." He looked at her. "You'll drive the truck. Can you get it out of the collective?"

She was already building a fire and getting the pot ready for the quick meal. She nodded. "You want a truck, my master," she said without looking at him, "Shirn will get a truck from my beautiful collective."

"Can't move a muscle," mimicked Bissa.

"I'll push *you* over the cliff," Raysta said, closing his eyes. He was asleep instantly.

Mikhail stripped, pulling off the old clothes. The skin around his waist was bright red from the grip of the fishing boat rope. He opened the medicine kit, found a tube of ointment, and spread it on the raw skin. Shirn took the tube and rubbed the colorless paste on the back where he couldn't reach it. His face betrayed no expression of discomfort.

"You should have a bandage on that." She studied him, standing nude except for his shorts, then she pressed a spot at his shoulder. "That's ugly. What happened?"

"A souvenir from the fishing ketch."

She touched his other shoulder, near the neck. "That's another one. How'd you get it?"

"There was a guard on board. He swung his pistol at me."

She stepped back, staring at him. "I didn't realize how strong you are. So hard. What did the Americans try to do, make a weight lifter out of you?" Her tone betrayed how impressed she was.

"They have a saying, 'Clean living and good booze.'"

"What?"

"Good liquor."

She looked at Raysta, asleep on the floor. "He should hear that." She turned reluctantly to her cooking.

Mikhail dressed himself in the uniform. When he was done, he turned to Shirn. "Major Ivan Kovelev of General Zagorsky's staff." He strapped on the belt and holster, slipped the army pistol into the holster, and snapped its flap shut.

"What are those things?" she asked, serious.

He laid them on the table, checked them, and began repacking them into the briefcase. "The black packages are superplastic, waterproofed with timers that detonate them." He held one up. "See the small string at the corner? They all have one. I can time the explosion to minutes by the length of the string I pull out. When I pull the string, it starts the timer embedded in the explosive. The more string I pull, the longer the timer works." He placed seven of the black packages into the briefcase, as if he were packing small books. "These," he said, lifting them in turn, "are four red flares and four smoke canisters."

"That looks like a radio." It was the size of a pack of cigarettes.

"Transistor. I'll listen to 'Voice of America' for instructions."

"How? I mean, how will they give you instructions?"

He didn't answer. He unfolded a small cloth travel kit and filled it with a shirt, shaving equipment, underwear, socks, and a book of poems. He put the eighth black package in a fishnet bag along with two books, a writing tablet, and a package. The package was different from the others. It looked like a gift. He stowed the makeup kit, the medicine kit, and two long cylinder explosives in the cloth carrying cases. He put the UPA-forged credentials in his tunic pocket.

"Your photo is on that military identification card," she said. "How did you manage that with the UPA?"

"They took shots of me in uniform in the States and mailed them to a go-between in Odessa," he said, grinning.

"What's superplastic?" she asked, busy with her cooking.

"A standard Russian explosive the Americans made more powerful." He didn't look at her. "I've worked with it a lot. Don't worry about it."

She regarded the briefcase dubiously. "I'll worry about

that damned thing." She brushed the hair from her forehead. "I'll worry about the whole damned lot of us!"

Colonel Gregorski stood stiff-legged, watching the four navy vessels gathered together offshore, their lights ablaze. The naval helicopters hovered overhead, the sound of them reassuringly firm in the thickening darkness. "They've found something on the bottom." He turned to look at Sergeant Timkin. "I knew this beach had some story to tell us." He turned back to watch the operation through field glasses. "So that's where they placed their secret, that far out?"

"We'll know what it is soon," Timkin said.

"Is it big enough to be the missing boat?"

"I'll check." Timkin switched on his battery-operated radio, which connected him with the GRU observers aboard the navy vessels. He exchanged sentences with one of the men. "No, it isn't that big, Comrade Colonel. It seems to be a strange mass of material wrapped around a tall rock at the bottom of the sea."

"A what?"

"He said a 'strange mass of material,' whatever that is."

"I want a better description."

Timkin reached for the radio and then pointed. "See! The divers are going down now."

The colonel was satisfied. He watched a black-suited frogman fall backward over the side of one of the vessels, then another, and a third. "Hold it. We'll soon see what they bring up." They carried underwater lights.

Timkin stared at the action far from shore. "Why would they put something out there?"

"The strangest mysteries have answers."

"If they came ashore here, they must've planned to come back and get whatever they left out there."

"When we find out what's at the bottom of the sea there, we'll have some of the answers we're looking for."

"They should be up any moment now," Timkin said.

The sea erupted in a fiery mass, shooting a geyser a hundred meters into the air and sending a furious sound across the water and the beach. The vessels disappeared into the maelstrom. A gigantic silver cloud of vapor burst skyward. A helicopter was struck down, crashing on its side weirdly. Bits of bodies and boats and debris from the sea rained down in a huge area.

One of the minute pieces to fall on the colonel and the sergeant was a fragment of Mikhail's frogman suit.

It was swept back to sea by the immense wave that roared onto the beach and inundated them as they struggled in the sand to get back to their feet.

"Two more days," Mikhail said. "It'll be over then."

Shirn, steering the truck down the rutted dirt road, kept her eyes ahead. The truck bore a faded sign identifying its collective, Kolkhosp 89, Silrada L-32. It clattered and clanked but it ran, and she guided it with a knowledge of its frailties and its age. A relic of nearly twenty years, its high two-door cab was fitted with a full-length wooden seat wide enough for three people. The van in back of the cab was dilapidated, a tall wooden box affair that sagged and swayed. At the front it had a small open window guarded by two rusty iron bars leading into the rear of the cab. A tall rear door at the end of the van also had a tiny square window, glassless and barless. A small two-step wooden stairway led from the van door to the ground. The drab black paint on the cab and engine section was scraped in many places, and a great deal of rust showed through. Its tired old engine made a loud, throaty sound of protesting metal, and a long shoot of oily fumes trailed behind it. "When will you kill him?" she said. "How will you kill him?"

"Don't ask questions," Raysta said through the van window.

"I want to know."

Mikhail was silent, looking at the countryside in the truck's headlights. The Ukrainian land away from the coast was flat, and he knew that without the darkness they would have been able to see thirty to fifty kilometers in every direction. "Get your cover stories firmly in your minds," he said. "The UPA's fixed us up with some good ones, and you're proscribed with the village to travel. Shirn has written permission to take the truck and go to Odessa for a medical checkup on her back. Raysta's been sent along to obtain special insulators for the new light line. Bissa's been okayed to go with you to see his wood carvings at the Odessa festival." With such cover it was obvious that someone in the village registration office was a hidden UPA sympathizer. Everyone in the USSR who travels must have his papers signed by his employer, he knew, and all employers represented the State in one way or another. The UPA was remarkably infiltrated in key spots. His respect for them grew as he realized the risks all the hidden ones were taking.

"Then why are we going to Nikolayev?" Shirn persisted, irritated because her questions about Gregorski hadn't been answered. "That's north of here. Gregorski is south, back at the beach. You said yourself when we heard the bomb go off a while ago." She darted a look at Mikhail. "Why aren't you there shooting at him?"

"We're going to Nikolayev tonight and Odessa in the morning because your commanders want a job done there."

"Work?" Bissa said anxiously.

"We're going to stir up a little trouble at the tracking station. It's one of the most important facilities Gregorski is supposed to protect."

"I don't understand," Shirn said, avoiding a large pothole in the dirt road. "If Gregorski is going to die, what difference does it make?"

"Don't ask questions," he said.

"I want to know."

Mikhail pulled a map from his pocket and studied it. They were on the main road to Nikolayev and had thirty kilometers to go. Shirn jerked the truck to the side of the road and jammed on the brakes.

"Hey!" Raysta cried. "For St. Cyril's sake!" There was a muffled noise from the van as the villagers went rolling around the floor.

Mikhail, unruffled, pointed to a spot on the map. "The tracking station is here." He pulled a folded sheet of paper from another pocket. "Your people have given us a map of how to get in and out.

"Damn you!" Shirn exploded. "How are you going to kill him?"

"Their map compares remarkably well with the satellite

photographs the Americans made of the place."

Shirn beat her fists on the steering wheel. "Damn you! You're not going to tell me?"

"What'd stop for?" Bissa said, his fat face peering through the open window. "What's matter?"

"Shirn lost her temper," Mikhail answered. He looked at her and his eyes were sober. "She's impatient."

"You came here to kill Gregorski! Why aren't you going to do it?" She folded her arms to stop the trembling of her hands.

"There is a plan," Mikhail said slowly. "Worked out by your people, the ones you call the commanders, and the Americans. I must stay with that plan. We're behind schedule because of the ketch, but with luck we can catch up before too long. If no patrols stop us."

Shirn was unyielding. "What is the plan?" She turned contemptuous eyes at him. "Or can you tell *us* that, Comrade Major?"

"I can tell you this. None of us will live unless we stick with the plan. Others are working with us. It's on a timetable. Things must be done under coordination. If we let these people down, they'll die and we'll die."

Shirn was silent. From the van Mikhail heard Bissa and Raysta breathing heavily. Bissa sniffed and Raysta coughed.

"The simplest thing would be to walk up to Gregorski and put a gun in his stomach," he went on. "After that, I'd have two, perhaps three seconds to live."

"Why don't you do it, then?" Shirn's words were icy.

"That's what I wanted to do. That's what I would have done. But your people and the Americans have some other things at stake. The Americans convinced me it would be a stupid waste to let Gregorski's death kill me as well. They agreed to help me come in only if I'd stay with the plan."

"To hell with your plan!"

"Gregorski will die. I told you that. What more do you want from me?"

"I want to be there and see you kill him!"

Raysta coughed again. "She's a damned hothead, that one." He spoke to Shirn. "What are you gettin' so burned up about? Mikhail's here. You saw what he did about the ketch and the underwater bomb. Now cool off. If he says there's a plan and we have to stick to it, then that's what we'll do."

Shirn turned her head and glared at Raysta and Bissa in the window, but she said nothing. She started the truck and steered it savagely back onto the road.

"Listen closely," Mikhail said. "I'll be going into the tracking station in another half hour. Each of you has a specific assignment." He pointed to the map. "When we reach here, we'll stop and I'll give each of you something from the cases in the van."

Raysta's voice held a note of amazement. "You're goin' into the Nikolayev base by yourself?"

Mikhail shook his head. "Major Ivan Kovelev, assigned to General Zagorsky's staff, is going into the base."

"Oh, sweet Cyril," Raysta said. "There must be five thousand soldiers and a hundred GRU men there!"

"What's he going to do?" Bissa asked.

There was a sound of Raysta slumping heavily to the floor of the van. "He's goin' to stick his fool head right into the open door of the furnace."

Bissa sat down next to Raysta. "Smart that's not," he said in his blunt way. "Hurt he'll get."

CHAPTER FIVE

Mikhail watched the truck drive away and felt immensely relieved. Shirn would drop off Bissa and Raysta at the spot marked on the map and backtrack part of the way to be at the high-voltage electric line junction in time for her own assignment. He shifted in his uniform in the growing heat of action. The rawness around his hips and waist bothered him, and his shoulder ached where the pistol had struck him. He pushed the body irritations to the back of his mind. There was no time for them now.

He put his carrying case down on the ground next to him and waited for the officers' bus that would pick him up at the entrance to the long winding road that led into the recently finished backup satellite tracking-and-command station. He turned idly to look at it, spreading under its lights in a giant neat pattern on the high ground west of Nikolayev. Its new tall steel towers, topped with radar cocoons and radio antennas, glistened under the floodlights. A high wire fence ran around the entire base, interspersed with guard posts built atop telephone posts thirty feet tall. Trucks rolled in and out, with a few uniformed motorcyclists racing in between them. He ignored them all, but he was impressed with the nighttime activity.

Inside was Colonel Rakoski, the base commander, due now for promotion to lieutenant general. A man the UPAs hated, a man who had executed eleven of their men in a stupid slaughter at a public square. Now he commanded this new base, linked to the older satellite tracking stations in the Crimea, linked to the cosmodromes near Pletsetsk, five hundred miles north of Moscow, and at Tyuratam on the Aral sea. With these facilities the Russians retrieved their spy packages by bringing their satellites' information

back to USSR ground. And Rakoski was readying the base
for its part in the celebration of Heroes' Day in the Ukrainian
Republic.

Rakoski had a surprise in store.

What had Shirn said to him in the cab of the truck as
he'd instructed her in the part she was to play in that surprise? "What kind of a man are you?" she had said in a
disbelieving voice. "You can't go in there alone! Do you
think you're *invisible?*" She'd clearly been shocked.

"Let me tell you what I learned when I got aboard a bus
with some kids in Washington," he'd said. "I was in a
strange land. I spoke pretty good English but with a Russian
flavor. The kids were laughing and scuffling with each other.
Then they realized I was somebody new on board. I dug
out some kopecks and said, 'See, comrades?' I was in. They
thought I was being clever with an accent and foreign money.
None of them thought to tell the teachers up front that I was
hiding in the back of the bus. They didn't believe I was a
Russian. I learned then that if you believe strongly enough
you're someone, like actors do, other people will too. If I
want to be a major on a general's staff, then I *am* that major.
Pretending to be what I'm not has become a way of life for
me, because it gave me life." He stopped because there
wasn't time for the whole story.

Her eyes had told him she thought he was a damned
idiot.

Mikhail turned away from the base. The Americans knew
it was one of the Soviet Union's newest tracking stations
for the control of the USSR hardware sent aloft elsewhere.
It could bring down from those soaring space units the
information they had collected, photographic maps of other
nations, weather data, electronic copies of other nation's
communications, valuable espionage bits and pieces that
would patiently be assembled by the Russians who labored
at that chore. He studied the dirt streets of the little settle-
ment built across from the main entrance road. The babushkas with their birch-twig brooms had swept the streets
that morning. The night air was clean and fresh, with a
gentle wind afoot. A hundred meters away, in a tiny park,
a group of old Bolsheviks huddled together on benches under

a light, their aluminum canes grasped in gnarled, aged hands, chain-smoking and talking. Talking of other days, he thought.

He wondered where the old Greek ruins near Nikolayev were. Kherson had been an all-Asian Greek colony at one time and Nikolayev had, long ago, been heavily populated by Greeks. The base had been built not too far from the site of the ancient ruins called Olvia.

The sound of music caught his ear and he turned back to the base. A unit was drilling under stadium-type lights on the long flat parade ground. Cadets from the Kharkov Military Academy marched smartly in formation, their khaki tunics and blue breeches neat and well fitting, their white-gloved hands swinging in rhythm with their steps, practicing for the celebration parade.

Past them, in the distance, he could see the lights of ships on the Yuzhnyy Bug, the broad body of water that came from the north, ran to the east of Nikolayev, and emptied into the bay that led to the Black Sea.

The same bay that led to the place where he had waited for the *Mother Russia*.

The bus came into sight, arriving from the city, and he picked up his cloth case and the small fishnet bag. There were no paper sacks in the Soviet Union. He boarded the bus when it stopped, as he'd been told by the UPA that it always did. He found a seat and settled back into it, not looking squarely into the eyes of any of the other officers aboard. The long road into the base departed from the main highway, where Shirn had left him, and wound through trees and across the Ingul River leading into the Bug.

He thought of Shirn. That girl! If only she weren't so hot-tempered. She had his briefcase and the rest of the equipment in her truck. She had two long cylinders, dangerous cylinders, and a job to do. He could only depend on the UPA training she'd had. He made himself relax and look sleepy. At the fishing village and in the contact with the patrols, she'd been cool enough.

Bissa and Raysta, if they kept themselves hidden, had a fairly simple job. Cutting down a large tree. Safe enough if they weren't discovered and didn't fell it a moment too soon.

At the inspection post he left the bus with the other

officers and filed with them through the long building staffed with satellite corps guards.

"Comrade Major," a lieutenant of the guard said as he handed him his army identification packet, *propusk*, and orders, "I apologize for detaining you." He shrugged. "We've been under the most strict orders." He read the documents. "You're a member of General Zagorsky's staff?" He raised his eyebrows. "But you came on the bus!"

Mikhail took the documents and returned them to his pocket, grateful that the Ukrainian Underground had such skilled forgers. He kept his face smoothly composed. "That was one of my orders, Comrade Lieutenant," he said in Russian. He let it go at that. The lieutenant could put his own interpretation on the inference. A sergeant joined the officer, and the two of them looked through the small overnight case, dumping everything out and then carefully replacing them.

"What do you have in the bag?" the lieutenant asked, shifting the net with a finger.

"Books." It was obvious. Two of the three items plainly visible in the fishnet were books.

"And the black package?"

"Book also." Mikhail opened the fishnet and handed the package to him.

"It's very heavy for a book." The officer looked at it carefully. "It has a name on it." He whistled softly and held the package for the sergeant to see. "Look at this."

"It's a gift for Colonel Rakoski," Mikhail said. "From the general."

"Yes, a very heavy book." The lieutenant hefted it in his hand.

Mikhail said nothing. He looked steadily into the lieutenant's eyes, knowing that the man was no fool. The slightest expression and the lieutenant would try to unwrap the package. It was triggered to explode when unwrapped. "The general does not give meaningless gifts," he said, reaching over and taking the package. He returned it to the fishnet. "I believe there's a personal message in it."

For five seconds neither the lieutenant nor the sergeant moved. Mikhail met their eyes, hearing the sounds of the other officers talking to their inspectors along the table.

"You know where the bachelor officers' quarters are?" the lieutenant said, breaking the silence.

"Yes."

"We will provide you with a car and driver." He handed Mikhail the overnight case.

"Nonsense. I'll walk."

"But, Comrade Major, the base is under extremely tight security."

"I'll walk. I need the exercise." Mikhail did not smile. "I want to take my time and study what you have here." He let a stern look come to his face. "There are no sensitive areas between here and the quarters." He went past the officer, moving with the others ahead of him. There was a narrow, crushed-rock sidewalk, and he followed this as a number of army trucks and sedans went by him. He looked around at the sprawling base and breathed deeply.

I am crazy, he said to himself. *What the hell am I doing here?* The sinking of the *Ustyug,* the ketch, and the explosion at the beach had been a sensation, he knew. They'll make no public announcement, but the military is on a sharp edge this night. The fishnet with the black package bumped against his leg. It's weight steadied him and he felt better. Then he remembered the slight hint of suspicion in the lieutenant's eyes as he'd left. What would the inspector-guard do?

He checked into the visiting bachelor officers' quarters, put his bag into the room, and removed the black package from the fishnet. He went down the wooden stairs to the orderly.

"I have a gift from the general for Colonel Rakoski. It is to be delivered at once."

The orderly was surprised. It was obvious that he was at a loss about what to do. "Our messenger left a half hour ago, Comrade Major. We can deliver it when he returns."

"When will that be?"

"Two hours, perhaps three. He was sent to the Nikolayev airbase to pick up three electronics specialists."

"They're here to repair the system?" Mikhail probed.

The orderly scratched his chin and studied Mikhail's GRU insignia. "I don't know what the trouble is over there. This is the second repair crew from Moscow this month."

Mikhail looked quickly at the clock on the wall behind the orderly and stiffened. Too much time! "The general asked that this book be delivered to the colonel at once."

The orderly reached for the telephone. "I'll call the messenger center. They'll send someone."

"It'll take too much time. I'll drop it off myself. Call the car pool and tell them to have me picked up immediately." He said it with such force that the orderly instantly obeyed. In five minutes a sedan arrived, and a woman driver, wearing the satellite corps uniform, pulled up before the quarters. He got in, saying nothing, and was driven quickly through the base. He showed his identification three times before the sedan stopped in front of the colonel's headquarters.

It was a low, ugly building, graced on one end with an unhealthy-looking clump of newly planted trees, and at the other with a short steel tower that held an array of communication equipment. It was the heart of the Nikolayev base, belly-full of the sophisticated equipment used for satellite control and data retrieval from space. There was a great deal of coming and going, with officers entering and leaving, cars pulling up and departing. "Remain here," he ordered the woman, and got out.

He was stopped at the entrance. Three soldiers, submachine guns strapped over their shoulders, looked warily at his identification papers. "Sorry, Comrade Major. Your papers do not give you special clearance for this building."

"I don't want entrance. I want to see that this book is delivered to Colonel Rakoski." He handed the black package to the nearest one, with the label at the top. The three of them studied the package. Mikhail turned and started back to the sedan. He held his breath. Would the soldiers take the package inside?

"Comrade Major!" the soldier holding the package called, coming after him. "We can't take the responsibility for this!" He held the package out, and Mikhail turned, fighting a bitterness. Damn these fools!

"What's this!" a voice said, and he turned to see a sour-faced lieutenant colonel getting out of a black Zim just behind the army sedan. "What's going on?"

Mikhail saluted. "General Zagorsky asked me to deliver this gift to Colonel Rakoski. These men feel it's too much of an imposition on the base security." He held up the package. "A book with a note of personal regards." He allowed a look of disgust to form on his face. "Tomorrow is the comrade colonel's first anniversary as base commander. The general wanted to recognize that fact with a small gift."

The lieutenant colonel reached for the package. "Give me that. I'll see that it gets to him." He brushed by the soldiers and went into the building.

Mikhail got into the sedan. "Now we will return." He sat back, tense, but refusing to look at the entrance and the guards, who were staring darkly at him. The sedan retraced its route, going back through the three checkpoints. Only when the bachelor officers' quarters appeared ahead did he breathe easy again.

But as he strode into the quarters his senses warned him a second before a voice said, "Comrade Major." He turned to see the lieutenant and the sergeant standing to one side. Their faces were strained. The sergeant was holding a machine-pistol tilted in his direction. In a second's time Mikhail knew where the safest spot was. He walked to it and placed his back against the wall, a wall between him and the colonel's headquarters building. He faced them loosely.

"We would like to see your papers again," the lieutenant said. He came toward Mikhail, holding out his hand. The orderly was behind his counter, leaning curiously with both hands on the top of it.

"Of course," Mikhail said, his hand moving to his pocket. He was smiling and he knew it but couldn't erase it. His fingers flipped his holster open, and his pistol swung up with a crashing sound. The sergeant, eyes wide-open, grunted and twirled as the bullet smashed into him. The lieutenant's mouth was open to shout, but before he had enough air in his lungs, the second bullet ripped into his throat.

Mikhail was turning, bringing the muzzle of the pistol around to his right to aim at the orderly when the black package exploded in Colonel Rakoski's office.

The blast started a chain of other explosions which in seconds destroyed the entire administration building and a large share of the satellite station control center. Glass from the window in the orderly room shattered and sprayed in deadly shards through the room, smashing into the orderly. Mikhail was hurled to the floor, sliding for several feet, his arms thrown out in front of him. Sirens began screaming almost as soon as bits of roofs and walls and bodies came hurtling back to the startled earth.

On the floor, face in the dust, Mikhail was still smiling. Then the smile drained as he heard his mother screaming on the other side of the locked door. He beat on the door, but he couldn't stop the screaming. He trembled violently at the sound.

He had to find a way to stop the screaming.

Shirn was jarred several inches off the truck seat when the satellite station erupted in the distance. Wide-eyed, she gripped the steering wheel, staring at the holocaust. Flames shot a hundred meters into the air, and smoke rolled angrily in shuddering white-gray clouds.

Instinctively she started the truck, turned on its headlights, and moved down the back road that paralleled the power lines leading into the station. Two small military trucks filled with guards raced past her on their way to the station. The faces of the guards in her headlights were white and horror-stricken as they looked outward from the speeding vehicles to see the terrible sign of destruction spreading into the sky.

She forced herself to concentrate on her assignment. Mikhail had been right. The first explosion ignited the highly combustible gases used at the command center. The pipelines for the gases spread the explosions as if they'd been giant, nearly instantaneous fuses. The road turned and went under the power lines. She stopped the truck, leaving the engine running, door wide-open, lights on, and took the two cylinders from the seat next to her. She ran to the high wire fence between the road and the tall double-brace poles that held the high-voltage lines. For a moment she paused. These were the junction lines that brought most of the electricity to the station. Small standby generator sets were everywhere on the base, and other power lines led in from two smaller power plants, but this was the main line, the aorta from the big power plant to the north.

And the guards had left it unprotected.

It was necessary to get the cylinders as close to the base of the tall poles as she possibly could. She steadied herself, pulled the small ring out of the end of the first, then pitched it over the high chain-link fence. The terrible glow in the night lighted the area. The cylinder landed two meters from the farthest double brace. She pulled the ring from the second cylinder and carefully lobbed it in a higher arc. It landed half a meter from the nearest double brace and rolled toward the poles, nearly touching.

She raced back to the truck and, without shutting the door, drove off down the road. Hunched over the wheel, she began cursing the Ukrainian Underground, the years of domination by the Russians, the fact that she was a woman, Raysta, Bissa, and the old truck. When she began cursing Mikhail, she suddenly slowed the truck and looked in the rearview mirror. Nothing.

What had happened to the cylinders? Why hadn't they exploded? Uneasy, she steered the truck, fighting a compulsive urge to go back and look at the cylinders. As long and as thick as her forearm, they were black and solid. What was supposed to happen? Mikhail had said the rings, when pulled, would set off a timer, which would ignite the detonator. And that would . . .

In the mirror she saw two of the poles, almost out of her vision, rise from the ground as if they'd been kicked upward in a bright shower of sparks and flashes. The thick wires snapped and went curling in giant arcs upward and backward. The second set of poles followed, looking like dark, lumbering missiles trying to get off the ground. A vast spray of dirt and smoke burst upward, covering the poles and the twisting wire.

There's no sound, she thought. No sound!

But it came, a swift moment later. A low, horrible, rumbling, gutty sound shook the earth under the racing truck and ran up from its tires to the steering wheel where it tingled her clutching hands. The road curved, and she bent against it as she guided the truck around the curve.

The thunder of the explosions burst past her and was gone, but echoes seemed to come from everywhere.

That insane Mikhail! What had he gotten her into? Where was Bissa? Where was Raysta? What was she doing racing the old truck down a back road away from the tracking station? Her hands shook, and she had a fierce struggle to hold on to the vibrating wheel. Why had she permitted Bissa and Raysta to go by themselves to make a roadblock? A roadblock! That had been part of the plan, a device to give them more time to get away.

Mikhail!

She heard his voice, and control began to return to her. She became aware of where she was and slowed the truck.

It was time to take the crossroad. She came to it, turned, and followed the narrow lane. It would bring her to a main road where she would find a small village and wait for her men to join her. At the railroad station.

Where had all of the guards gone? The area she'd left was usually tightly patrolled. Had the Underground been busy there without her seeing them? Had the UPA helped decoy the guards away from where she'd thrown the cyl- inders over the fence?

The village came into sight, and breathed relief. She found the spot where she was to park the truck and did so. She got out, her legs unsteady and weak. She wrapped her bright red scarf over her head, feeling damp and clammy, and walked to the tiny railroad station perched alongside a double set of tracks.

Everything comes in twos today, she thought, looking around. What was wrong? She studied the village. Then it came to her. Not a person was in sight!

A car screeched to a halt, and she turned at the sound of running feet. Two men in uniform stopped in front of her.

"Remain motionless," one of the men said roughly. "I wouldn't want to blow your pretty head apart."

He was pointing an army pistol at her face.

"I don't like this," Raysta said. "Why doesn't the UPA do its own damn dirty work?" They stood in the lonely darkness of the road.

"Us to do it Shirn wants."

"That Mikhail wants us to do it, damn him."

"Stop we could?" Bissa asked hopefully.

"The hell we can. We're in this stinkin' mess too far."

Raysta nodded his head in the direction of the satellite station in the far distance. "You saw. The madman did what he was to do."

"Shirn did too! You heard it. Heard it I did. The explosions!" Bissa's pale brown eyes were watery with excitement.

"We should be back at our village safe and sound, not out here cuttin' down a damn tree."

"We going to die, Raysta?" Bissa said quietly.

"Who the hell knows?" Raysta swigged from the vodka bottle. In the other hand he held the old crosscut saw.

"You sorry we're in this?"

Raysta put down the bottle and wiped his mouth. "You know what I'm sorry about?" His dark eyes were focused in the distance. "In the war there was this girl I met. She'd been burned in a buildin'. The shitty Germans airbombed it, and she was burned before she got out."

Bissa was amazed. "Us you never told about her!"

Raysta shook his head. His stringy black hair flapped with the movement. He squatted, hanging the bottle by the neck between his legs. "I met her in a hospital. A stinkin' crappy tent filled with the dyin' and the dead. She was the prettiest thing there. I helped a corpsman bandage her. When I could, I helped feed her." His voice melted into a low whisper. "She was burned all over except her head. She put a rug over her head and ran out through the flames. In the tent she was bandaged everywhere but her head. She had the most beautiful eyes I'd ever seen, and long golden hair. And the softest voice. I used to sit on the ground next to her cot and wipe the sweat from her face. The tent was an oven." His voice stumbled.

"What happened?"

"What always happens? They put me back in the line again. I was shot a week later and ended up in the same tent."

"She there still was?"

Raysta's eyes cooled and the lids nearly closed. "Nearby. They buried her with the others on a little hill under the hot sun. She was eighteen. I never stopped lovin' her."

Bissa rubbed his fat hands together in confusion. The conversation had unsettled him. His friend was suffering, and he decided to change the subject. "Done it almost is, Raysta." He pointed to the large crosscut saw and then to the cut almost two-thirds of the way through the tree. A wedge was thrust in the open end. They moved and sat on the ground, hidden from the road by a screen of dense bushes. The UPA had concealed the tools for them in the thick underbrush. The tools were branded with the army insignia. "What is it we're supposed to do?"

"You slab of lard!" Raysta was coming back from the past. "Can't you remember anything? When the train whistles, we're goin' to finish this cut."

Bissa nodded. "Now I remember. The tree falls." He pointed again. "There across the road!"

"And across those telephone lines."

Bissa felt better. "Then the trucks and cars down the road can't get." He looked at Raysta. "Why they down the road can't get?"

Raysta slapped him across the back of his stubby neck. "You dumb bastard!" he said in his old detached manner, "because that tree'll block the road."

Bissa smiled brightly. "Now I remember." This was more like it.

And it would. The road narrowed where it went through the stand of trees. When the tall, thick tree fell, it would jam into others on both sides of the road. It would be an effective block until it was power-sawed and dynamited out of the way. That would take hours.

"That road leads to the satellite station. Mikhail and the commanders want it blocked and the telephone lines brought down. They want to delay the rescue machines."

In the distance they heard the screech of the approaching train. Raysta rose instantly, his hands reaching for his end of the saw. Bissa scrambled in an ungainly way to his feet, his boots slipping in the grass, and wordlessly they began surging the saw through the remainder of the thick tree trunk. In a minute the tree groaned and leaned against the undercut. They worked desperately until the tree surrendered. A torrent of creaking, splitting protests came from its severed trunk and it fell, coming earthward with a great *swoosh*, striking the road with a mighty roar and bouncing once in its dusty death throes. It was jammed into the trees on each side of the dirt road like a monstrous green wall.

Raysta was already running, his straggly hair flying in the breeze. Bissa followed, clumping heavily behind, his short arms held close to his fat belly, concentrating on keeping close to Raysta's flying boots.

They boarded the train as it paused at the dimly lighted station, trying to act nonchalant, wiping the sweat from their faces with their jacketed forearms. They paid the conductor their kopecks and found places to sink onto the wooden benches bolted to the sides of the passenger car. They didn't return the stares of the other passengers. They sat, waiting for the train to pull out and the security man to come and check their papers.

"Raysta—" Bissa began.

"Shut up," Raysta hissed between closed teeth.

The train started and was nearly out of the village when there was a commotion on the road alongside it. Two army trucks raced in the direction of the tree they had left at the far edge of the village. A dark green army sedan careened in their wake. It was filled with officers.

Raysta turned from the window and leaned back, eyes closed, sitting upright, his neck against the cool window glass. Bissa sat huddled, his hands folded, engrossed in the twitching of one of his thumbs.

Someone stopped in front of them, and a stern voice said, *"Propusk!"*

They stared in relief at the officer who stood looking down at them.

It was Mikhail.

"I know these men," Mikhail said to the security man. He held up their papers. "They have passes, but I suspect they are not in order. There's something strange about them." He looked at Raysta. "This scarecrow was on a labor crew at the station." He looked at Bissa. "This one is a common drunk."

"Drunk? Me?" Bissa said puzzled.

"Shut up!" Raysta ordered, nudging him with a sharp elbow.

"I'll take them off at the next stop and check on what they're doing," Mikhail said to the guard. "With the explosions at the station we can't take chances on our security."

The guard's relief shown on his dullish face. "Yes, Comrade Major, that would be best." He looked at his watch. "We'll be there in five minutes." He left, going down the swaying coach in a practiced stride that compensated for the movement.

"You," Mikhail ordered. "On your feet. Come back here to the door. I warn you. Make no attempt to escape." He herded them to the rear of the car. Few of the passengers turned to look their way, but he knew they were listening carefully.

The train came to a stop and they got off. There was a swirl of uniformed men around the small station. Mikhail stopped a soldier going by.

"What goes on here?" he asked.

"Comrade Major, something happened at the satellite station," the soldier said, standing stiffly. "The security officers have arrested some suspects."

"Where are they?"

The soldier pointed at a small procession of uniformed guards and villagers. "There."

Mikhail, Bissa, and Raysta watched the procession. There were four men and one woman marching between the armed soldiers. They were headed toward a large enclosed van that had a state security emblem on its door. The woman marched with her head up. In the station lights the braids in her long black hair shone under the red scarf, which fluttered in the breeze.

"Shirn!" Bissa squealed, and then Raysta's hand was clapped over his mouth.

"You, there!" Mikhail said quickly, moving toward the sergeant in charge of the detail. "What is this?" The procession stopped at his words.

The sergeant saluted, his eyes careful and suspicious. "Our officers found these people in the village, Comrade Major. They don't live here, and they can't explain why they're here."

Mikhail looked at the four men. "What do they say?"

"They say they came here to catch the train."

"And the girl, what does she say?"

"She said she was to meet her boyfriend here. I don't

believe her. She's from a village south of here, near Ochakov, on the sea. What's she doing so far from home?"

"You have their papers?"

The sergeant produced them from his tunic. Mikhail studied them and handed the papers back, except Shirn's. He opened his tunic pocket and showed the sergeant his forged credentials. "You are right to suspect the girl, Comrade Sergeant," he said. "I've taken these two men into custody for questioning. Give me the girl and I'll take them back to Nikolayev."

"But I'm under orders to bring in anyone who acts suspicious," the sergeant said in dismay. "My officer commanded me to bring these four in for questioning."

"Do you contradict the GRU?" Mikhail said nastily. "The girl answers the description of a suspect we have at Colonel Gregorski's headquarters." He gave the sergeant an out. "What is the name and unit of your commanding officer? As soon as I return to Nikolayev I'll contact him and explain what happened."

The sergeant was relieved. He explained that something had happened up the road and the officers had raced off to investigate, leaving him with the suspects. He rattled off the officer's name, rank, and headquarters and seemed to dismiss the affair, although his eyes lingered on the silent Shirn for a moment before he turned away and barked a command to get the four men into the van.

"Move over there," Mikhail ordered Shirn, motioning to Bissa and Raysta. "How did you get here?" He said it loud enough for the curious passengers to hear.

"A truck." Her voice was defiant. "I have permission!"

"Then we will leave here in that truck. Show us where it is." He unholstered his pistol, and with it swinging in his hand, he marched the three of them to the truck. He motioned for Shirn to drive and put Raysta and Bissa in the van in the back, locking the door loudly. Pistol still in hand, he got into the cab next to Shirn.

As soon as the village was behind them, he had the map out and studied it by flashlight. "Turn left at the next road and drive as fast as you can." A dense cloud of black smoke hung behind them, to the north and east.

After a long time Shirn said, "How did it go with you?"

"It went well. I had luck." He held the map loosely in his hand and put the pistol away. "After the explosion I found a car and drove out, right to the train station. It was a matter of getting out of the car and onto the train."

"Was there trouble on the train?"

"None. Bissa and Raysta got on not a moment too soon. Luck for them."

"The lines are down."

"I know. The electricity went off right on time."

"Was the roadblock necessary?"

"Of course. They'll need heavy equipment to dig out. Your commanders said it's all stored in a special motor pool, and that road is the shortest way to get the equipment from the pool to the station. Otherwise it has to go over the river."

She nodded, understanding. "Then the station is down."

"It's burning beautifully. The main thing is that we've given the commanders what they wanted, and we've given Gregorski something more to chew on."

Her voice turned bitter. "He's at the beach. Why aren't you there? You came to kill him. Why aren't you trying to kill him, then?"

"He's not at the beach."

She was surprised. "How do you know that?"

"He'll be in a helicopter coming to the station. Perhaps he's there now." He turned the light on to study the map again.

"Are we going back to the station?"

"No." He put his finger on the map. "Turn left at this intersection."

She did and said, "Where are we going?"

"Odessa."

"Odessa? Why there?"

"Because in the morning that's where Gregorski will be."

"Does he tell you these things himself?" she said bitingly.

"It's the way the GRU works. There'll be a board of inquiry and he'll be present."

"Why?" Raysta said from the window.

"He'll have to explain why the satellite command station blew up while he was getting his boots wet at the beach."

He grunted. "Your papers will get you into Odessa."

Shirn turned to look at him, and her eyes held green fire. "Mikhail," she said softly, her red scarf fluttering in the breeze from the open window, "if you don't kill him in Odessa, I warn you."

"Warn me?"

"If you don't kill Gregorski tomorrow, I will."

CHAPTER SIX

Colonel Gregorski faced the board of inquiry.

The eight officers, summoned hastily, had heard three officers testify, would hear seven others, and now they were deep into their questioning. It was an old familiar situation. He had been before many boards. But the difference this time was brilliantly contrasted to the others. As he turned in his chair he saw behind them, through a series of narrow, closely set windows, the midmorning scene of the Odessa military complex. The last hours of the day before had been vicious!

At the beach, then walking like a dead man through the horrible destruction of Nikolayev, and now here in this brutal morning with these grim-faced senior officers of the army, navy, air force, and State security. Two observer political commissars sat alert at a separate table placed discreetly to one side. The atmosphere in the long room was dry, electric, dangerous. His uniform clung to him like a sheet of thin plastic, hampering his moves, suffocating his skin. He adjusted his pince-nez glasses, aware of his naked hands and discomfited that he had forced himself to discard his beloved gloves. This was no place for his affectation.

"We are told the command station will be in limited operation within a week," he said. "Equipment is being flown in and the crews are being assembled to install it." He returned their stares, sending his cold, scrutinizing eyes along the line of their faces on the other side of the table. At his elbow was a smaller table heaped with documents. "We are stunned as to how this could have happened. There are questions. Why was there just one explosion which in turn started others in the administration building and the control center? Why was there not a single person in this highly restricted area who did not belong there?"

He paused, aware that his face was set in similar intensity. He knew his jaw jutted forward, almost uncontrollably, a device to help him maintain his own belligerence. "What caused that explosion? Why did it occur in Colonel Rakoski's office?" He rose from his chair and walked around the table, thumping a stiff finger on one of the aerial views. "We know it was deliberately planned. Today would have been the colonel's first anniversary as commander of the base. He died a hero's death! He was developing one of the finest installations in the Soviet."

He held up an aerial photograph taken in the first morning light. "These power lines were destroyed a few minutes later. Blown off at ground level by someone who threw explosive material over the fence. Here, at this point, a tree was cut to block the road to prevent the rescue equipment from being brought in quickly from the storage depot." He looked at them coldly again. "A lieutenant and a sergeant were shot in the bachelor officers' quarters, away from their duty at the entrance check. There is no question that they had become suspicious of someone and had gone there to investigate."

Looking down at the photographs, he flicked one with his finger and picked it up. "This is where it started. Here, this one taken at the beach near Ochakov." He raised his head and adjusted the glasses on his slippery nose. He studied them quietly, all in turn. "It started with the Turkish submarine. Why? It staged a pattern of coming close to our international line and dumping its garbage in weighted bags at the same spot. It did this for weeks." He walked around the small table again, rubbing the fingers of one hand together as the photograph remained held by the other. "Then it changed the pattern. Yesterday it approached as usual, in the hours after midnight, dallied, dumped its garbage, and left. Our submarines and surface ships charted it under strict procedures. When we sought to find the garbage, it wasn't there."

He paused again for effect. "Something left the submarine. What? We picked up the sounds of a school of fish, not at all unusual. But the school went toward shore, not out to deeper water. We found aluminum strips in the water. Something went toward shore under the cover of that decoy." He dropped the photograph and slapped his hands together in a quick motion, startling the officers.

"A frogman! He left the submarine and somehow, even though its nearest inland position was too far for normal frogman operation, he made it to this beach. We suspect he had some type of underwater propulsion equipment. We haven't discovered that, but we did find his personal gear, at the bottom of the sea not far from the shore. And it was booby-trapped! They wanted us to find it! We lost eleven men, two small boats, and a helicopter."

He was interrupted by the officer directing the inquiry, a major general of the army, the Minister of Defense, who said in a low, rumbling voice, "This frogman infiltrated our shore defense in the night, and the same day he was able to plant an explosive device in Colonel Rakoski's office? Is that what you're saying?"

Colonel Gregorski went to the table and picked up a map. "Here is the beach where there were heavy footprints, indistinct, but enough to show in pictures a helicopter took that at least one large man was on that beach with two others. Here, offshore, was the booby-trapped frogman gear." He jabbed the map viciously with his finger. "Here, in the cove a few kilometers to the east, is where a very strange fishing boat was sunk."

"We are aware of that. The boat that was seized, its crew allowed to go, then the boat disappeared while under guard last night." The major general's voice was heavy with sarcasm. "Can you give us your opinion as to how it escaped?"

The colonel placed the map on the table. "Somehow the frogman helped the boat to escape because there was something on the boat he wanted. The crew had forged papers. The real people whose names were used were fishing elsewhere and were not involved. There was a guard on board. When they brought him up this morning, we found he'd been throttled."

"Then there was a very large man."

"A trained killer. We can assume that he got what he wanted from the boat and sank it. We can assume it was the explosives." He rubbed the top of his nose, not meaning to. "He came ashore. What was he wearing? Did he bring clothes with him? How did he know where the fishing boat was? Our patrols brought it in that morning because it had tied up alongside a Turk supply ship for repairs the night before. It's all too obvious what happened. The Turks concealed explosives aboard that boat. They fitted it with a system of small incendiary bombs that blew out its bottom when the frogman had gotten from it what he wanted. He came ashore again, in a rubber boat which he hid poorly."

He made a show of checking through the photographs again, flipping from one scene to another. The remains of the frogman gear, the hulk of the old ketch, the rubber boat. "We conclude that the Turks and the frogman wanted us to find these things. They wanted us to know he's ashore."

"Is it your theory," another officer said, "that one man did all of this?"

"No. He had help. The power-line poles were deliberately sabotaged to cut off the major electricity line at a crucial moment. The tree was felled across the single road leading to the construction- and rescue-equipment depot. All in different places at different times."

"This explosive material at the base," the major general said heavily, "was it a small nuclear device?"

"There were no traces of fissionable material, nor any radioactive debris at the site. The first explosion ignited the cooling gases and these in turn destroyed the center."

"What type of explosive was it, then?"

"Our experts are diagnosing it, but the first clues show it to be a more powerful version of the very same type of heavily concentrated plastic material that we have in our own explosive depots."

"You're saying the station was blown up by some of our own explosives?" The major general was even more sarcastic.

"I'm saying it's the same type. Other powers could duplicate it."

"Comrade Colonel," the major general said, shifting his weight, "my curiosity extends itself to why these things have happened in your district. Nothing like this has happened before. Now, here, on the day you arrive from Moscow to become commander of the GRU, these things happen?" It was a deliberate thrust. He'd been expecting it.

"That is our mystery. Why? But all mysteries have threads and we have one. A Major Ivan Kovelev."

"You haven't mentioned him before. Who is he?"

"He entered the station and had proper papers. He walked to the bachelor officers' quarters. He said he had a gift for Colonel Rakoski. The entry inspectors who survived recall him vividly."

"Then he delivered this gift to the colonel?"

"We don't know. A car was dispatched from the pool to the bachelor officers' quarters to pick him up. He went through the checkpoints, we know that."

"Can the driver testify? Why don't you have the driver's statement?"

"The driver is dead. A woman. She was going past the administration building at the time of the explosion."

"The orderly on duty at the officers' quarters? Where is his testimony?"

"He was found mutilated. Glass from a window nearly severed his head at the time of the explosion. A few feet away were the lieutenant and the sergeant, both shot by regulation army ammunition."

"But the major, what happened to him?"

Colonel Gregorski shrugged his thin shoulders. "There was a great deal of confusion. Guards left their posts, people ran in circles. Cars and trucks were left unattended, gates were unguarded." He stopped, looking at them carefully. "The major left a small bag with a shirt, underwear, a shaving kit, and two books of poetry in his room, nothing else. He would not have any trouble leaving the station. The electricity was off in many places. Telephone lines were down. It would have been easy for him to mingle with the rescue crews and to obtain anything that he had come to obtain."

The officers were silent, digesting this information. The major general spoke. "You obviously feel that the explosion was a distraction. What was it this man came to obtain? Was it the death of Comrade Colonel Rakoski?"

"That is the sharpest part of our mystery," the colonel

said softly. "That is what we will find out."

"If he has this object, if that was what he sought, then he will be attempting to leave with it?"

"What we can safely assume is that a skilled organization is operating in this district," the colonel said. "These dangerous saboteurs will make a mistake. We've tripled our security at every military center. All of our GRU people are aroused and fully alerted."

A third officer, silent until then, said, "Could these assassins be from the Ukrainian Nationalist Underground? Your predecessor had a great deal of trouble with the UPAs."

The colonel allowed a frosty smile to form on his face. "These UPA agitators are dim-witted. What they have done before has been child's play. Stupid little things. No, this is the work of highly trained professionals."

Another officer pointed to the map. "How did these professionals get from the beach to Nikolayev in such a short time? Where did they come from in the first place? You said only one man came from the Turk's submarine; now you say there is a group of them?"

The major general's voice rumbled out of his chest. "And what about the submarine? Won't they be trying to get back to it to make their escape?"

The colonel picked up the latest computer reports and made a show of reading the last statements in them. "It's doubtful. They have something else in mind for their escape."

"Why do you say that?"

"The submarine is no longer offshore. In fact, it is quite far away. Our navy is following it. It appears to be going back to its port in Turkey."

"Why don't we board it?"

The colonel shook his head. "It was joined this morning by three surface vessels, all Turkish. It is extremely well protected. We would have something very hot on our hands if we tried to sink it or capture it."

There was another silence. "No, the submarine did its part. I suspect it brought in the ringleader. This Major Ivan Kovelev."

"Is there a possibility that he is a defector?"

"He's a complete fraud. He speaks fluent Russian. He

has false papers." The colonel slapped his hands together. "He is passing himself off as being on the staff of General Zagorsky."

The major general was amazed. "He's insane!"

"My very thought, indeed," the colonel agreed.

"He must be captured at once!"

"We are waiting for him. We have the men we need. We have helicopters and photo-planes for overhead. On the ground we have infrared and radar for night. We have all of the navigable waters patrolled, all airports under tight security. We have installed the most sensitive sound- and electronic-detection equipment in every strategic location."

"Then you feel you have set your traps so that he can't escape?" A long pause. "What about the sonobuoys? Why didn't they pick him up when he left the submarine and got to shore?"

The colonel said nothing. He merely nodded. It was a question that had plagued him all morning. He had no answer.

The major general leaned forward, his massive face pinkly tinged with emotion. "For the security of our country and for your future, Comrade Colonel, this man had better be caught!"

The colonel nodded agreeably. "He will be caught, and so will the others." He held up one of the computer reports. "We will clear up another mystery surrounding the submarine."

They waited.

"The freighter, *Ustyug*. In some manner which we don't know, the frogman must have placed an explosive on her. We know their courses intersected at roughly the same time. We know it blew up two hours later, after it left that intersection area. We want to know how he accomplished this."

The major general leaned forward on his thick arms. His eyes were steady under the black spray of eyebrows. "I wonder if you realize how incredible your testimony is, Comrade Colonel?" he said slowly. "I have never heard anything like it in my life. Would you have this board believe that one man could do all of these things?"

It was a question he didn't care to answer.

The major general persisted. "Leave a submarine far at

sea, guide a submersible unit close to shore, make it disappear, tie his gear to the sea floor and booby-trap it, come ashore, make a fishing boat disappear from a guarded harbor, remove his explosives from it, send it to the bottom, row ashore again in a rubber boat, appear at the Nikolayev station in the uniform of a major, shoot two men, and magically make a bomb explode in the heart of one of our best-protected centers?" It was a long question, and the general was nearly out of breath. But he left no room for misunderstanding his disbelief.

The colonel again had no answer. "Everything points to one man."

The major general looked around at the other senior officers. "If one man can do these things, then we must give thought as to how well organized our GRU district is." He turned his chilly stare to the colonel. "We will continue the inquiry, and you are dismissed for the moment." He paused. "Unless you have more details you wish to add?"

He shook his head, feeling a choking sensation in his throat. Damn it! It *had* been one man!

"I suggest you report immediately to Comrade General Zagorsky," the major general said leadenly. "The question now is, where is this man who has done so much destruction?"

He rose, not liking the way he was being dismissed, unable to think of more points to press his case.

"There is still one other unanswered question," the hulking officer said in the same leaden voice. His eyes were like gunbarrels. "And that is *why* one man came to this area to do these things. At this time? Such a strange coincidence that you both arrived nearly on the same day."

He knew that every eye in the inquiry room had followed him as he left, and he exited from the building in quick, nervous strides, setting his mind to work on the unsolved, razor-sharp riddles. As he neared the staff car where Sergeant Timkin waited alert at the open door, he pondered harshly. Where was this Major Ivan Kovelev? Where were the men who'd toppled the tree and blown up the power-line poles? How had the major gotten out of the satellite command station? What had been in the fishing ketch? How had the *Ustyug* been sunk? He got into the car and watched Timkin shut the door. As the sedan moved away he stared moodily at the military complex.

Where were these destroyers?

Why were they attacking in his district?

What were they really after?

From the jumble of his thoughts a small, pressing realization arose. Nothing resembling *this* had been done in any of the other districts. Was *he* somehow involved? Why had these things happened so quickly on his arrival in the Ukraine? Who in the Ukraine was working with these professionals? He thought of Vera. Were his enemies trying to get at him in some strange, insane way? Was Vera to be another target? He pushed the thought away. Vera was a young girl. She meant nothing to his enemies.

But for the first time that he could remember, there was a cold, uneasy sensation wiggling in the depth of his groin.

He snapped at the sergeant to drive him to General Zagorsky's office. He had no doubt that even then the general was being briefed about the board of inquiry. He sat back and put on his gloves from the car seat where he'd left them as a precaution. He rubbed his gloved fingers together, enjoying the soft feeling of the warm, thin leather.

He removed a small notebook from an inside tunic pocket, seeking some mobilizing force to repair the damage that had been done within him at the inquiry. He flipped to the last page. It was a death sheet filled with a cipher that he had long ago devised and which only he could read. It held the intimate history of the lingering death of his mother.

The death of his mother, nearly twenty years before, was a very personal thing to him. He had never revealed his hatred of his mother to anyone. But even now he could rejoice in recalling every small detail of her death. He could still hear her voice.

"I tried to make a man out of you," she said, staring at him from her bed the night before she died. Her room was on the third floor of the old stone home built in Czarist times, and even then a relic of the forgotten, ignored past.

"You tried to make a puppet out of me, an automaton who would do everything you bid!" he countercharged harshly.

"No, a *man!*"

"I needed a father, not you."

"Your father was a very busy man before his death. You were three years old. It was up to me to raise you."

"Then why didn't you? Why did you send me to boarding school? Why did you pay so many other people to raise me for fifteen years?"

"I had important things to do! The revolution! Lenin gave us an entire new world!"

"If you'd tried to be more of a mother and less of a revolutionary . . . !"

"You indict yourself. What a stupid thing to say!"

"I had to break away from you. I got married against your wishes. I became a father, and that enraged you, didn't it, because you didn't give me your permission? You kept me penned up, you kept me away from people when I was a boy, and when I cried, you punished me. Is that what you mean by making a man of me?"

"You were always crying."

"I was a child, and I was always alone with people I didn't know."

"Are you saying I deserted you? How dare you! I had work to do. Do you think it has been easy, this work for socialism?"

"Just once. If you had been a real mother to me just once!"

"You talk to me as if you had been a real son."

"They told me you were dying. That's the only reason I came back. My wife thinks I came in sorrow. I came because I wanted to see you die."

"What a splendid display of gratitude."

"Why should I be grateful? You tried to destroy me!"

"Destroy you? I wanted a dozen children, and all I was given was *you*. I wanted you to be someone very special."

"You wanted me to be a vegetable."

"If that is so, then I succeeded," the thin, whispery voice said from the pillow.

"You're insane!"

"No, Rykan Antonovich, not me. Perhaps I was strict in your training. I wanted you to be like your grandfather, a *real* Russian. But it is not *I* who am insane." The faded blue eyes had glittered in their flickering intensity. "The insanity is your problem."

He had laughed, a brittle sound. "You'll be dead soon," he had said, "and I'll be free of you."

The vaporous voice had come to him, floating in the dry, unmoving air of the unpleasant room that smelled of harsh disinfectant. "You'll never be free of me," his mother said. Her skeletonlike hand, still wearing the diamond-and-ruby ring, rose from the white covers. It made the final sign, a brush of dismissal.

She died, starting her death battle almost as the new day had begun at midnight, and lingering until just before the new sun rose. Then the big house, once richly attended, once meaningful, was silent, and the funeral preparations by strangers went on. Rykan Antonovich Gregorski had gotten drunk, as drunk as he had ever been, and he had celebrated for four days until he had become ill and had to be cared for in an army hospital and nursed back to health. He hadn't gone to the funeral and had never been to her grave.

He put the notebook away, grateful for the restoration of his spirits it had accomplished. He was in trouble, serious trouble, but he'd been there before. Success in finding the assassin would bring him to the attention of those in Moscow and save him from the torch in the Ukraine. He *would* win! He had his immense GRU machine, and it was only a matter of time.

His thoughts of Moscow made him think of Beria. There had been a *real* Russian! A man who knew how to protect Russia from its enemies. He had learned a great deal from the master. He found himself relaxing. He watched the buildings of the huge base move past the window of the army sedan. When he had his hands on the man who came ashore at the beach, things would change swiftly in his favor. He began to hum.

He knew how the hum sounded. Exactly like the low snarl of an unleashed wolf, and he was pleased when he saw that the hair on the back of Sergeant Timkin's neck rose in uncontrollable alarm.

* * *

Mikhail put on a pair of sunglasses and pulled the old peaked cap down over his forehead.

Ahead on the sidewalk was a kiosk, and he stopped and bought a newspaper, the *Radianska Ukraina*. There was a vague statement in it about a freighter in trouble but nothing about the satellite command station, nothing about the beach. The columns instead were filled with comments about the sixty and more years of progress the Ukrainian Republic had made. A political commentator cast scorn on the NATO powers. A Soviet scientist boasted about the achievement of establishing a new communications satellite. A small story reported how one collective had once again achieved more than its quota.

An entire column was devoted to the Odessa Heroes' Day celebration, which had been under preparation for several days. Speeches, proclamations, dedications. Special observances at the factories and parades of the Komsomol, Young Pioneers, and other local groups.

That evening there would be a special dance festival in the center of the city. During the day there would be a great musical festival.

He shook his head. How long had it been since he had danced? He thought of Detroit and the dates with the mini-skirted girls, the officers' dancers at the sprawling American bases, the officers' parties in Washington. Long, long ago.

He wondered vaguely if Shirn could dance American-style. The thought of her fulsome body in his arms was pleasant, and he let himself daydream for a moment, standing there in the passing crowd on the sidewalk, pretending to read the paper while his thoughts flew aimlessly. Shirn! Her green eyes and full red lips were bewitching. But her eyes had held only anger when she'd left him a short time before to check in at the clinic as the plan called for. What had she said?

"You and the stinking commanders!" she'd cried in the cab of the old truck as they'd entered Odessa. "You want to make a battlefield out of our Ukraine! You killed a lot of innocent people back there." She'd slapped the steering wheel in disgust. "If I'd known it was going to be like this, I'd have taken a knife and gone after Gregorski by myself!"

"Those were Russians at the station, Shirn, not Ukrainians. They don't allow Ukrainians in the administration building or the control center."

"They're dead, aren't they? They're dead and he's alive."

"Not for long."

Her lips curled unpleasantly. "I don't believe you. You said that last night and you said it this morning. Men have died but not him."

Mikhail looked around the street. A black Chaika sedan rolled by, its curtain half drawn. A small group of muzhiks walked on the other side of the wide street, talking noisily with each other. Another boy and a girl, walking close together, held a small transistor radio between them. He could hear the strains of music coming from it. They were expensively dressed for the August day, children of someone important, that was obvious.

Bissa and Raysta were on their way to a rendezvous with representatives from the commanders. He had no idea where it was. They were all to meet Shirn again at the truck in an hour, and the updating information from the UPA was vital for the next two legs of the plan. Finding his father and getting the microminiature computer.

He shifted in his Ukrainian clothes, uneasy, thinking of the problems of getting Shirn, Bissa, and Raysta through two more days.

Something inside him clicked into place, and he felt a wonderment. The gnawing uncertainty disappeared, and a fine new sense grew in him. What was it? He stared at the people on the sidewalk as if he'd just been introduced to each of them at a backyard barbecue.

Hell, he thought, what was I worried about? I belong here. These people aren't much different from the Americans. They do what they can for themselves. They keep it down so they won't be noticed, but they do their thing the best way they can. They care less about who runs the place than they do about what they'll eat tomorrow.

He looked at their placid Ukrainian faces, returning their unmoving stares. They want a quiet life. What they concentrate on is getting some of the better things, more food to eat, radios, TV, refrigerators, cars, better clothes. They're the world's greatest goof-offs on the job, doing just what they have to to get by and no more, and they steal more from the government than any others in the world. But hidden in this crowd are the ones who never forget. The Nationalists.

They've got firebrands here, just like in the States, and thank God. He couldn't do anything here without their haters. He looked around the crowded streets and felt a smile spread itself on his face.

I'm with my people, he thought, *the haters.*

He folded the paper, stuck it in his jacket pocket, and fell in step with a group of Odessans going his way. They walked past blocks of new military off-base apartment buildings, all alike, all constructed in recent years, but all looking in need of repair. He left the group and entered one of the buildings, stuffing his sunglasses in an inside jacket pocket. He saw how poorly the doors fit their framings. He shook his head at the shoddy workmanship as he went up the stairs to the third floor. The building seemed empty. He heard few sounds. A radio was on somewhere. A child's voice came through one of the doors. He went down the hall, careful to step soundlessly, and found the number he sought.

The apartment of Colonel Rykan A. Gregorski.

The key the Underground had relayed to him through Bissa was in his hand. He put it in the lock, turned it, and went in. He closed the door softly behind him. The apartment was empty, dull and uninteresting. He stood silently, looking around at the cheap furniture, smelling the dank odor. Where would be the best place?

He took the thin packet from his pocket and studied it for a moment. Inside the water-sealed cover was a CIA document. In code it reported changes in the method of transmitting military information from within the GRU to U.S. outposts near the Black Sea. It was a sheer fraud.

He went to the wall switch and studied it carefully. He grunted softly and pulled a knife from the leather sheath clipped to the inside of his pants top. With its point he unscrewed the plate. He bent to look inside the small receptacle. It would do. He took the packet, wiped it of fingerprints, folded it, slid it into the area, and replaced the cover plate and screws.

Two doors led from the living room, and he went to one,

opening it slowly and easily. It was the colonel's bedroom. As rapidly as he could he searched the colonel's effects but found nothing of importance. Where did Gregorski keep his papers? Locked in his headquarters safe most likely. He would expect the apartment to be searched, either by the GRU or by the competitive KGB.

The second door intrigued him. The colonel's daughter had joined him. Where was she? The Underground knew little about her except that she worked for Intourist. He stared at the door, then decided against it. He was halfway across the living room, heading to the hall, when the second door opened.

Vera Gregorski walked into the living room, and it was a moment before she noticed him. In that moment he saw her sober face, her incredibly blue eyes, and her braided long blond hair. He reached her before she could make a sound, his left arm encircling her and turning her away from him, his right hand bringing the knife point up to her throat.

"Be quiet!" he hissed between his teeth.

She twisted her head, and her eyes held a shocked look as she tried to see him. He smelled the fresh sweetness of her hair and the tantalizing fragrance of her perfume.

"Who are you?" she said, struggling for breath.

"Be quiet!" He looked around the room. The thing to do was to press the knife home.

"Don't hurt me. Do you want money?"

He couldn't press the knife. His hand shook with the effort. Sweat rolled into his eyes and he blinked. He let his right hand fall away.

"I won't hurt you. Promise not to . . ." He was whispering.

"I won't scream, if that's what you want." Another whisper.

"That's what I want."

"Then let me go."

Something about her sudden calmness jolted him. He released his left arm, and she moved away from him, rubbing her throat with both hands. She turned to look at him.

My God, he thought, *I nearly killed this girl!* He stared at her eyes, lost in their blueness. "You're Vera?"

"What are you doing here?"

Her voice was like music, he thought. He shook his head. "You're not his daughter?"

She studied him. "Are you going to stand there with that knife in your hand?"

He sheathed the knife. "I'm sorry."

She walked to the center of the room as he watched her. She's five foot three or four, weighs about one hundred and ten, has the bluest eyes, and her hair is real blond, he thought. He felt sick. Was this Gregorski's daughter?

"Are you Vera?"

"I'm Vera Rykanova Gregorski." She stood simply, her hands at her side. "Did you want to see my father?"

Uneasily he moved toward her. How would he play this? "I don't want to see him. I'm here because I thought there might be something worth stealing."

"I was robbed in Moscow once," she said. "It was unpleasant. I was frightened."

"I didn't mean to frighten you."

"Well, you certainly did."

"I'm sorry."

"You said that."

"What are you doing here? It's the middle of the morning. Why aren't you at the beaches?"

"For a thief you seem to know a good deal." She studied him carefully. "You know my father. You know we've just moved in here. You knew my name."

"It's my business to know things."

She accepted that. "But you haven't stolen anything."

"There was nothing. I thought a colonel coming from Moscow would have more than this."

She let herself sink into a chair. "Why don't we drop this silly pretense? You're not a thief. If you'd been an apartment ransacker like they have in Moscow, you'd have torn up this place. You'd have gone out that door like a whippet when I came in." She motioned to a chair. "Sit down. Unless you're uneasy and want to leave."

He was captivated by her calmness. "I don't think you frighten easily at all." He sat near her in a wooden chair that sagged under his weight.

Her small hands made a fluttering motion. "I've been frightened all my life. What's your name?"

The suddenness of the question took him back. "Ivan."

She laughed. "I don't believe it."

He shrugged and said nothing.

"Are you GRU?" she asked.

He found himself laughing.

"Then you're KGB?"

"You think I'm here to spy on the colonel?"

"I do. Give me a better reason."

"There are better ways to spy than poking through an apartment."

"Still, it's standard procedure. Father's done it countless times."

"I'm neither one."

"And you're not a very good liar."

He scratched his head and found that he was still wearing the cap. He took it off and tried to stuff it in his pocket. The pocket was filled with the newspaper. He put the cap in the other pocket. "Let me ask some questions. Why are you here?"

"My father ordered me to come." It was a simple statement, but it was colored with obvious bitterness.

"You wanted to stay in Moscow?"

"I wanted my vacation in Sochi."

He sighed, a strange sound from him. "I've never been there. I hear it's wonderful."

"It is if you're with the right people. If you can have fun, a good time. If you can laugh."

He looked at her. "What's it like to laugh? To really laugh and not care?"

Her eyes were suddenly compassionate. "It's been a long time for both of us, then?"

"A long time." He shifted uneasily on the chair, and it groaned. Then he stood, feeling that he had to get away from this strange, small girl. He glanced at his watch and was startled. He'd spent too much time in the apartment.

"You're going?" she asked.

He went to the door, and she rose and followed him. She put a hand on his arm.

"The knife," she said. "Would you have?"

His eyes met hers. "I didn't have to."

"But would you have?"

He put his hand on top of hers and shuddered inwardly at its warmth and softness. "No." He looked at her hair, at the stark blueness of her eyes, the gentle curve of her cheeks, and fought a strange desire to reach out and take her in his arms.

"Will I see you again?" she said. Her voice was low, gentle, with an odd note in it that he couldn't understand.

"No. I won't be in Odessa much longer."

For a precipitous moment he almost bent down and kissed her. He turned, opened the door, and went out into the hall. He heard the door shut softly, and he stumbled as he walked. He was at the stairs when his senses returned. GRU? KGB? The daughter of Colonel Gregorski would be aware of the hidden, dark recesses of counterespionage, of counterrevolutionary work. He stopped, stiffening, his mind alert and working at top speed. The apartment! Had it been bugged? Had someone been listening to them? He felt a sourness sweep through him. They would put the colonel in a place where they could observe him. The Underground had no trouble learning where he was placed by General Zagorsky's staff. He let his mind shift through the meaning of the apartment and came to a conclusion. If the apartment was bugged, there had to be a listening post. Where?

He went down the stairs easily, without a noise. At the basement level he turned into a dimly lit hallway. The post would be directly under the apartment, where the wires could most easily be led. He paced off the distance. The doors were unmarked. He listened at one, standing motionless, then moved to the next. The smell of cigar smoke halted him. He knelt and breathed the air coming from under the ill-fitting door. Someone was in this room! Hand on the knob, he felt the door give. It was unlocked. Slowly he opened it a crack. Enough to look through. He could see the room, bare where his vision fell. He opened the door a touch more. The edge of a table, the legs of a chair. Even more. The back of a man.

He opened the door enough to pass through. He kept moving, and as he moved, he pulled the knife from its sheath. The man was replaying the tape, the earphones tight to his head, the recording machine working smoothly and soundlessly, only its low hum showing that it was on. Next to the recorder was a small portable battery-operated short-wave radio. A clipboard with a log sheet was at the man's right elbow. Cigar smoke hovered over the equipment.

Suddenly aware of the movement behind him, the man twisted and half rose, reaching for a flat automatic in his hip pocket.

Mikhail's knife thudded into his chest at the heart. The earphones fell off and swung wildly by the wire from the table.

Mikhail held him the head and let him sink to the floor. He removed the knife, jerking it loose with a sharp motion. He cleaned it with the man's shirttail and replaced it in the sheath. He turned to the recorder and picked up the earphones, placing them to his head. He heard Vera's voice. "I've been frightened all my life. What's your name?"

He turned the machine off and removed the tape. The cigar had fallen on the floor. He ignored it. He found the matches in the man's pocket. Nothing else. No identification. A few rubles and kopecks and a cigar pouch. He put the pouch in his own pocket. Quickly he unspooled the tape, letting it roll out into a tangled pile on the cement floor. Then he lighted it with a match. The room filled with an acrid stench. The tape curled, burned, and turned to ashes. He ground it into dust with his shoe. He wiped his hands and looked around the room. It was obvious that they had just set up the equipment. No extra comforts had been brought in. One man had been detailed because it was daytime, and only the daughter was there. Mikhail looked at the log. It was noted there. The operator had been on duty only three hours, not quite that. His relief wouldn't come for another three, perhaps four hours. But the radio! He would be making check-ins by the radio. The radio was to be used to summon more men if anything unusual happened in the colonel's apartment.

Had an alert been sent out?

Mikhail reached for the radio and stopped. There might be an outside watch, another man in a car keeping an eye on the apartment building entrance. He couldn't walk out into daylight carrying the radio. But it was an invaluable thing. It had the well-guarded frequencies of the GRU, and if not the GRU, then the KGB.

He pulled the newspaper from his pocket with one hand and his cap with the other. He put the cap on and unfolded the paper. He wrapped the radio in it, wadding up one section of the paper to camouflage the shape of the radio. He put it under his arm and left the room. On the steps to the main floor he put on the sunglasses. When he was on the sidewalk, he moved casually, loosely, as if he had all the time in the world. But he looked from the corners of his eyes as he walked. He saw no one seated in the few cars parked along the curb. Buses and a few trucks went by, and three youths on motorcycles. Children played in the small park across the street with the voices of the babushkas raised in warnings about running too fast or getting clothes dirty.

He was a block away from the building when a black sedan raced down the street. He turned his head to watch it. It came to an abrupt halt before the apartment building and three men, all cut from the same stocky form, burst from it and ran into the building. He shifted the newspaper-wrapped radio to his other arm and kept walking, not breaking his easy stride.

He was several blocks away when he realized what had been in Vera's voice as she had touched his arm.

"Will I see you again?" she had said.

And she had said it with a deep note of loneliness and despair.

CHAPTER SEVEN

Raysta glanced at Bissa's wristwatch. "You're sure you know where to meet him?" he said crossly. "You're sure about the time?"

Bissa, trudging alongside him on the Odessa sidewalk, waggled his head happily. He pointed playfully at a group of white-bearded grandfathers playing chess in a small open spot between ramshackle buildings. He rolled his eyes to indicate that he'd never learned the intricacies of the game.

They crossed the street, dodging a truck, and headed down the long Primorsky boulevard toward the park where Bissa was to meet his UPA contact. The midafternoon breeze brushed the elms and limes, and from somewhere came the sound of an accordion. A group of vacationers passed them, all men and all looking like workers from the same plant. Some of them had pipes, and the air around them was filled with the stink of native green tobacco, *makhorka,* a mixture of leaves and stems cut up together. Bissa wrinkled his fat nose and looked skyward with his eyes imploringly until the group was gone and the odor had diminished. They walked by a sign near the Pushkin statue that announced "Glory to the Communist Party" without looking at it. Farther on was a red-and-gold one that read, "Odessa salutes the Heroes of the Ukrainian Republic." The next block held food markets, graced with chickens tied up by their legs and hanging on outward-braced rods in a way as to almost engulf the sidewalk. At the end of the block was a war monument, a battered weapons carrier set on a wide, flat concrete platform. It looked antique. A long column of trucks moved by the next intersection, and they waited, standing in the cloud of dust the caravan made, ignoring the dirt that fell on their Ukrainian jackets and trousers. Their boots were dirty. One of Bissa's heels was loose and flapped uneasily as he plodded along. When they finally crossed the intersection, they found themselves pushing through a crowd of people alighting from an intercity bus, a mixture of Ukrainians, Byelorussians, Moldavians, Georgians, Uzbecks, and Moslem Turkmen. A handful of swarthy-faced Armenians, sticking together in a strange city, all seemed to have noses made from the same mold, and Bissa stared at them curiously. Another group passed by, and Raysta squinted at them. Ukrainians but with heavy doses of Iranian blood left over from invasions centuries ago. All were in Odessa for the celebration.

"Damn it," Raysta said. "It's a bus station." He propelled Bissa into the old building and headed for the public bathroom. They relieved themselves, squatting casually over holes in the floor in full view of the other unembarrassed male travelers. They cleaned up, washing their hands and faces in evil-smelling Russian soap. Exiting, they were checked by bored militiamen who barely glanced at their *propusks*. At an open counter near the Opera House they wolfed down sandwiches of cheese and meat and gulped glasses of greenish beer.

Raysta wiped his mouth with the back of his hand. "Now, you sack of cow's teats, it's about time. Go meet the man."

Bissa's happy expression turned to a blank one.

"Sweet Cyril," Raysta said softly. "You remember how you're supposed to make the contact, don't you?"

Bissa's eyes began to water.

"Remember! How did they tell you to do it before we left the village?" He slapped Bissa sharply on top of his round head.

"Now I remember!" Bissa said, ducking another blow. He scampered down the sidewalk as fast as his stubby legs would take him, his jacket fluttering behind him, his soiled pullover shirt bottom jogging up and down with the movement of his broad hips. Raysta followed him, melting through a throng of Russian *kolchozniks* who nearly filled the sidewalk. Many of the tourist farmers wore huge beards. Bissa, not looking back, crossed another street and disappeared into a block-square park heavily shrubbed and laced with paths. High in the center stood a statue of Lenin.

Raysta came to a halt and stood uncertainly. He wasn't

to go any farther with Bissa. He was to wait and make certain Bissa got back safely to Mikhail with the information the UPA had gathered since the meeting near the village the previous day.

Babushkas with their grandchildren in tow wandered past him, and he sat down on an old stone bench. He saw that the women looked at him with distaste, and he brushed the stringy black hair from his face, smoothing it back as best he could with his fingers. He buttoned his jacket against the brisk sea breeze racing damply through the park. He crossed his legs and saw how muddy and dirt-stained his boots were. He wet his fingers and attempted to rub some of it off, succeeding only in smearing the boots. He tried to sit nonchalantly, legs crossed, arms folded, his thin body bent forward.

A jeep with four young soldiers in it rolled by, and he looked at them distantly, thinking how it had been in the other time when his own uniform rotted on his back. He blinked, shielding his dark eyes from the light for a moment. He never liked to think of the war. Other days, a long time ago. An unwelcome sound made him raise his head. A tank? It was only a long, ugly lowboy truck coming down the street, heavily loaded with steel girders and growling with the strain.

There had been another sound, in another time. The low, thunderous, chilling noise of the German Panzer tanks rumbling down the Ukraine road toward Raysta and his rifle and his comrades. They lay in the tall grass and smashed bushes, pressing their faces into the rich black earth, the *chernozem*, waiting. Rifles and grenades and Molotov cocktails against the Germans in their murderous steel monsters.

And as he fired his rifle, aiming at the small slits where the gunners' eyes were, others of his company dived under the tanks with grenades, pulling the pins and thrusting the explosives into the clanking treads.

He ached for a bottle of vodka and looked around desperately. He had to wait! Bissa depended on him. Fat, childish, irresponsible Bissa. He fought an impulse to get up and run and forced himself to stay on the stone bench, which now seemed cold and inhumanly hard. He made himself forget the other days. He thought instead of Bissa and how he met the boy, surrounded by a bunch of jeering village kids, taunting him, tossing pebbles to see how many they could make land on the top of his rounded head.

"The poor son of a bitch was laughin' right along with them," Raysta said aloud. "He didn't know." He sniffed and rubbed the bottom of his long nose with a knuckle. "He's never known." He blinked again. Bissa had known little about reality since he'd sat for hours near the bodies of his dead parents after the explosion that erupted through the plant where they'd both worked. Bissa with the scrambled brains, whom sympathetic Nationalists had arranged to be brought to the village and placed under his care.

He sighed and uncrossed his long legs. He spat at an ant crawling by and missed. He tried again and missed. He lifted a boot and ended the ant's journey. "Screw you," he said in irritation.

He looked up, suddenly very much alert, and his irritation changed swiftly to alarm. Two men in ill-fitting suits with felt summer hats pulled down over their foreheads came from the park and walked heavily along the sidewalk toward him. He looked around quickly. Where was Bissa? Three trucks rumbled by, trailing a foul odor of poorly refined gasoline. He stood up and started across the street, away from the park. Away from where Bissa was meeting the UPA contact.

"You there!" one of the men shouted. "Stop!"

He faced the men, head lowered, looking at them with darting eyes. There was no uncertainty about who they were. Security police. KGB. It was written all over them.

"Propusk," the other one said, holding out his hand.

He produced his dirty, creased pass and travel identification paper.

"What are you doing in Odessa?" the first man, said, reading the papers over his partner's thick shoulder.

"You have to have a reason to come to this park on Heroes' Day and see Lenin?" he said, forcing his face into blandness.

"Yes, you have to have a reason," the second man said. He tapped the papers in the fleshy palm of his left hand. "You're a long way from your village."

"I'm goin' back tonight," he said, putting his hands in

his pockets. "As soon as they load the insulators on the truck."

"What insulators?"

"I'm an electrician. I was sent here to bring back insulators." He twisted his face into what he hoped was an engaging smile. "You know how hard it is to requisition anythin' these days. I was twelfth in line. They told me to come back later." He pointed at the papers. "See, I have on the papers about the insulators."

"He's right," the first man said. "It's in his travel papers."

The security officer handed the papers back to him. "You should stay with your truck and not wander around the city, celebration or no celebration."

Raysta stuffed the packet into his jacket pocket. "But it's such a great statue, comrades." He turned and looked lovingly at Lenin standing high above the trees and shrubs. "In our village we have no such wonder!"

The men looked at each other blankly and pushed him to one side roughly. He watched them walk down the sidewalk, arms swinging in unison. Then he spat in their direction and hitched up his trousers.

"Screw your mothers," he said choppingly.

But he said it softly.

Bissa nearly panicked.

Looking around the interior of the park, he was unable to remember what it was he had to do. He rubbed his fat hands together in despair, then slapped his broad cheeks to stir up the memory in his head. A bird fluttered down near his feet, looking for seeds, and he brightened. The bird reminded him of the cabin with Shirn inside cooking borscht and Raysta coming down the path humming an old army marching song. The courier at the village had patiently told him which bench to look for and who would be seated on it, waiting for him at this time, at this park in Odessa.

Slowly he walked, counting the benches, and when he came to the right number, he looked with glee at the old woman seated on it. What was next? He rolled his eyes upward. He was to say something. What was it? Then he remembered the little game the courier had taught him.

"I a dip in the sea would like to take," he said, reciting

his part carefully in his hesitant way. He bent down a little
to see the old lady's face better. She wore a white shawl,
and her long white hair was braided and piled on top of her
head. A bag of knitting was at her feet, near her long skirts
and her worn boots. Her face in the shadow was a creamy
pink, heavily lined, and small eyes were an intense brown.

"A walk in the sand is better," she answered. "It the legs
makes stronger." She knew of him and talked in his way.

He patted his hands together happily and danced a small
jig.

"See!" he cried. "I remembered!"

She nodded to the empty space on the bench next to her.
"Well, you did," she said. "Me you will join?"

He plopped down delightedly next to her, bending forward to see under the edges of the shawl, which capped her
braided hair and covered her shoulders. She continued to
knit as she studied the park area near them.

"Me you can hear?" she asked softly.

He nodded vigorously. This was a fine game! He interlinked his fat fingers across his belly and rocked back and
forth.

"The big one. You a message must take to him."

"Mikhail?" he asked, then looked around quickly. He
remembered he wasn't to use names.

"He about his father must know." The soft voice was
perfectly clear to him, although it carried no farther than
his ears. "In the Dombosky Prison is. A map I will give
you him to take."

He sat motionlessly. Mikhail's father? He was in a prison,
and Mikhail would want to know. Slowly, laboriously, he
began to memorize the things he must tell Mikhail, Shirn,
and Raysta. The granny, as if reading his mind, talked to
him carefully and with emphasis as she continued to knit.

"Old the prison is. Well guarded. In the small building
at the back the father is. Electricians' tools you we will
give. An old deserted *dacha* we have ready for you tonight.
A map also is made you to show where. At the *dacha* the
tools and papers and food."

Bissa's lips moved silently as he repeated the information
to himself. She waited, looking at her knitting but seeing
the people coming and going through the park. The wind

blew a tree branch, and her face was lit harshly by the sun. It seemed incredibly old.

"At the *dacha* under boards in the old stable uniforms are for you. There, maps you need for the thing that flies in space hidden are."

He knew what she meant. The little something that Mikhail must take from the Odessa military complex. When would Mikhail take it? After Mikhail saw his father at the prison? He frowned, concentrating as hard as he could. He resumed his gentle rocking, his arms held tightly across his belly, his ankles crossed. Despite the breeze, sweat rolled down from his curls, dripping into the crevices of his fat face.

"When out the father is brought, at the *dacha* you must hide him. We will come help if hurt you are." She didn't turn her head. "You this have heard?"

He was jolted. He'd heard it all. He bent forward, but he couldn't see her eyes. She was looking down the path at a group of young girls coming their way. "I remember!" he said stoutly.

"The big one tell the plane will be ready. Tell the decoy explosions will be ready." Her words were hurried to beat the arrival of the girls. "The sedan also ready will be, at the *dacha* will be hidden."

She stood up, gathering her knitting. So swift was her motion that if Bissa hadn't been looking directly at her hand, he wouldn't have seen her slip the folded papers into his jacket. It was all he could do to prevent his hand from going into the pocket to touch the papers. She was standing between him and the approaching girls. Behind the girls were two matrons, obviously escorting the group. "Warn the big one, they are stirring as a snake and dangerous are. No move must lightly be made."

Then she was gone, and he stared after her until she disappeared along an adjoining path. The girls passed in front of him, chatting gaily, all wearing the same school uniform, brown dresses and black pinafores. The matrons glanced at him with unevasive eyes, and he rocked back and forth and looked up at the treetops. Where had the little bird gone? One of the girls stopped in front of him and giggled. He brought his eyes down to her and then rolled them impishly, and other girls put their hands over their mouths to stifle their laughs.

"Girls!" one of the matrons admonished. "Move along!"

Bissa looked at her and winked, and she grinned and looked away coyly. The other matron was unimpressed. "What you don't see in the park these days!" she said acidly. "You'd think they'd take a bath before they came to the city!"

He watched them with interest as they moved away, then looked down at himself. Bath? What was she talking about? He'd had one the week before.

He got up and retraced his steps, counting the benches until he came to the main path, a wide, blacktopped sidewalk, and followed that to where Raysta was waiting. He skipped a little as he went.

"You sack of cow dung!" Raysta said to him, growling when he came out of the park. "What took you so long?"

Bissa was surprised. "I long didn't take. I quick came."

"Was he there?"

Bissa dissolved into a shuddering laughter, holding both hands over his mouth, doubling over in glee.

"What's so damned funny?" Raysta said, alarmed.

Bissa wanted to say it hadn't been a man but an old granny. But in the little game that was his secret. "It a tiny bird was," he said, choking happily on the blunt words.

"Oh, sweet Cyril," Raysta intoned. "And they send you to do this kind of work!"

He started off across the street. It was late, and Shirn and Mikhail would be waiting at the truck. He looked around cautiously. The security men were nowhere in sight, but they could come back at any moment. The thought made him scurry faster.

Behind him Bissa's heavy boots made thumping noises.

"A little bird!" he said between giggles.

Shirn came out of the clinic and found Mikhail waiting for her. He was lounging against the wall of the building, his cap pulled low, his sunglasses hiding his eyes in the late-afternoon sun. He fell in step with her, carrying his package.

"How'd it go?" he asked.

"They told me I'm alive, healthy, my back's all right and to go home and not bother them anymore."

He grinned. "You don't look too well to me. You look as if you swallowed a handful of tacks."

She held up the slip of paper. "I have this certificate to prove I was here," she said caustically. "What good will it do?"

"It's part of the plan. You may need it."

"I don't need a slip of paper. I need to see Gregorski in his coffin!"

They walked wordlessly the remaining distance to where the truck was parked. Mikhail got in under the wheel, placing the package on the floor near his feet. She handed him the keys and sat staring through the windshield. He started the truck and drove through the Odessa traffic, headed to the spot where they'd pick up Bissa and Raysta.

"What were you doing while I was in the clinic?"

"I was in Gregorski's apartment."

"You killed him!"

"No. He wasn't there."

"You planted explosives?"

"No, I planted some evidence that will be hard for him to explain."

She was incredulous. "Evidence? What will he have to explain if you kill him?" She released her hands, balled them, and beat them on her knees.

"It's part of the plan. Why can't you understand? There's more at stake than just killing him."

"I wish you'd just go back to wherever you came from. You and your stupid plan!"

"Easy now."

"I don't see where you're doing any good at all."

"Shut up and listen to me," he said brusquely. "That's the reason you weren't chosen by the commanders to be our contact. You lose your temper too much. They didn't pick Raysta because he was a soldier and there may be a time when he'll have to make a choice of killing a man in uniform. They picked Bissa as a go-between because he's the least affected and will do anything because he loves you, because no one would suspect him."

"They're my family, both of them."

"The plan is simply to force Gregorski into a corner where he can't get out. He'll die. Will you believe that?"

"When I see it."

"There's another thing. I'm here for two reasons. Gregorski is one. My father is the other."

She was stunned. "Father? You never said anything about your father! Where is he?"

Mikhail drove for a while, marshaling his thoughts. "When my mother died in Washington, my father was back with the engineering crew at the Dneiper dam. He was an important man, one of the best electrical engineers in the Soviet. He buried mother and demanded to know what had happened to cause her death. They didn't tell him. He went to Moscow to demand an investigation. Instead he was arrested."

"Why? Just for asking?"

"Gregorski was on a highly sensitive assignment in the United States. He was trying to steal plans for the Americans' computers and nuclear submarines. They didn't want him uncovered."

"But your father! How long was he in jail?"

"They dummied a trial, convicted him, and put him in prison, Shirn."

"My God!"

"It was supposed to be for a short time. They wanted to keep him quiet."

"What happened?"

"Gregorski had friends in power. He arranged for my father to be kept in prison."

"For fifteen years?"

"Can you see why I hate? Can you see why I'm here and why there's a plan? I'm going to get my father out of prison and take him with me."

She reached over and placed a hand on his, and the touch made him think of Vera. Vera!

"Why didn't you tell us this? It would have helped us to understand."

"And if any of you had been captured before this, you might have talked."

"Never!"

"The GRU has ways of making anyone talk."

She fell silent. "Where is your father, Mikhail? What prison is he in?"

"We don't know. The Americans traced him to this area. The UPA is trying to locate him."

"What will you do if you find what prison he's in?"

"I'll go in and bring him out."

"Mikhail! How can you do that?" She was huddled against the corner of the door, looking at him strangely. "You, with just Bissa, Raysta, and me? How can it be done?"

"That's why I'm working with your Underground. They'll help me locate him."

"Will they help us bring him out?"

He shook his head. "The UPA had a deadline of this afternoon to find him for me. I have a deadline of tomorrow to bring him out." His words were like knife thrusts. "And I will bring him out."

Shirn shuddered and hugged her arms across her chest.

The truck was hidden in the ramshackle stable next to the weather-beaten *dacha*.

The small frame house with its faded Ukrainian decorations was set away from the main road, connected to it by a winding dirt path that ended in its clearing surrounded by tall trees. It was ancient and looked abandoned. The UPA said it was scheduled to be torn down in a week and replaced with a larger *dacha* for a favored commissar. Night had arrived on the heels of a short evenglow. The windows were covered with heavy pieces of old cloth.

Bissa, standing importantly in the center of the main room of the house, held their attention. The scraps of their meal littered the table, and a half-filled bottle of vodka rested at the edge, near Raysta's hands.

"You elephant's belly," Raysta said pleasantly, his high voice fogged from the drink. "Get on with your report."

"I remember!"

"Then shut up and finish the report," Raysta said illogically.

"He's gone over it five times," Shirn said. She was curled on the bed, boots off, a cup of tea in her hands.

Mikhail sat in a chair with his bare feet propped up on the table. He held a glass of vodka in his hands and sipped at it easily. "Relax, Bissa," he said.

"I remembered everything!" Bissa announced for the tenth time.

"Listen to me," Mikhail ordered. "We're all out on our feet. We've got to get some sleep." He looked at them in turn. "We go to the prison early in the morning."

Raysta's face darkened, and he poured more of the yellowish fluid in his glass. Bissa sobered and sank to the floor, his thick back propped against the bedpost. He stared at Mikhail.

"Dombosky Prison." He held up the map. "We know where my father is. The UPA gave us electricians' tools and workmen's uniforms. More forged papers. We'll be able to get in." He paused, sipping at his vodka. "We have signs to paste over the truck. Shirn will wait for us and we'll bring my father here." He cleared his throat. "Then we'll be on the last lap."

"What does that mean?" Shirn asked.

"Once we leave the prison, all hell is going to break loose around here. We've got to move on to the microminiature computer before they get back on their feet."

"Mikhail!" Shirn protested. "If you get your father out, why don't you run for it! Get out of the Ukraine!"

He avoided her eyes. "We're going to get the microminiature out of the Odessa military complex."

"Walkin' into a death trap," Raysta said thickly. "Thousands of soldiers and God knows how many security police."

"What good is this microminiature computer?" Shirn pressed. "Can't you leave it to someone else to get?"

"For two reasons. The Americans want it. If we get it, that means Gregorski doesn't have it to protect." He studied his glass. "There are some things you don't know. It's the heart of a new orbiting missile space station the Russians are working on."

"A what?" Raysta said, fascinated.

"A space station orbiting the earth. It'll be armed with nuclear warhead missiles. They could fire the missiles at any other satellite in outer space."

"If we get this crappy computer, that'll stop them?" Raysta scratched his hair.

"They need microminiature computers to control the space

station. The computers have to be very small to conserve space and weight. They have to be accurate or the Russians could blow up a lot of their own cities."

"Why is it here, Mikhail?" Shirn said. "All the big electronics centers are up north."

"The Americans said it's a crash program. They have seven centers working on finishing the microminiature units."

"Then if you get this one, they'll still have the other six?" Shirn rose to a sitting position on the bed. "What good will it do to take one if there are six still left?"

"Put yourself in their place. If one working model still under test is taken, it'll slow them up, worry the hell out of them. They'll know another country has some of their secrets." He looked steadily at her. "And the man who is supposed to guard the unit is going to be in even more hot water. Scalding water."

Raysta reached for the bottle. "Somehow our village doesn't seem so bad," he said.

Mikhail examined the UPA diagram of the complex. "Right. The computer is in a special laboratory on the second floor of the headquarters building. Directly over the GRU district command center."

Raysta whistled drunkenly between his teeth. Bissa examined one of his thumbs, which was twitching uncontrollably.

Mikhail rose and went outside of the *dacha*. The night was warm, touched with a little clammy dampness from the nearby Black Sea. He felt dried and uncomfortable, and he stood with his back to the building, letting his eyes become accustomed to the darkness. The door opened and Shirn squeezed herself out, shutting it quickly behind her. No light came from the heavily draped windows.

"It's quiet out here," she said softly, coming to him.

"Like your village. Do you miss it?"

"It's only been a day, Mikhail."

"It seems longer. Much longer."

"You need sleep. You haven't slept at all."

"Tomorrow's going to be a bastard. We'll all need our sleep tonight."

"I don't think I can. I'm too much on nerves."

He was silent, looking at the sky, and she came closer

to him, her shoulder next to his arm. "You're a strange one, Mikhail. I can't believe you do the things you do."

He didn't answer.

"It has to be done, is that the way you feel?"

"I wish it were some other way, Shirn, and it was someone else, if that's what you mean."

"It has to be you?"

"No, it could be anyone else."

"A man like you. A man who hates very much." She put her hand on his arm. "I hate, Mikhail. I hate because of what Gregorski did to me, but I could never hate the way you do." Her voiced faltered. "It makes you do insane things."

"They don't seem insane when you're doing them. Only afterward."

She shuddered lightly. "For a long time I accepted what happened. In part of my mind I did. In the Soviet you get used to what happens. But I never really forgave, never really forgot. When I heard he was coming here, all the old bitterness, the old hate came pouring out. I had to see him get what he gave my mother and father. I could never forgive myself if I let him live when he was so close to me." She looked at the treetops, stark against the sky. "You had a choice. You didn't have to come."

"Choice? There was an army career if I wanted it. I've a degree in chem engineering. Once I thought I might go into chem research." He paused, his eyes half lidded as he searched through his thoughts. "No, I couldn't have picked either of those. The hate's been in me too long." He moved closer to her. "It's strange how you know there are things you must do. Like you said about yourself. I always knew, even when I was a kid in Detroit, that I'd have to come here. When I got older, I knew I had to do something. I couldn't go through my life wondering if I were man enough to do what my hate told me to do." He shrugged. "So, there was never a choice. The madness in me wouldn't have it any other way." He slumped slightly. "Madness is something you don't negotiate with."

From inside the *dacha* came Raysta's voice, singing an old resistance song. It was a high, clear, but not powerful voice:

"Forest is our father, night is our mother,
Rifle and sabre our whole family.
Cossack, leave your girl and go to the UPA,
Burpgun is your sweetheart now."

Mikhail made a move but Shirn held him. They heard
Bissa's loud shushing and Raysta was quieted.

"Will you tell me about your mother?" Shirn said when
it was apparent that the scarecrow villager had fallen asleep,
filled for the moment with his sugar-beet vodka.

He put his arm around her and she heard him sigh deeply.
"I want to tell you about it, Shirn."

She waited, pressing against him.

"There was this celebration, an American celebration
called the Fourth of July. The embassy was almost empty.
We children were supposed to stay in our beds, but my
mother hadn't come in to kiss me good night. We were
going to look out the window and watch the fireworks in
the sky. I lay in bed wondering where she was and why she
hadn't come. I went looking for her."

Shirn swallowed, imagining the boy searching through
the embassy for his mother. A nine-year-old boy.

"I went straight to her room. I heard my mother's voice.
I stood outside the door listening. I knew she was in trouble.
I trembled and cried, and I didn't know what to do. Almost
every adult in the embassy was attending an American party
somewhere."

"You were a child!"

"I heard her beg someone to stop." His voice thickened
until it was a growl. "The door was locked. I beat on it
with my fists until blood splattered out of my fingers. I
heard my mother screaming, and the sound froze my heart."

"Mikhail!"

"There was nothing after that. I threw myself against that
door. I kicked it with my feet. I hit it with my hands and
my head." He stopped, almost choking, and she felt the
sweat pouring down his body. "The door opened, and Gregorski walked right past. He brushed me out of the way as
if I were a fly. I'll never forget the look on his face. His
eyes were a strange yellow. His face was twisted and
scratched. Blood ran down his cheek."

"Your mother!"

"I ran into the room. The chairs were knocked over. The bed linens were ripped and bloody. There were little whips on the floor. The window was open. I ran to it and looked down." He stopped, his voice fading to a whisper of air. "My mother was in the courtyard below, curled there as if she were asleep, laying on the cement under the lights."

Shirn closed her eyes and turned her head in silent agony.

"I ran down and tried to wake her but I couldn't. I put my face to hers and her cheek was still warm. It was covered with blood." He took a deep breath into his lungs. "Some men came and there was a lot of shouting, and they carried my mother away. I heard them say, 'She jumped. That's the story to tell the police.'"

Shirn opened her eyes. "Why would she have jumped?"

He shook his head. "She was trying to get away from him. I think she got to the window to shout for help and she fell."

She couldn't believe it. "At an embassy! What kind of a madman is he?"

"They ordered my mother's body sent back to Russia without waiting for my father to come to Washington. They were to take me to the airport with the coffin. I saw an American newspaper. My mother's picture was on the front page. They said she was a suicide."

"Yes, the Russians would say that."

"I ran away, Shirn."

"In Washington? Where did you go?"

"It was in the morning. We were going to the airport. My mother's body was in the hearse ahead. A man from the embassy was in the car with me. There was an accident in the park we were going through and everyone had to stop. The driver and the man got out. When they weren't looking, I got out the other side and walked up to the hearse. I could see the coffin inside. I stared for a while, I don't know how long. Then I heard sirens coming and I walked away." He breathed deeply, and his body shook with the effort. "There were buses and children around a tall monument. The Washington Monument. I fell in with the largest group of boys and someone called them to get into a bus. I got in with them. I sat in the back where I could slide down and hide. The bus left with three others." His voice trailed off.

"Couldn't they tell you were Russian?"

"The kids were mostly my same age. I showed them some kopecks. I talked to them in my limited English. Later I told them I was hiding, and they helped me. They thought it was a game."

"Where did they take you?"

"There were two teachers in charge of the bus with mothers, chaperons. They talked to each other the entire trip and never seemed to know I was there. We drove overnight to a big city on a huge lake. Detroit. When they got home in time for breakfast, one of the boys finally had to tell on me."

"They sent you back to Washington?"

Mikhail shook his head. "It was a school group, informal. There were hundreds of parents waiting for the buses. One of the boys I'd gotten acquainted with took me with him. He told his parents about me."

"What happened, Mikhail?"

"I told them the truth. I was Mikhail Karlov, a Russian. My mother had been murdered. They didn't believe me. They thought it was a prank. Then someone found a paper with the story in it. It shook them up. They held a family council. They had three children of their own and they were concerned about me. They decided to try to get in touch with my father. They went to the State Department, and it was weeks later they found my father had been arrested, tried, and put in prison."

Shirn gasped. "Mikhail, oh, Mikhail!"

"They had a mess on their hands. Their CIA found that Rykan Gregorski, who then was a major in the counterintelligence service, was the one who'd put my father in prison."

"The Americans didn't arrest you?"

"They were afraid I'd be killed or put in prison. The Russians were trying to find me, looking everywhere. The Americans solved it by doing nothing. The family, the Lordbrynas, told people I was a relative. They enrolled me in schools. They gave me their name. Michael Lordbryna. They raised me."

"But you speak Russian and Ukrainian so well."

"They found immigrants for me to talk to. Detroit is full of them. They spent a lot of time with me. I studied Russian at the university, along with German. Later the CIA sent me to Canada, near Winnipeg, to learn Ukrainian."

"No one in the United States knew who you were except the Lordbrynas and the CIA?"

"Their other security people knew, and they made all the cover arrangements. I got to know some of them very well. They came often to check on me." His grip tightened on her shoulder. "It was sometime in high school that I began to really brood about Gregorski, think about him day and night. Like you, I'd sort of pushed him out of my mind before that, what you do when you've had a nightmare. When I went to Purdue to study chemistry, it became almost an obsession. I started to bug the CIA people about coming back to get him."

"Mikhail, you should have forgotten him."

"When I graduated, I went to them with a proposition. I wanted them to train me so I could come back. They told me to forget it. Then I saw a picture in *Newsweek* about the Mayday parade in Moscow. He was in it with a group of officers. After that, I had to come back. I told the CIA if they didn't help me, I'd come back on my own."

"They were foolish to help you. They shouldn't have listened to you."

"It made sense to them. I worked a year in their Department of State, in the Russian department. They taught me to be a pilot, they taught me underwater demolition, they taught me about the Russian military apparatus, about explosives. I worked a year in West Germany in their Russian evaluation section. When they heard Gregorski was being transferred to the Ukraine, things fell into place. They wanted the microminiature computer. The UPA wanted Nikolayev and Rakoski. I wanted Gregorski."

She leaned her head against his shoulder, exhausted. Her legs were trembling and her bare feet were icy. "It sounds like bad Russian fiction. I can't believe it. It's like a crazy dream."

"It's real, real as it is when I see my father tomorrow."

"Mikhail, Mikhail," she said softly. "You're the only

thing that's real. The only thing." She paused. "At first I thought you were just a cold-blooded American assassin. Now I know you."

He put both arms around her and pulled her to him. "I have trouble telling what's real and what isn't anymore."

"Don't let me go. This is the first time you've touched me."

"You're real. I can tell that." The harshness was leaving his voice. He felt drained, dazed, detached.

"I don't believe you ever think of that. You're a machine. Have you ever had a girl?"

"It's none of your business."

"That means you haven't. If you had, you'd boast about it."

"Have you ever had a man?"

She laughed, a strange nervous sound as she trembled. "Thousands. All sizes and shapes. All of them lousy lovers."

"Now who's boasting?"

She fell silent. "No, there weren't any. I'm off-limits to them. I just hear they're lousy lovers." She raised her head to look at him in the darkness. "Mikhail, we could be dead tomorrow, couldn't we?"

"Don't think of that!"

"I have to think of it. It's my life. What we do is so dangerous. Anything could happen."

"We're in it. We can't get out now."

"We have tonight, haven't we?"

He was puzzled. "We have tonight?"

"Let's not waste it." She raised herself on tiptoes. "Now, right now, let's not be insane. Tomorrow we'll be as insane as we can, but let's keep now for ourselves."

He bent to kiss her, tasting her lips hungrily, holding her taut body tight against his.

"It's ours. It might be all we ever have."

He kissed her again and again.

General Zagorsky was red-faced.

"You talk about getting organized," he shouted at Colonel Gregorski. "We've lost a freighter bound to Cuba with top priority missiles! We've lost a satellite command station for who knows how long! We have more than eighty of our men dead and a terrible loss of equipment, and you sit there and tell me you have to get organized!"

"General, I've only been here for a little more than a day." Colonel Gregorski was depressed.

"Your own apartment was entered. Your daughter reported it at once. A man entered and she frightened him off. One of your own men was killed at his listening post."

"I might point out, Comrade General, that it was a listening post on my own apartment." He felt he had to make a point of that at least.

"The post was set up for your own protection," the general said, unmoved. "After all, you are in a most sensitive position."

"My daughter could have been killed."

"But she wasn't."

"When I said organized, I meant that this district has many military targets. It's taken most of our GRU units to cover them. That has left us vulnerable in patroling airports, harbors, highways, and other areas where these saboteurs might be intercepted."

The general got himself under control. "Would you like me to tell you what Moscow said today?"

"My imagination provides a clear picture. The board of inquiry made it very plain this morning."

"Moscow is at the point of relieving you of your duties."

The colonel was shocked. He rose and stood, shaking with anger. "Relieve me! I won't stand for it! They must give me a chance to bring these men in!"

"You won't stand for it? Come now, Colonel. What would you do if your orders come through to that effect?" The general's face was decorated with a Cheshire cat smile.

The colonel walked around for a few steps. "Why? Why would they assign me here and then, because I can't solve this thing in one day, remove me?"

"Very simple. They feel that somehow *you're* the reason these explosions have happened?"

"Comrade General, I haven't been on duty in the Ukrainian Republic for six years. The time before that was nineteen years ago. Why would I be the lightning rod now for these subversives?" His voice turned cold. "You know the submarine put a man ashore. I suspect he's an American-trained agent. You know what was done at the satellite station was the work of professionals. Explosives, forged credentials, knowledge of the place. It wasn't the work of hotheaded muzhiks taking potshots from behind a haystack. These men are professionals and we'll capture them because they are."

"I'm understandably relieved to hear you say you will capture them. How?"

"This phony Major Ivan Kovelev will show up again. He'll figure he got away with it once, he can do it again. Every post in the Ukraine is alert for him."

"Strange that this man, if he is an American, speaks such fluent Russian."

"He's a defector of some kind, I tell you that. He's working with them. Our problem is, we don't know why. Why was the satellite station his target this morning? We don't know. If he removed something from the station, we don't know what it was because of the tremendous damage that was done. There had to be a reason for that explosion."

"Where do you expect him to strike next?"

The colonel raised his hands and rubbed them together. "Another military post. No doubt about it. They're all on full alert. We're working extremely close with the KGB and the militia. Anything even slightly out of the ordinary will be reported at once and we'll move in."

"It's late, Comrade Colonel," the general said, standing. "I will say only this as you leave. Moscow has given you a few more hours. The pressure is on you to bring these men in." He shrugged. "If you don't, they will recall you for a full inquiry."

He wanted to argue, but the expression on the general's broad face stopped him. "I understand. If I were in their position, I would do the same." He also understood what would happen if the KGB caught the men before he did. The thought sat like a sharp-edged rock in his rounded belly.

He was dismissed and he went back to his office. Captain Prokov was busy with the large pile of teletyped reports. Soldier clerks were everywhere, bustling around, decoding and coding more messages, handling telephone calls, radio messages. The entire GRU Ukrainian Southern District Command was going at full speed right through the night.

"Anything new?" he asked the captain.

"Nothing we can put our fingers on." Captain Prokov dug into the pile and fished out a teletyped sheet. "Here's a strange one from an army sergeant. He was sent with a detachment to a railroad station eleven kilometers this side of the satellite station immediately after the explosion. His officers arrested a number of suspects, four men and a girl."

"Where are they?"

"The men all proved to be citizens in normal activities."

"The girl?"

"A major got off the train with two other male suspects in tow. He took the girl."

"Where?"

"The sergeant said they were going back to the station, but we checked that. They're not at the station."

"Who was the major?"

"The sergeant saw his credentials, but with so much going on, he didn't write the man's name down. He recalls that he was assigned to General Zagorsky's staff."

Gregorski was silent, thinking it through. "It could be our Major Ivan Kovelev, but that would mean he left the station after the explosion, boarded the train, had two men with him, and for some reason wanted the girl as well." He paused. "This railroad station, is it the one where the road-block was caused?"

"The one just after that."

"Then the two men could have been the ones who felled the tree?"

The captain nodded. "But the girl? How'd she get into the picture?"

"That's what we want to find out. Get that sergeant in here and question him. How did this group leave the railroad station area? What did the major look like? Get descriptions of the girl and those two men." He looked sharply at the captain. "We may have our best lead on Comrade Kovelev." He turned to leave. He had to find some relief from the growing depression that was plaguing him. He couldn't afford to allow the KGB to find these assassins before his GRU network hauled them in! Why weren't events working *for* him?

"Comrade Colonel, where will you be?" Captain Prokov's face held a bland look.

"I'm going to check security at a number of places. I'll be back in two hours, no more. If you need me, you can raise me on my car radio. Sergeant Timkin will know where I'm at every moment."

The streets were nearly empty. Timkin guided the sedan without effort through the banner-draped Odessa outskirts. The banners proclaimed Heroes' Day. From time to time there would be patrols of white-jacketed, white-capped militia walking around, and groups of youths with red armbands with DRUZHINNIK spelled out on them. They would stop talking at their intersection cliques and turn to stare at the sedan. Spotting the staff car and the uniforms inside the people's squads, they turned back to their animated conversations.

He began to relax as he thought of Julien's. It was risky going there with the district in full alarm, but he needed it more this night than he had in years. Was the place still open after six years? They denied him nothing at Julien's. He paid well and he got it. When Timkin pulled up before the building, he got out.

"Keep the radio on. Come inside and get me if there's a call."

The building appeared not to have any lights on. It had been six years since he'd been in Julien's, but he couldn't believe the place was closed. It paid off to the right people. Then he saw a subtle movement of a drape as it was pulled apart a crack. He pressed the button at the door. It opened almost instantly, and a tall Armenian stood to one side to let him in. The Armenian was dressed in a Parisian flic's costume.

What a ridiculous sight, he thought as he handed his cap to the man. Who would believe that this swarthy, mustached man even remotely resembled a Paris policeman? He looked at the man coldly and went up the stairs. Lucien met him at the top.

"Ah, *bon soir*, Monsieur Gregorski!" the tiny swish said. "It has been such a long time. It is so good to see you again."

"What have you for me tonight?"

A faint flicker of concern showed itself on the small

man's face, then Lucien smiled and in the smile was all of the degradation the Colonel sought.

"Oh, she is so young!" Lucien said, hugging his small chest in mock ecstasy. "You will adore her."

He nodded and followed the male madame into a room. "Monsieur Gregorski, please meet Mademoiselle Helene." He held out his hand and the colonel filled it with a roll of rubles. "Ah, how nice it is to see you together, you two, on such a lovely evening." He held the money in both hands as if it were a trapped butterfly. "Now I leave you to your pleasure." He left, and the colonel heard the lock snap shut.

"Helene," he said to the girl, "help me undress. How old are you?"

"Seventeen."

His fist shot out and struck her on the left cheek. She twirled and fell against the bed in a shocked heap. She looked up at him and he was delighted to see the fear in her eyes.

"Why did you do that?"

"You're not seventeen. Get up." He watched her stand and rub her cheek. "How old are you?"

"Twenty-three."

"That's more of the truth. Come here."

She obeyed.

"Take that ridiculous gown off." She let it drop to her bare feet, and he studied her. He guessed she was a Byelorussian, not too well built. Her shoulder bones protruded, her hips were wide, and her legs had a definite bow to them, which she tried to hide by using the model's stance. Her breasts were small and high. Her stomach was only a bit rounded.

"Undress me." It took her awhile but she managed. He stood nude before her, and it was her turn to judge him. She said nothing.

"Hand me the belt," he commanded. She undid the belt and gave it to him. He saw that there was an even greater fear in her eyes. "Kneel!" he barked, and she did.

Lucien, standing at the end of the long hall, holding hands caressingly with the Armenian, winced as the screaming started.

It did not stop until a long time later.

CHAPTER EIGHT

Mikhail walked slowly toward the prison gate.

Behind him, at the truck parked in the small zone maintained for nonentry vehicles, Bissa and Raysta were unloading the large toolbox. The truck bore the seal of the Oblast Security Electric Service pasted artfully over the old collective designation. They wore the gray uniform the State Security Electricians sported on important occasions.

Mikhail looked down at his uniform. The UPA, aware of his size, had stolen one that fit reasonably well. He pushed his sunglasses back on his nose and stared at the massive structure ahead of him, a relic of the Bolshevik days. Several of the older buildings had their small, narrow windows boarded up. The more recent ones, those built during the Great Patriotic War, housed the several hundred remaining prisoners, all of them skilled.

His eyes went over each of the buildings. His father was in the farthest one.

He was going to get his father out of it.

The wire fence surrounded the prison in double runs set well apart. It was topped both with barbed wire and electrically charged lines, rusty and dirty-looking. The fence had lost its purpose of standing straight and taut. It rested in many places, showing fatty paunches and backsides down the lines. Behind the fence were the guards, a handful of well-armed but immensely bored middle-aged and teenage remnants of what had been a very large guard force at one time. Ten million people had been destroyed in prisons like this, he reminded himself. Prison wire and guards were commonplace, and Dombosky once had been a most feared place for Ukrainians.

Before the morning light, the UPA had slipped a note under the *dacha* door. Shirn, the first awake, had found it. The real electricians had been diverted. They were to have connected a new bay of computers that were being installed in an addition to the administration building. The telephone and power lines to the prison would be cut a kilometer up the road as soon as the first alarm was heard from the prison. A new contact would be waiting for Bissa at the same park, at the same place, but five benches down. The sedan had been delivered to the *dacha* before daylight and was concealed in the trees a short distance away. First-aid supplies and medicine had been hidden under the floor of the barn.

Mikhail thought of the note and of Captain Pell. The intelligence officer would be pleased with these nationalists and the way they went about things. They'd found his father; now they were helping in every way possible. Nikolayev had made them more than grateful and enthusiastic.

"Good morning," he said in Russian to the two guards who came out of the entrance shack to stare dully at him as he approached.

"Stop right there," one of them ordered. "Your papers?"

"Of course." He pulled the papers out of his jacket and watched as the guards read them. He tugged his workman's cap down over his forehead.

"You're an electrician?" the first guard asked. His round face was thickly pitted. It looked like pink-tinged sponge rubber.

"A good one," Mikhail answered, accepting the beautifully forged papers and putting them back in his pocket.

"We need more of everything around here," the second guard said. "The place is falling apart."

"I can see that." Mikhail glanced at the dilapidated buildings. "Don't you have your own electricians here?"

"We had two of them until yesterday," the first guard answered. He swung his AK-47 rifle onto his back, looping an arm through the leather sling. "I don't know what happened to them."

"They're drunk somewhere," the guard said. "Everybody drinks around this zoo." He held his shotgun crooked in his arms. Bissa and Raysta came, carrying the heavy toolbox between them.

"You'll get an escort," the first guard said, checking their papers in turn. "Go to the administrative office. Someone there will take you to wherever the work is."

"We ought to look into that box," the other guard warned.

Mikhail opened it. The first guard shook them down while the other examined the toolbox.

"What are these things?" the guard asked, holding up two black packages.

"Electrical tape. I keep it wrapped in plastic paper to keep it fresh. The stuff dries out if you don't keep it wrapped." Mikhail held his breath.

"It's heavy."

"You'd be surprised how much of that stuff I use in a day," Mikhail said dryly.

The guard let the packages plop back into the metal box and shut the lid. "Tools, nothing but tools."

"What about them?" the first guard said, pointing to Bissa and Raysta.

"My helpers."

"They don't have toolboxes."

"We all work out of this one, Comrade."

The second guard snickered at Bissa. "This fat one's an electrician! Maybe they won't let him out. They've got plenty of work in there for a fat-ass electrician."

The first guard swung open the steel-mesh gate. "It's the chance you take, comrade electricians." He guffawed. "If you're not out in two years, we'll come looking for you." He waved them through.

They walked along the narrow cement sidewalk and into the depressing administrative building. Mikhail removed his sunglasses. A small wiry man came toward them, and Mikhail was surprised to see that he wore the Leninesque goatee and glasses.

"Ah, comrades!" the little man said in Russian. "What a miracle it is that you came." He bowed slightly, a quick, dipping motion from the hips in the way a bird drinks water. "I am Borlan Ivanovich Markov. I am staff assistant to the administrator. It was I who requisitioned you. I am relieved that you came so promptly. We don't know what happened to our own electricians. They disappeared! We are in serious trouble here with the electricity. Please follow me."

Mikhail followed in the man's wake. He guessed Markov was in his sixties, a retired Georgian who helped out in running the tired, ancient prison. Markov would be a Party member. He cleverly effected the Lenin-like makeup because his facial features closely resembled Lenin's. Despite his short stature, Markov had an air of authority. Mikhail reasoned that it was from decades of work for the Party, not for the prison.

"Comrade Markov, it would be wise if my helpers and I could learn of the trouble."

"Ah, a thoroughly conscientious young man!" He stopped and looked closely at Mikhail. "I think I like you!"

"Thank you, Comrade."

"Let me tell you the situation." They were in a large room filled with men who obviously were bookkeepers or accountants. Records were strewn over the desks along with adding machines and other data recording equipment. "We have a balky electrical system. The wires are old. The fuse protections are old. Yet we are installing new data processing equipment. Our men were working diligently on this project when, *zoosh!* they do not show up for work yesterday."

"We're honored to be permitted to help, comrade."

Bissa and Raysta remained near the door, looking carefully at the layout and the exits.

"May I be permitted a question, comrade?" Mikhail said.

Markov's eyes were wary. "Something troubles you?"

Mikhail swung a hand to indicate the area beyond the administration building. "This is a very old prison. It's falling down. Why are you putting new computer equipment in it?"

Markov relaxed. "Ah, so perceptive! Yes, of course. The prison is being phased out. Soon there will be no prison. All torn down. In its place one of the great data processing centers of the Soviet Union!" His sharp eyes reflected his eagerness. "What you see here is just the start. A pilot operation. Before the end of the year we will have many new buildings." He patted his hands together happily. "We will handle all of the expanded data processing in the Odessa District. We will be connected even to Moscow! So my bright young electrician, you see the importance of it all, don't you?"

"What will happen to the prisoners?"

Markov's smile faded abruptly. "So few of them. Some will stay. Others will be moved." He shook his head. "Not our concern, is it?"

"No, comrade. I was wrong even to think of it."

"The new equipment is in this special room," Markov said, leading the way. "You must connect the new wiring system our men started. The new computers are to be tested tomorrow." He raised his small hands in supplication. "How can we do this when we do not have the electrical connections?"

Mikhail recorded every detail of the room in a sweeping glance. Shiny new computer banks were spread out along three walls of the windowless room. The installation and operation manuals were placed on top of the main machines. A bored guard, armed with a rifle, sat in a chair near a pile of computer tapes arranged neatly on a small metal table. A large empty storage closet, its door open, was in a corner.

Mikhail, walking around the room, managed to read the hand-printed labels of the tapes. LASER BEAMS, TANK MOUNTED. TEST REPORTS: RADAR SENSORS AND SIGNAL PROCESSING EQUIPMENT. TEST FINALS: ELECTRO-OPTICAL SENSORS. TEST FINALS: ROBOTICS FOR MILITARY MACHINE MANUFACTURE. LAB TEST MICROCHIP 500 MILLION.

He turned to Markov, who was anxiously dogging his steps. "I must see the master diagram for the power lines," he said.

Markov's head bobbed up and down. "I will get it for you. I should have anticipated your need." He left.

Mikhail motioned Raysta to follow him out of the room. "I don't believe this!" he whispered in Raysta's ear. "They've left computer tapes in there guarded by one man! There's a tape for a microchip that can process five hundred million calculations a second! It's for a computer to design space-based weapons. They can model a weapon like that on a computer using this superfast technique before they even build it!"

Raysta blinked, understanding some of it. "What do you want me to do?"

"After Markov returns I'll get him out of here. Take the guard. Put him in that closet in the corner. Tape his mouth, hands, and feet. Grab those manuals and the tapes. Dump the tools in the closet and put the manuals and tapes in the toolbox." He looked around at the empty corridor. "I'm going back in and get the explosives. I'll take one and hand you the other. Yours goes inside the control panel of the unit with the red top, that's the master set. Pull the string out as far as it will go. Be careful. It'll be armed when you do that. It has a vibration detonator."

He reentered the room with Raysta behind him. He removed the two black packages from the toolbox, stuffing one in his pocket and handing the other to Raysta. The guard barely noticed them, so complete was his boredom.

Markov returned with the master electrical plan, and Mikhail unfolded it. He found the section he was looking for and traced it with a finger. "I want to make a check of the lines here," he said. "I'll have to cut the power at this transformer in order to tie in the new computer area circuit-breaker box."

Markov looked at the diagram. "That's by the work buildings. I'll give you a guard. Hurry, please! I must go now to attend to other duties." He strode out, and Mikhail breathed again. He glanced at Raysta, standing near Bissa, and their eyes met. He left the room.

Minutes later he walked through the prison yard with a portly Russian dressed in an undersize prison guard uniform. The guard carried a pump gun. He wasn't the slightest bit interested in Mikhail.

Mikhail headed for the work building at the end. The guard at the door opened it for Mikhail and his escort. Mikhail went in, followed by the silent guard. The long, low-ceilinged building was poorly lit. Men worked in groups around a vast array of electronic equipment. Workbenches were jammed with test equipment and production tools. Mikhail walked down the center aisle, looking at the faces.

He'd seen prisoners before but none like these. They were middle-aged or old. Most of them had gray hair or balding pates. They kept their eyes on their work, refusing to look at him and his guard. But from the way they worked he knew they were experts. He felt slightly ill. These men were educated. Scientists, engineers, technicians, probably some had been professors. Men whose views and those of the State hadn't matched, and they'd found this prison waiting for them.

There wasn't a shifty-eyed criminal in the lot. They looked to him like a collection of American businessmen who had found a group hobby to work on, on Saturday mornings. Except for the miserable prison uniforms, the thin, hungry faces and the unmistakable cornered attitude that cruel confinement stamps on men. He found his fingers tightening into fists, and he turned to the guard.

"The line goes from this building to the next. I want to see it."

With unchanging expression the guard led him from the long building to the small separate wooden building adjacent to it. He pushed in the door, Mikhail behind him.

There was no guard in the little building, and Mikhail was surprised. There was one person in the place, and he sat at a machine, dully inserting squares of metal into a stamping device that thumped up and down noisily.

"What is this man making?" he said.

"It is forbidden to talk to the prisoners," the guard said in a flat intonation. His voice was as fat as his belly.

"Comrade, I'm not talking to the prisoner. I'm talking to you."

"He makes electrical connectors the others use," the guard said evasively.

Mikhail unfolded the master diagram. "I'm to make a check of the electrical load on these circuits. Can you find this switch here"—he marked it with his fingernail—"and turn it on and off three times for me?"

"I'm not supposed to do things like that."

"Then why did Comrade Markov send you with me? You're supposed to assist me as well as guard me."

"If I leave you to turn the switch, how can I guard you? It's in the other building."

Mikhail motioned to the prisoner. "Am I supposed to fear this man? You'll be gone no more than three minutes."

The guard looked around, shifted his shotgun, and left to find the switch. Mikhail turned to the withered man at the machine.

"What is your name?" he asked.

There was no response. Mikhail put his hand on the man's

frail shoulder and shook it. "Father," he whispered, "are you Karl Stepanovich Karlov?"

The man turned his head, cocking it as if he were listening to a faraway sound. His eyes sought Mikhail's, and when they met, Mikhail shrank within himself.

He was looking into the vacant depths of an empty soul.

"Are you Karl Stepanovich Karlov?" he persisted.

A twisted smile came to the man's face, and he began to hum a mindless tune. Mikhail stared at him, memorizing the blank eyes from which came no message, no communication to the living. The silvery hair was shaggy, unkempt, untended. The deep creases in the skin were dirt-ingrained. The once-handsome face betrayed the ravages of beatings, of starvation and disease. Large scabrous sores covered his neck and chin. The mouth was firm, almost defiant, but the eyes had long since lost their contact with the world. Before him was a mockery of the robust, pleasant man whose photograph his mother had kept in her room at the Washington embassy.

But it was the same man.

The lights in the section blinked on and off three times. Mikhail stepped away from the man, his eyes not leaving him, and took the black package from his jacket. He moved to a point where he was hidden from the door and glanced at his watch. Nine minutes to ten. He placed the package in a well of the machine and pulled a short string to trigger its timing device.

He heard the heavy steps of the guard. "That was against regulations," the man said. "I'll have to report it."

"That's your duty."

"Yes, it's my duty."

"Why is this prisoner allowed to work on this machine alone in this building? He looks as if he's out of it."

"Him?" He made a motion to his head. "They get that way, comrade. They get that way in prison."

Mikhail took one last look at the vacant-eyed man, then led the guard to the entrance and down the path to the administrative building. "This is a tough job you have," he said over his shoulder to the plodding guard.

"It's tougher than it looks, comrade," the guard said. "This is no Young Pioneer Camp."

"Some of them crack under the strain?"

"You get beat like some of them have, you'd crack too." The guard was breathing heavily.

"These men are scientists, engineers, brainy ones. What did they do to get in here?"

"They angered someone."

Mikhail left him at the entrance to the administrative building and went inside, going past Markov, who emerged suddenly from a room. He went to the computer room and nodded to Raysta. Raysta pushed the control panel shut and tightened it with a screwdriver. Bissa hurriedly picked up the toolbox. He rolled his eyes to indicate that the manuals and tapes were in it already. The guard was missing, the closet door shut.

"What's wrong?" Markov said anxiously, coming into the room.

"It's a more difficult job than I thought," Mikhail said. "We'll have to go to the truck and get another set of tools." He motioned to Raysta and Bissa, and they left, carrying the toolbox.

"Oh, that's terrible! You must hurry." The little Lenin goatee trembled. "They are coming tomorrow. You must understand! These are very special computer models. Some extremely important scientists are coming from Moscow, and the computers must be hooked up and working by tomorrow morning." He was agitated. "Please," he implored, "hurry. There are many highly secret military devices in the computer tapes, and they are to be reviewed by the officials. It is most important!" So agitated was he that he did not notice the missing tapes and manuals.

"We'll hurry," Mikhail said, leaving quickly. He was out of the gate and was nearly to the truck when the first explosion came. It lifted the roof of the little work building twenty meters into the air and sent its walls flying outward. The electric lines, ripped skyward in the midst of the fire and eruption of smoke, shot great showers of sparks. The second explosion came a split second later, sending the computer building into a maelstrom of swirling bits and pieces.

The gate guards were blown forward, and when they got to their feet, they found Mikhail running toward them.

Wordlessly he swung his big fists, and they went down
again. He picked up the shotgun, tossing it to Bissa. He
grabbed the AK-47 and the clips. The fence guards were
running toward them. He stood, spraying bullets through
the wire fence, hot sweat pouring down his face so hard
that he had to blink to see. The guards tumbled and fell as
if they had struck unseen wires stretched across their path.

Mikhail felt a hand slap him across the cheek and heard
Raysta's voice screaming. "The towers! They're shootin'
from the towers!"

He ran with them to the truck, and Raysta jerked wildly
and fell to the ground. Mikhail grabbed him with one hand,
holding the rifle with the other, and dragged him the rest
of the way. Bullets splattered in the dirt around them, and
Bissa let out a long, high yell as he struggled to help Mikhail
haul Raysta into the back of the truck.

"Raysta!" he cried, "hurt you are!"

"Help me! Put your shoulder under my arm!"

The three of them struggled the few remaining steps,
Bissa grunting and Raysta breathing in whiny gasps as each
step took its toll.

"You're not going to die?" Bissa shouted in sheer terror.

Then Raysta was in the back of the truck, ducking the
automatic rifle that Mikhail threw in over his head and
rolling in pain on the floor. Bissa was on his knees next to
him, pulling Raysta's legs from the door so that Mikhail
could slam it shut.

"You fat bag of gas!" Raysta said grittingly. "When I
die, I'll die for somethin' important. Not for a damned pain
in my gut." Tears streamed down his dark face and bubbled
at his mouth as he talked.

More bullets sprayed around them as Mikhail dived behind the wheel and started the truck, racing it down the road
away from the prison. The prison sirens began to wail and
then abruptly stopped.

The UPA had cut the wires. The guards had panicked
and forgotten how to aim their weapons. The prison was in
flames.

And he was leaving without his father.

He had difficulty driving the speeding truck. He nearly
went off the road a dozen times. On a curve he did, bumping

and rattling and scraping a low-hanging tree. His vision was swarming, and he blinked his eyes to see the road.

He could see only the lifeless eyes of his father.

"Are you Karl Stepanovich Karlov?" His voice echoed over and over.

"Father, don't you know me?"

"I am Mikhail, Father."

"I am nine years old and I am afraid."

Shirn, running out of the door to meet the truck, saw Mikhail's face as he swung down from the cab. "What happened?"

Mikhail brushed past her and went into the *dacha*. She turned to Raysta. "My God! *Tell me what happened!*"

Raysta's long, triangular face was pale. He limped, bent over in pain. "His father's dead."

She was stunned. "Bissa," she implored, "tell me what happened!"

Bissa was strangely unresponsive. He held the shotgun and the rifle in both arms like fire logs.

"It went as we planned," Raysta said, stopping near her. He was breathing deeply and clutching his thin stomach. "We got into the shitty prison. Mikhail went to find his father. He was going to bring his father to the gate and blow it up if he had to, for us to get out." He grimaced. "But his father was dead."

"Dead?"

Bissa rolled his eyes hideously and let his tongue hang out. His intent was all too apparent.

Shirn felt ill. She put a hand against the truck to steady herself. "You mean Mikhail's father was insane? Is that what you mean?"

"Mikhail came back by himself. He'd seen his father."

"Why didn't he bring him?"

Raysta's eyes were half lidded and his face was drenched with sweat. Drops of it hung on the end of his long nose. "On the way back we talk to him through the window. He kept saying over and over his father was a shell. An empty shell." Raysta tightened his grip on his belly. "You know what happens in prison. The bastards leave the man alive but they cook his brain."

"Raysta! His father was an idiot?"

"Had to be that. What else?" Raysta's eyes closed briefly. "He left the explosive in the shack where his father was. We got out just before the stinkin' thing went off. It set off the other one we planted in the administration building. The whole crappy place is burnin'." He turned and went into the barn. Bissa followed him, trudging slowly. At the door he stopped and looked at her. Tears were in his eyes. He placed the weapons on the ground inside the door and lifted a fat hand and pointed a finger at his forehead. He tapped his forehead and rolled his eyes. Then he disappeared into the darkness of the barn.

Shirn was cut adrift. Raysta was hurt, although he wasn't bleeding. She wanted to go to him to help. She went to the door of the *dacha* but she hesitated. She didn't hear Mikhail inside. She sat down on the wooden steps, shocked and unable to think, unable to understand what had happened.

The mission to the prison had failed because Mikhail's father was insane. And Mikhail had buried his father. That much was clear. Half of Mikhail's reason for coming to the Ukraine was ended. The other half lived: Gregorski. She understood why Mikhail had wanted to get his father away from the prison first. If he'd killed Gregorski, there would have been such an uproar in the security police networks that getting into the prison might have been impossible.

The assault on the Nikolayev satellite command station had been demanded by her Underground leaders. That much was clear too. The commanders wanted their bill paid first. Before Mikhail went after his father. Before he killed Gregorski.

Her trembling stopped, and she felt the tightness in her shoulders lessen. Mikhail was tougher than even she had understood. A hard-minded man who followed the plan relentlessly. What came next? Would Mikhail leave? Would he invade the Odessa military complex to get to the colonel? The secret device the Americans wanted, was that the next price to be extracted from Mikhail for their bringing him to the Ukraine?

The questions rambled through her mind, and she was so lost to them that she jumped when the door opened and Mikhail came out.

"Where's Raysta?" he asked.

She stood up, unconsciously smoothing down her skirt and brushing her hair from the sides of her face.

"He's in the stable with Bissa."

She followed him and watched as he knelt next to Raysta, curled up on an old blanket on the floor.

"How do you feel?" he asked.

"Like a cow kicked me in the gut," Raysta answered.

"What was it? You weren't hit. You're not bleeding. What the hell happened to you?"

"A war wound it is," Bissa said from the corner where he sat propped up, Buddha-like. "It him all the time hurts."

"Shut up, you loaf of stale bread," Raysta said through clenched teeth.

"Don't be a damned fool," Mikhail said sternly. "What's wrong with you?" He lifted him to a sitting position. "Damn it! What's the matter?"

Raysta's dark eyes began to clear. "How the hell do I know what it is? Am I am goddamned doctor? All I know is when I get excited or run, my gut is on fire." He sniffed, wiping his nose with a sleeve. "It burns like hell."

Mikhail glanced at Shirn. "Get the medicine kit."

She found it, brushed the dirt from it, opened it, and began laying out the articles on the edge of the blanket.

"It's some form of an ulcer," Mikhail said. "Look for an antacid. He needs something for his stomach." He began reading the labels on the bottles and found one. "It's either a stomach ulcer or chronic gastritis." He turned to Raysta. "How long have you had this?"

"All my stinkin' life."

"Be serious. How long?"

"Started in the war. Get nauseous. Vomit. Couldn't keep food down."

Mikhail selected one bottle. "It's what happens when you're tense all the time. Nervous."

"A war wound it is," Bissa said from his corner.

"I'll give you a war wound," Raysta growled.

"Take these." Mikhail handed him two tablets.

"What are they?"

"Tranquilizers. Shirn, get him some water."

"Get me some vodka."

"With a hole in your stomach, that's the worst thing you can do."

"I need a drink worse than I need these."

"What are you worried about now? It's over."

"Those dirty bastards were shootin' at us!"

"What in the hell did you expect? They were lousy shots. They didn't hit anything."

"The hell they didn't!" Raysta held up his sleeve. Two bullets holes were neatly placed along the edge of his left jacket sleeve.

Shirn, bringing the water, gasped when she saw the holes. "You could have been killed!"

"When those blasts went off," Raysta went on, "I damned near let my water go." He took the pills.

Bissa giggled.

In the silence Shirn said, "What do we do now, Mikhail?"

He stood up, easing the strain on his legs from the kneeling position and looked at them in turn. His face was serious and still pale.

"We're running out of time. It won't take Gregorski long to find out the name of the prisoner in the little shack."

Shirn sucked in her breath. Mikhail had killed his father and could talk about it this way! She cocked her head, staring at him.

"He'll know it was someone connected with my father. He'll run a check on all known contacts. It will remind him of the son." He studied the trees through the open door of the stable. The noontime sun was bright, and very little breeze was blowing. "The GRU will be boiling. They can't find the man who came ashore from the submarine. They've found the ketch at the bottom of the Black Sea, but they don't know what happened. They're still poking through the Nikolayev explosion. They're on to us as a group because they'll have a report from the sergeant at the railroad station."

"What're you gettin' at?" Raysta said.

"Now they're at the prison. The manuals and computer tapes were taken, the computers destroyed. The specialists are on their way from Moscow." He returned Raysta's look. "Do you get the picture?"

"I do! I do!" Bissa said eagerly.

"Shut up, you goat's ass," Raysta said irritably. "You don't know nothin'."

"Given enough time, they'll suspect that the Odessa space computer is the real target," Mikhail continued. "They'll put an even heavier guard around it. We must get in there tonight before they reach that conclusion."

Shirn was jarred. "What if they've already thought of it? That means you won't be able to get near the computer room."

"If we move tonight, we can walk in, take what we want, and walk out." He said it so casually that she couldn't believe him.

"Damn you!" Her temper flared. "You'll walk into a death trap!"

"I'll be Major Kulish from Moscow. He's the chief security officer for the computer development program."

"It's a terrible risk. They know Kulish. They won't let someone walk in, say he's Kulish, pick up the computer, and leave with it." Despite herself, she added a thrust. "That's insane!"

Mikhail nodded. "That's why it will work. Tonight. Tomorrow he may very well be here himself."

"How can you be this major?" Raysta said. He sat on the blanket, his long legs crossed, his hands over his belly. It was obvious even in the shaded light of the barn that he felt better.

"The Americans have a dossier on him. On everyone. I know enough about his background to get by on. They took photographs of me made up like a number of them. I have copies of his papers and contact lenses to change the color of my eyes to his." He pulled a packet from his shirt pocket and selected a small print. "We'll get this to the UPA and have them make a pass to the headquarters area with this picture on it."

"But you don't look like him," Shirn protested. She grabbed the print and studied it.

"That's where the makeup kit comes in, hair dye and the contact lenses. You'll help me. Kulish has an old burn on his right hand at the wrist. We'll touch up my hand to give me a fake burn." He looked at her steadily. "The UPA must get me the proper insignia for the uniform. If they're really good, they can find out where Kulish actually is right now. He's scheduled to come to Odessa." He crooked a finger at Bissa. "Shirn will drive you in the truck. You make the contact in the park. Can you remember the things I've said?"

Bissa rose and came forward, nodding his thickly necked head. His eyes were shining. He could play the game again. "I remember!"

"Tell the contact that we go in tonight. That doesn't give them much time. The stuff must be delivered here, including clips for the rifle, and fast. We've got the sedan, so we're that much ahead. But they need a time schedule for the street decoys."

"What's that?" Shirn asked.

"We'll need a lot of noise going on around the city at the time we're going into the complex. The UPA'll set off small explosions and flares all over Odessa. If the security asses are all stirred up, we won't be so noticeable."

"Oh, good God," she said.

"And the decoys must be ready when we come out. It's a matter of extraordinarily good timing. We'll need a place to hide for a few hours before we go to the airport."

"What airport?"

"Dal'nik, where the out-tunnel plane is waiting for us." He took out a pencil and a sheet of paper and, with the paper placed against the barn wall, began writing.

"What are you doing?" Shirn was puzzled.

"The time schedule. Bissa can't remember all of this. We'll have to take a chance and write it out. We go in at ten minutes after eight. We come out no later than thirty five minutes after eight. We'll need a hiding place between the complex and the Dal'nik airport. We'll take our clothes and change from our uniforms when we're in the truck. You'll have the truck waiting for us no farther than ten kilometers from the complex. We'll leave the sedan and switch to the truck. When we come out of the complex, they'll start more decoy bombings and more flares." He scribbled quickly on the paper.

"Sweet Cyril," Raysta said, getting to his feet and grimacing. "You talk like a stinkin' general. When you say *we*, do you mean Bissa and I are goin' into that complex with you?" His narrow forehead glistened with sweat, and there was a sparkle of fear in his eyes.

Bissa bounced happily. "I the shotgun get to carry?"

"Don't do it, Mikhail," Shirn said in desperation. "Three men can't do it. You'll be captured!"

Mikhail finished his writing and handed the paper to Bissa. "Who else do we have? The plan was built on us. Shirn, you'll wait with the truck."

She clenched her fists and looked as if she were going to strike him. "And if it all goes as General Karlov plans, what do we do at the airport? Stand on the ground and wave good-bye to our hero?"

"You come with me."

Her temper boiled over. "The hell we will! We're going back to our village!"

"You're damned right," Raysta put in. "You're not gettin' this cossack in any stinkin' airplane!"

Mikhail's voice was definite. "Now that they have the sergeant's report from the railroad station, how do you think you can go back to your village? He saw your name on the *propusk*. They have descriptions of Bissa and Raysta. When they get around to checking the village, which could have been anytime, how long will it take them to tie the three of you together with a phony Major Kovelev? Your truck will be reported overdue before long." His face was marked with deep concern.

Shirn walked in a small circle around the stable floor. She beat her fists together. "You knew this all the time," she said bitterly.

"No, if you hadn't been stopped at the station, we'd have made it without exposing you." He shrugged. "You've known it too."

His logic was undeniable, and she wilted. She'd known how difficult it would be. She hadn't wanted to face the truth because it was easier not to. She stared at him. This was a man who'd destroyed the shell of his father, who'd sunk the *Ustyug*, who'd turned the Nikolayev base into a disaster area, who was ready to assault the largest military installation in the Odessa area. She felt faint and leaned against the barn door for support.

"Now that we've remembered who we are and what we're here to do, let's eat something and then get to our jobs," Mikhail said. He slapped Bissa on top of his rounded head as one comrade does to another. "Get our uniforms," he said. He took Raysta by the arm and led him to the door. "Do you feel well enough to go?"

"I'd just as soon face the tanks again," Raysta said.

There was no doubt in his voice that he meant it. He hobbled into the *dacha*, but he moved better and the color was back in his face. Shirn watched him go and gave Bissa a hand at uncovering the package of uniforms hidden under the loose timbers of the stable floor. She dusted her hands and found her voice. She had to swallow twice before the words would come. "Mikhail, can't we just stop?"

She saw that his eyes were uncomprehending.

"I mean, we've done so much. Let the Americans get their own stinking computer."

"We can't stop. It's what we need to put Gregorski away once and for all."

The way he said it frightened her with the enormous finality of the decision.

"I don't want us to die," she said slowly and softly. "I just found you and I don't want us to die." She put her hands over her face because suddenly the light seemed too intense to bear. She wanted a darkness to hide in. She felt his arms around her, heard his voice as he spoke into the top of her hair.

"We have to try," he said patiently to her, "or what is left of our lives would always be a question mark."

The GRU patrol surrounded the old cabin, the headlights of four army vehicles aimed at its sides.

When no one obeyed his shouted commands to come out of the unlighted *khootir*, pistol in hand, the lieutenant approached the door cautiously. He saw the rusty padlock and motioned to one of the men to break it. A soldier fetched a crowbar from a truck, and the padlock housing was ripped from the old wood. Other soldiers kept their rifles and machine guns aimed at the door and windows. Taking a torch from the nearest man, the lieutenant went through the door. He played a light around, pistol at ready. Another motion and three soldiers entered on a run, all carrying torches. The lieutenant saw the single light bulb, found the switch, and the light came on.

A soldier came out of Shirn's room. "Comrade Lieutenant, there's no one here."

He waved a hand. "Search the woods. They may be hiding. They heard us coming and ran." Then he thought of the padlock. He looked at the uneaten food on the table. He felt the stove and teapot. Cold. It had been some time since anyone had been in the cabin. He stood, thinking of the other *dachas* and cabins his patrol had investigated. They had found no strangers, had been told nothing about strangers. All were citizens with proper papers.

He looked at the cossack statue on the table, at the other wood carvings hanging by strings on the wall. He went into Shirn's room. On the table was an amazingly good wood carving of a man and a woman, holding hands. He held it up to his torch. Then he searched the room, finding only a few woman's clothes and toiletries. A soldier came in to report that there was an old shack in the back where someone lived, but it was empty.

The lieutenant shrugged. This was the place where a truck driver from the collective lived with two men. It was recorded as such on the papers he'd been given when his patrol got the assignment to search all the living quarters around the beach. He picked up the man and woman carving and left the room, reaching for the cossack on the littered table. At least he had some excellent souvenirs.

In the cab of the bouncing truck as it left with the others to continue the checking of all the area's residences, he wondered where the three *khootir* dwellers were. Then he sighed. They could not be the ones who blew up Nikolayev, who helped the saboteur come ashore at the beach. Anyone who lived in such a simple place could not possess the intelligence to aid such a skilled professional.

He reached for his report book and, in the light of the torch, began writing a short report of his investigation of the miserable old cabin. It would be radioed in with the others.

* * *

Captain Prokov patiently went through the reports from the patrols, ignoring the hurried goings and comings of other officers in the command center.

Eyes tired from the long day, he shifted in his chair, squinting under the light at the computer printout sheets. Patrol reports, radioed in, had been collected for his review. He came to the one about the old cabin. A woman and two men? Something fell into place. There had been that young girl at the railroad station, the strange major with two men! He turned to his computer video terminal and called up information on those citizens. As it raced across the green screen his spirits rose. He reached for the phone and talked to the collective's security man on night duty. Then he called the village commissar. He sat back, looking at his notes.

He had them! They had passes for Odessa, all for different reasons. Why were these three in Odessa? Then he reached for his tunic and pistol belt, rising. He would not inform the colonel. He would contact his KGB link. He had no idea where the three were spending the night, but in the morning he would have KGB agents scouring the city. He picked up his notes, stuffing them into a tunic pocket.

He checked out and headed toward the waiting car and his driver. They drove toward the bachelor officers' quarters on the base, seeing the heavy traffic on its streets even at the late hour.

He knew he was grinning. He felt alive and revitalized. Tomorrow, on Heroes' Day, he would add another accomplishment to his record. He would concentrate on the young woman. She would lead him to the saboteur!

He thought of the dour colonel and laughed.

The sedan came to a stop in front of the quarters, and he bounded in, going straight to his room. He poured himself a drink and sat for a long time planning what he would do on Heroes' Day.

He picked up the telephone and called his KGB link.

They lay naked under the blanket, on another stretched on the hard *dacha* floor, listening to the loud snores of Bissa and Raysta in the adjoining room.

"My father was thirty-five when my mother died," Mikhail said. Shirn lay next to him, her head in the cradle of his arm.

"She was thirty-one. Beautiful. Dark hair, blue eyes, very buxom, intelligent, well trained. Born in Leningrad, like my father. She'd been a member of the Communist Youth League. Her parents had broken up. Lived apart. My grandmother on her side had been a Communist, and my grandfather didn't like it. He became a drunk. After my mother died, I was told by the CIA, they were hounded by people who said she'd committed suicide in the embassy. They're dead now, but I don't know how they died. I have relatives up north and I know some of their names. I can't go visiting them."

She stirred, moving a touch closer to the warmth of his body. "Tell me about your father."

"He was really in love with Mother. He was so proud of her. She was number one in her class at the cryptographer school the KGB runs in Moscow. She learned English. When she was sent to Washington, he was sent on a string of new field trips. He had his parents look after me while he was gone, in Kalinin, where I was born."

He moved restlessly. "The last full day I was with him, he took me out to fly a kite and have a picnic. In the hills. He was jovial, handsome. We had a great time. I loved him very much. But I was lonesome for Mother, so he arranged for me to have a holiday with her. He took me to the airport when the papers cleared. That's the last time I saw him. I've never forgotten the hug and kiss he gave me. I saw his love for me in his eyes."

They were silent for a long time. "I remember my father, before Gregorski came to arrest him," she said. "He was worried about the plant. The idiots from Moscow were doing things he couldn't control. I heard him talking to Mother about it. He took us to a circus that last day. I was in heaven, it was so good. When we got home, *he* was there with his GRU men, waiting for us. My Mother screamed when they threw Father in a car and drove off. She went running after them, still screaming." Her voice was soft, muted by emotion. "You and I, Mikhail, we live with the screams of our mothers."

His arms closed around her, and she felt his tears against her face.

She closed her eyes, knowing why his strong body was trembling. *I thought he was an assassin. I thought he was a machine. Now I know who he is and what he is.*

And I love him.

Tears came to her own eyes.

CHAPTER NINE

Odessa was alive with two sounds.

One was the music and dance festival that was being held in ten of the city's parks.

The other was the more quiet but ominous sound of the security forces at work, with an extraordinary number of motor patrols and teams on foot. All entrances to the city were checkpointed with traffic tied up for long distances as trucks and autos were investigated.

Shirn, stopped twice as she'd driven the truck into town from the *dacha*, was relieved that they carried the proper travel registration papers from the village. They'd parked the truck on a side street, and now, watching the massive crowds in downtown Odessa for the celebration, she worried about getting back to the *dacha* and Mikhail. The security measures were the strongest she'd ever seen. Impulsively she turned to Bissa and Raysta and pulled them to a small clearing along the tree-lined sidewalk. She looked into each of their faces.

"Listen," she said softly, still holding them tightly by the arms, "you know how dangerous all this is." She stopped to swallow, which she did with difficulty. "I'm sorry I got you involved in it." She looked around to make certain no one was eavesdropping. "Third ears" were always around, fink informers who made a career out of listening to others. No one paid any attention to them. "I want you to know how proud I am of you. You've done so well." She swallowed again. "You're my family." She found the words she hadn't used in years. "I love you. I love you both very much."

Raysta's long face suddenly softened from its dark homeliness. *"Moia zironka,"* he said gently, "your love is our life."

"My little star she is also," Bissa said possessively. "What you do, we do with you, *moia zironka.*" He turned to look at a group of Russian vacationers nearing them. Shirn released their arms and stepped away.

Raysta, looking at the sky, said, "It's goin' to storm again."

"It feels that way," Shirn agreed. "It always rains when it's this hot and humid." They turned and walked through the crowds toward the park. "That's all we need, another storm." She looked around. "Where's Bissa?"

Raysta exploded. "You pile of chicken beaks, get back here!" he yelled at Bissa, who had stopped behind them on the sidewalk to watch a group of dancers doing the *kozachok* in pairs in the street. His big boot was stamping up and down in time to the music of the accordions and the *kobzas,* stringed Ukrainian instruments. He paid no attention to Raysta.

Shirn walked back the distance and took Bissa gently by the arm. She led him to the main entrance to the park, threading through the heavy crowd of people who were watching another group of dancers performing the *metelytsia.* From all over the park came the sounds of singing and musical groups. A large wooden platform had been built near the Lenin statue, and a group of young girl dancers from an Odessa school were midway through their *podolianochka.* She pulled Bissa to her as Raysta glared angrily at him.

"You must remember everything." She looked into his pale brown eyes. "You know how important it is."

He nodded his head vigorously, completely happy in the welter of sounds and aware that he could play the game again.

"Raysta will wait right here for you. I'm going to buy some medicine for his stomach. Do you understand?"

He nodded again, but he was watching the colorful dancers in the street. The men wore the old national costumes, *sharavary* trousers, *vyshyvanka* embroidered shirts, and the high boots, *tchoboty.*

"I'll meet you at the truck." Shirn turned to Raysta and handed him the key. "You keep this. I don't want to take a chance on losing it." She shoved Bissa. "Hurry, please! There's so little time left."

Bissa moved jauntily down the path, shouldering through the stream of people, his bulky shape seemingly stirred with a sense of mission.

Shirn sighed. "This is a terrible place for a contact," she whispered to Raysta. "All these people!"

"They must know what they're doin'. They set it up."

Her green eyes took in the merrymaking, and she sighed again. All this business with Mikhail was making her jumpy. Next she'd see monsters lurking behind the elms and limes. Reluctantly she left Raysta, leaning against a tree, the traces of discomfort still on his dark face and went to find the medicine.

It took her longer than she'd planned. Only one small shop sold the bottled antacid that Mikhail had suggested. She bought two. Mikhail! He was at the *dacha*, fixing the uniforms, dying his blond hair brown, getting his explosives ready for the military complex. Readying himself for the role of Major Kulish.

She saw herself reflected in a shop window, her bright red *khoostka* scarf, white *sorochka* blouse with embroidered front and sleeves, simple *zapaska* wraparound skirt and sandals. It was an outfit the UPA had sent with the courier. Was she pretty enough to make Mikhail fall in love with her? Did he feel the love she felt for him?

Glancing nervously at her reflections, she walked along the sidewalk, hurrying toward the place where they'd parked the truck. Just a short distance farther. She was a few minutes late. Bissa and Raysta should be there waiting for her. She bumped into two boisterous drunken men, and her crimson scarf came loose. She stopped to tie it tighter around her head. She was engrossed in holding the medicine and tying the *khoostka* and didn't hear the car stop at the curb near her.

But something alarmed her and she turned quickly. She was looking into the delighted eyes of Captain Prokov, who had a triumphant expression on his pink-cheeked face.

* * *

Bissa and Raysta, coming from the park, were nearly at the truck when they noticed the commotion down the street. As they pushed through the crowd they could see Shirn's scarf and hear her voice screaming insults that even in their village were rarely used.

They began to run toward the scene, but the crowd was dense and the crimson scarf disappeared into a State Security sedan. The sedan pulled away before they got to it, its horn blowing a strident warning. It disappeared into the people in the street, making its own quick path through them, and was lost to sight.

Stunned, they stood on the sidewalk. A smashed bottle, its gooey white contents splashed on the concrete, lay half out of its newspaper wrapper. Four members of the militia were shooing people on their way.

Raysta picked up the unbroken second bottle, grabbed Bissa's arm, and propelled him back to the truck. "Don't look around and don't say nothin'," he growled into his ear.

"Shirn!" Bissa said, his fat chin trembling. "Shirn!"

"It was a captain who took her, that's all I saw. We'll get Mikhail."

In the truck, as Raysta started it and moved slowly through the heavy traffic and the people on foot filling the street, Bissa said, "Shirn! They took Shirn!" He began to cry.

Raysta didn't answer. He concentrated on the task of driving the truck, but he blinked back his own tears.

His stomach was on fire again, and he fought to keep from doubling over, trying to recall exactly what Mikhail had told him to do in such an emergency.

Vera Gregorski walked along the beach, looking at every male face. She was disappointed. She'd hoped to see the big man who'd held the knife to her throat. Had it been a hint he'd made, about going to the beach? Now she was both disappointed and annoyed. The dancers and musicians and the crowds that had come to see them filled the city. How could she find one man in this mess?

She knew she was being foolish, but he *had* mentioned the beaches and this was the nearest one to the apartment building. This was the one he'd come to if he really wanted to see her again. Now there were not only Russian vacationers everywhere but thousands of Ukrainians enjoying the festival as well.

As she walked in the sand she knew two security women were stalking patiently behind her. She'd seen them the moment she'd left the apartment building hours before. It was nothing new. She'd been followed many times when she'd conducted Intourist trips. Part of her Intourist training had been conducted by KGB officers in a special school known as Intourist Guide so that she'd know how to co-operate with the security forces. She knew that many of her fellow guides also served as spies, a role she'd been able to avoid so far. She could tell each time her father was in difficulty. The security people who trailed her would seem more desperate and more determined to stay close to her. She knew all of their procedures.

She didn't care about the two beefy women behind her. She cared about the tall, handsome blond rogue who'd entered the apartment. He was all she'd thought of since she'd seen him. What was there about him that captivated her so? She didn't know, and she swung her blond braids impatiently. She had no doubt that he was a KGB man sent to spy on her father. And, whatever was going on with her father, it was big. She'd never seen him so shaken as he'd been when he'd returned late the night before. And he'd gone out early in the morning. She had no idea what was happening, but she knew he was under tremendous pressure. He seemed to have aged overnight. She'd made a quick breakfast for him but he'd barely touched it. A stream of telephone calls had come all during the night, and Sergeant Timkin had knocked on their door as the colonel was halfway through his cup of tea.

Depressed, she took a last stroll around the beach, avoiding the sunbathers jammed onto almost every available foot of it, and started back to the apartment. It was nearly two o'clock and she'd been in the sun longer than was good for her. With her light complexion she burned easily, and she'd forgotten to bring suntan oil. She'd even forgotten her sunglasses, and the sun, even though it was shielded by a light ground haze, was brutal. Someone had said a storm might be coming, and it felt like it. Her thin dress was stuck to her body from the humid heat. Her eyes felt baked from staring so long into the faces of the crowd.

If her rogue was there, he was well hidden. She hadn't seen him. She took her time walking back to the apartment. The place was under the usual surveillance. Whatever had happened, someone wanted to know every move she and her father made. No one told her what was going on, but they never did. A man was found dead in the basement of the apartment building, and she'd been interrogated afterward by six different officers for a period of three hours. She'd told them everything, because one side or the other knew who the intruder was. Why deny that a man had been in the apartment? She'd called her father as soon as the rogue left, because she had to. Still, she wished she hadn't. She wished somehow that he hadn't left, that he would come back, that they would find something to laugh about. Whoever he was, he'd had nothing to do with the dead man. Of that she was certain. He could never use that silly knife. There was so much interplay between the security services that it could have been anyone. Even a plot to get her rogue into trouble. The Russian mind worked in fantastic ways, and she was particularly skilled in knowing how security minds worked.

She glanced behind her as she went up the wooden steps from the sand to the sidewalk and the street. The heavyset matrons were not far behind, keeping in step with her. The obviousness of the surveillance irritated her. A colonel's daughter being followed as if she were a common spy! Damn it, she had a perfect record at Intourist. They should know she wasn't a dangerous person.

She decided she'd had enough. She entered a store by one entrance on the corner and left immediately by an entrance at the side. An old dodge. A bus pulled up to the curb, and she got on, putting her kopecks into the box. She left it two blocks later, looking down the street. The matrons, caught off-guard, hadn't moved fast enough. She was away from them! A smile broke on her face, and she flounced her head, making her blond braids twirl. She almost skipped. She'd go to the apartment, anyway, because there was nowhere else she wanted to go. A narrow street ahead provided a shortcut, and she took it because it would keep her out of sight of the matrons a bit longer.

A truck came up behind her, and even though it stopped, she moved to one side to make room. A hand came from behind her and was clapped over her mouth. Strong arms lifted her from her feet, and she was carried to the rear of the truck. She was hauled inside and the door slammed shut. A fat little man held her tightly. He was trembling, and it frightened her even more. A high-pitched voice said from the cab, "Don't struggle! We aren't goin' to hurt you."

The truck started up again, and she bounced on the floor in the immensely strong grip of the fat one who had his hand over her mouth. She fought to free herself.

"Stop that!" the fat one's voice said. "A hostage you are."

She was able to bite the plump hand, and it was jerked away. In that moment she said, "I won't scream. Keep your hand from my mouth. It's too hard to breathe that way." She tried to see them, but in the darkness of the van, she could make out very little of the man. His body stench told her that he hadn't bathed in a long time. "What do you mean, I'm a hostage? Who are you?"

"Angry we are, that's all you need to know," the voice said. His loglike arms held her so firmly, she couldn't move.

"I'm angry too. You have no right to do this. I haven't done anything."

"Your father he has."

She was suddenly chilled. "What do you mean? What has he done?"

"Our Shirn prisoner he has taken," the blunted voice said. "Now our prisoner we've made you."

The interrogation room was unusually large.

Originally it had been a warehouse room where records were stored, but in the giant expansion of the military complex, it was freed for other uses. It served now as one of eight interrogation rooms, complete with tape recorders, lights to be shone in eyes, and soundproof walls.

"Who are your accomplices?" Colonel Gregorski said. He sat erect behind a large wooden desk, his pince-nez firmly on his nose, his arms folded. His voice echoed strangely in the fortresslike room.

"We've been all over that," Shirn answered in her imperfect Russian. She sat loosely, her hands in her lap. "There are no accomplices. Just me. I came to the clinic to have them check on my back."

"You look healthy to me."

"Do you drive a truck? If you did, you'd have an aching back."

"Don't be impertinent. You're here on serious charges."

"I'm here because of a sore back."

"What were you doing at the railroad station?"

"I wasn't at a railroad station."

"We shall see. The sergeant who took you into custody is on his way here. He'll identify you."

"Then he has a good imagination."

"Where is the truck you say you drove from your village?"

"I told you. Right where I left it."

There was a long pause. The colonel's voice was even. It went neither high nor low. Interrogation was an old game to him, and his voice indicated it. "Then why can't we find it?"

Shirn refused to let her face show how the news affected her. The truck was gone! That meant Bissa and Raysta had returned. Then another thought came to her. Was the colonel baiting her? Suppose the truck was still there where she'd parked it? She could not trust a word the man said. She studied him as she would a snake coiled in front of her. They'd brought her into the empty room and thrust her on the stool in front of the single desk, the captain who'd grabbed her smiling broadly. The colonel had made a dramatic entrance, surrounded by six guards. Three of the guards remained with them. At that moment, when their eyes first met, there'd been not the slightest indication that he knew her. Her mind raced with thoughts. Her *propusk* carried her village name, but Shirn was a nom de guerre from the beginning. She'd chosen it because it had no Ukrainian meaning at all. Her real name was unknown in the village, even by Bissa and Raysta. Raysta, with his influence, had been able to get her a name and a village registration. She knew their real names. On missions they lived by code names. Shirn, Bissa, Raysta. How much did the colonel really know?

So this was the man who'd murdered Mikhail's mother, imprisoned his father, who'd sent her mother and father to the New Lands to die in a prison camp. A man who testified that her father was a parasite of the State because the military engines hadn't been made fast enough to suit some Moscow idiot? She watched him warily across the desk as he read through some papers. He'd had too many years of not showing his emotions to let any recognition show in his eyes. He'd seen her, but it had been six years ago. He was making her wait, testing her. What had Mikhail told her about his training last night as they lay under the trees behind the *dacha?* What had he said?

"The Americans trained me for a month on what to do if I'm captured. They made a Russian prisoner of me."

"I don't understand."

"They wanted me to know what to expect if I were picked up. They put me in a cell and treated me exactly like the Russians treat the prisoners they want to break. Guards yelled obscentities at me, taunted me, spit at me, urinated in my cell. They brought me a bowl of lukewarm soup once a day. It had fish eyes and scales in it."

"Oh, God!"

"I drank the whole thing. They ran tape-recorded noises all night long to keep me awake. They routed me out, stripped me naked, and searched me five or six times a day. Women guards stood at the cell door and taunted me with the damnedest sex suggestions they could think of. They kept a bright light on me twenty-four hours."

"For a month? The Americans must be sadistic!"

"They've learned how it works inside a Russian prison. Unless you know what's coming, you can't make it work for you. The thing to remember is, don't fight it. Move along with it. Reduce yourself to the lowest common denominator. The game is to survive. What they'll try to do is break you so you'll confess to anything. What you must try to do is survive, not confess the truth. You have to outlast them."

Her mind raced with other thoughts. Mikhail had said the Soviet Union had more than seven hundred thousand people in its internal security forces. Eighty-five million people had died in lands controlled by the Russians since the revolution of 1917. The Moscow plan had always been to isolate the people from each other, to make them distrustful and suspicious of everyone else. Out of two hundred and seventy million people only eighteen million were in the Communist Party. One thought tumbled over the other, wildly.

What filled her eyes now was brilliant evidence of everything she'd heard from the UPA about the brutality of the KGB and the GRU. How many Ukrainians had died in rooms like this? She steeled herself against a tremble and fought it to a standstill.

Mikhail and his training! How could he know it would be her and not him who needed it most? Her eyes focused on the colonel, head bent over the table, reading through those ridiculous pince-nez glasses. He was losing his hair. The long threadlike scar on his cheek looked ugly . . . had Mikhail's mother put that scar there? His eyes looked wolfish, sadistic. She took stock. She was captured. The colonel was seated across the desk from her. She was in an interrogation room at the military complex. The truck probably had been found as well. Raysta and Bissa were free. Her task was to survive until Mikhail came.

Would Mikhail come?

She thought again about what he'd said about his prison training. She thought of him going into the old prison that morning and what he'd done. "I would have brought him out if he'd been reclaimable. They left me nothing to reclaim, Shirn." She thought of what he'd said about the military complexes, the computer, and Colonel Gregorski. She thought of the way he'd made love to her, hungrily, completely.

Mikhail would come.

She pushed the thoughts of him from her mind and concentrated on the man in front of her. If only she had a gun, a knife, even a club to strike him with!

He let the paper slide from his fingers and raised his head, looking at her coldly. "I'm waiting for your answer. Why can't we find your truck from the collective?"

"You'd better find it," she answered. "It'll go hard on me if I don't return with it."

He rubbed the bridge of his nose with a gloved finger. "You'll not see your *kolkhoz* again."

"What am I charged with? Since when has it been a crime to come to the Odessa clinic for a physical examination?"

"You came for more than that. The clinic gambit was a cover."

"A cover for what?"

"The clinic records show there was nothing wrong with your back."

"Then why does it hurt when I lift heavy things?"

"The X rays showed there was nothing wrong."

"You lift heavy things and see how your back feels."

He placed both of his hands flat on the desk and leaned toward her. "We will stop this foolishness. You can save yourself a great amount of pain if you'll tell us who is behind this plot and where they are."

"Why don't you check my collective? They'll tell you who I am."

"We have done that. You have a strange record. You must be aware of that. You've been there only the last six years. Your name is suspect, your past is unknown. You're kept by two village hoodlums. You live in a *khootir* with them."

"One sleeps in the stable at the back."

"These hoodlums, where are they?"

She shrugged. "Who knows?"

"They're nowhere around the village. The old one is registered to be in Odessa getting electrical supplies. The fat one is supposed to be here peddling his wood carvings. They both were registered to travel with you in the *kolkhoz* truck."

She forced a laugh. "They drink a lot. They could be anywhere."

His eyes glittered behind the little glasses. "Strange, the descriptions of your two drunken protectors are identical to the descriptions of two men who were also seen at the railroad station."

She waited.

"Who was the major they were with?"

"I don't know any major."

"Yet there you were, all three of you, at the station, and you left with the major."

"That isn't true."

"The sergeant remembers you very well."

She waited again.

"If you tell us what you know, you'll be well taken care of."

"I've already told you what I know. Do you want me to invent things just to please you?"

He stood up and motioned to the guards. They left the room, and he pulled open a drawer of the desk. He removed a long leather strap and wound a part of it around his right hand. He came from behind the desk and stood before her.

"Too much is at stake for us to play games," he said.

Her eyes were on the strap. "You're very brave, Comrade Colonel. What do I hit you back with, my braids?"

"Get off that stool and kneel!" He barked the order.

"The hell I will!"

He kicked the stool with his boot, and she went sprawling on the cold cement floor. Her red scarf fell next to her. She looked up at him as he stood over her. He raised his hand high over his head.

I won't scream, she said to herself. *His eyes are those of a madman. I won't scream for him, no matter how much it hurts.*

As the strap came flashing toward her she was thinking of Mikhail's mother.

CHAPTER TEN

The thunderstorm was forming.

The skies over festival-decorated Odessa were thickened with clouds that held the summer afternoon's muggy warmth tight against the city. The revelers on the rock-littered beaches watched apprehensively as the skies darkened. The more cautious of them began gathering their things to head back to the resorts, sanatoriums, and their homes. Noisy flocks of gray-headed crows flew over the city, acting as heralds to the coming storm. Flags of warning flew over the port jammed with ships and boats. The city rose one hundred fifty feet high above the sea, as if trying to avoid getting its feet wet. Vacationers, loitering in the old, weather-worn resort areas, began to feel uncomfortable.

There was a curious foreboding in the air. A group of sailors, boisterous when they started to climb the Potemkin Stairway, their uniforms white and crisp, found that they were unusually depressed and damp when they reached the top of the long climb. An aquafoil ship, arriving from Kherson, moved quickly into the harbor, and they watched it silently.

It moved past six swift little P-4 boats tied to a floating dock, past two gray Kresta-class destroyers equipped with guided missiles, and docked near the berths of a super gunboat of the Mirka class and two cruisers of the Sverdlov class. Overhead there was the drone of a squadron of Tupolev-16 bombers and higher, escorting them, a flight of old SU-7 fighters, all returning from an aerial exercise. The shipyards were visible, the newly laid keel of a helicopter carrier the newest event to attract attention. The fumes from the fertilizer plants helped brace the air with peculiar odors. The granaries were taking in the wheat from the summer harvest, and the chaff from the biggest single grain crop of the Ukraine hung in the air, tickling nostrils and misting eyes.

Atop the old Odessa stock exchange the statues of Mercury, the god of commerce and shipping, and of Ceres, the goddess of fertility, looked with concealed amusement at the people on the streets below. Seabirds rose from the mud and brine of the estuaries, lower than the level of the sea, and began their flights ahead of the approaching thunder and rain. The arc lights were quickly turned on at the immense railway yards as the weather-wise trainmen hurried their loading and unloading.

Mikhail sat in the back of the black sedan, waiting. Raysta, in the front seat, sat hunched, staring straight ahead. They were in full military uniform. Mikhail had put on the makeup, darkening his skin and making him look older, like Major Kulish. He wore contact lenses to change his eyes to brown. On his right hand was a purplish scar from an old burn. It looked incredibly realistic.

"She's been in there a long time," Raysta said from the corner of his mouth. "Time enough for that bastard to kill her."

"He won't kill her. She won't break, not her. She's a lot tougher than that."

"You know what kind of a man he is."

"He'll want her to lead him to us. He'll keep her alive."

"We've got to go in!"

"We'll go in when the plan calls for it. If we don't, she will die, Bissa, you and I will die."

Raysta fell silent.

"Another few minutes. Hold on that long." Mikhail's eyes were half lidded, his face grim and unmoving. He glanced from time to time at his watch. At his feet was the regulation army briefcase. In his pockets were the forged papers that named him Major Kulish. The sedan, stolen the day before by the UPA, had official army markings painted on it. His palms were damp, and he wiped them on his thighs. The briefcase carried the KGB NOT TO BE SEARCHED label.

"Bissa'll screw it up," Raysta said. "We made a mistake. We shouldn't let him go in there on his own."

"He'll make it."

Raysta sighed. "The dumb kid doesn't know what chances he's takin'."

From the port there was a massive eruption of sound. A cloud of black oily smoke shot upward. From everywhere there came the sounds of ships horns and klaxons blaring a cacophony of distress signals.

"It's started," Mikhail said. "That's the UPA's first. Let's move out. It's eight ten." Raysta drove the sedan through the street toward the military complex. Around them in the city they heard fire engines racing toward unseen trouble spots where mysterious fires had broken out. The skies to seaward were dark and threatening, and the first great flashes of lightning streaked across the black mass.

The Underground had the truck with Vera tied inside it. They'd be waiting ten kilometers down the escape route to switch the truck for the sedan.

"The UPA's doing its job," Mikhail said as they neared the main gate of the complex. "Now we'll do ours."

The guards holding Sudarev submachine guns stopped them and took their papers. They turned repeatedly to look at the skies and to listen to the strange sounds from the city. Mikhail studied the gate. It was wide-open to through traffic. The vehicle bar was raised and locked into its upright position. There was no serious block to bar a speeding vehicle coming *out* of the complex.

"What's happening over there, Comrade Major?" one of them asked. "It sounds like all hell's broken loose."

"I suggest you pay attention to what you're here for," Mikhail said harshly, "and that is to guard this gate."

A captain approached, and Mikhail beckoned to him. "I am not happy with the way this entrance is maintained," he said, looking at the man coldly. "I will put it in my report."

The captain examined the papers and handed them back. "We're all on edge, Comrade Major. There've been some crazy things going on."

"My business is the Computer Center, as you can see from my orders. I request an escort to take me there."

The captain waved Raysta on and shouted an order to a soldier on a motorcycle. Raysta followed the cyclist, going by the giant T-64 and T-72 tanks stationed at strategic spots near the entrance. Russian soldiers, their heads shaved under their garrison caps, marched in patrols along the perimeters of the vast complex. The barracks buildings were the typical two-story frame military type. The concrete apartment buildings for the officer corps were modern, rising to five stories but presenting the same drab unimaginative look-alike architecture. In the distance was the military airport, jammed with aircraft. Mikhail, in quick glimpses through the areaways between the buildings, spotted MiG-25s, SU-15 fighters, and old Tupolev-16 bombers. Mi-24 helicopters were rising as the military went to see what was happening at the Odessa port.

The cyclist stopped in front of the huge two-story brick-and-stone structure that housed the military command headquarters, the GRU offices, and the Computer Center. It was alive with people coming and going. Echoes from the thunder over the Black Sea beat against it, and the streaked glass windows shook visibly in the dimming light. Raysta got out, opened the door for Mikhail, and said, without moving his lips, "It'll be hard waitin'."

"Watch your time. We can't be back a minute too soon or too late."

Raysta shut the door. "Luck," he said, and turned away to pretend to wipe the windshield.

Mikhail went into the building, carrying the heavy briefcase by its handle, stopping for another security check. This time there were three officers. Each of them looked casually at his papers. "What's happening out there, Comrade Major?" one of them asked, returning the papers.

"Just a summer storm, but I'd guess a fire has broken out somewhere in the city."

Another officer nodded soberly. "Those crazy vacationers from the north set three fires last year. They damned near burned down a sanitorium at Arcadis. My aunt was there and had to get out in her nightgown."

The third officer studied papers on the desk. "Major Kulish," he said, "we have no record that your arrival was anticipated here." He looked at the special label.

Mikhail stared him down. "I am not always anticipated. My trip from Moscow was not planned until this morning." He allowed a faint look of disgust to show on his face. "I wouldn't have to come if someone in this district would discover how to keep our security under control."

"I'll take you to the Computer Center," the first officer said.

"That's not necessary. I can find it easily." Mikhail walked away from them, the briefcase held tightly and respectfully in his hand. He threaded his way through the stream of military personnel flooding the corridor. The entire building seemed to be on a war footing. He set his mind to recalling every line of the layout the UPA had sent him through Bissa. He brought his left wrist up and looked at his watch. Thirty seconds off time. He hurried up the stairs to the second floor and the Computer Center. The UPA diagrams were perfect. He knew exactly where everything was. At the heavily guarded entrance to the Computer Center he was checked again.

"Kulish?" the officer in charge said. He ran his finger down the list of persons cleared to enter the Center. "Yes, Major, you're on the list."

"I should be," Mikhail said stiffly. "I made the list myself." The real Kulish *had* made the list.

"The sergeant will go with you," the officer said, unlocking the door. Mikhail and the noncom entered. The Center was three long, spacious rooms linked together. The computer development night-shift teams were everywhere. The rooms were manned with an incredible array of equipment.

"The microminiatures," Mikhail said. "Just the microminiatures."

"This way," and the guard led him to a small room at the far end. Their passage through the three rooms evoked little attention from the busy engineers and technicians. Army officers were sprinkled throughout the rooms. One more made no difference. "In here," the guard said, motioning for the machine-pistol-equipped sentry at the door to open it.

The microminiatures were alone. They occupied the center of the unwindowed room. Bright lights from the ceiling killed virtually every shadow. Mikhail's eyes darted from item to item. "Why are these left unguarded?" he said severely. Around the walls and in jutting-out bays were scores of test stands and development equipment, everything needed for the research and prototype production of the tiny space computers.

Something struck the side of the building, and Mikhail turned his head. The rain! It was beating against the windowless wall in frantic torrents.

The sergeant was puzzled. "Comrade Major, there is only one entrance to this room. There are no windows. We are on the second floor. There is a sentry at the entrance." His eyebrows rose. "No one is allowed in here without proper clearance. They do not work in this room this night."

"I don't like it. These units represent a great step forward in our space program." Mikhail walked slowly around the equipment and placed his briefcase on a small table against the wall. "Do you know Colonel Gregorski?"

"The GRU commander? He is in the interrogation room, Comrade Major."

"I want him brought here at once!"

The sergeant was uneasy. "I must have a written order for that. They are very strict."

"At once! There is no time for written orders. My superiors will be displeased at the lack of proper security for the microminiatures." Mikhail kept his eyes boring into those of the sergeant.

"I'll report to my commanding officer."

"There is no time to waste. This has top priority." He watched the noncom leave. As soon as the door shut behind the man, he had the briefcase open. He removed four small black packages, six inches square and two inches thick, pulled the timing strings, and placed them under the test stands, hidden from sight. He went to the center unit, the computer that was the star of the space station program. A tiny but fantastically clever brain under development, a small book-sized unit designed to work for a very long time hundreds of miles above the earth, receiving ground commands and functioning in the intense cold of the outer void. He unplugged and lifted the microminiature, placing it carefully in the briefcase, in the spot vacated by the four black packages.

He snapped the briefcase shut and went to the door. The

sentry turned to him. "Where did the sergeant go?" he asked the surprised soldier. The sentry pointed to the far end of the three long rooms. Mikhail retraced his steps through the rooms, looking neither to the left nor to the right. He attracted no more attention than he had when he'd entered.

He stopped at the checkpoint. "I've no time to waste," he said to the officers. "Take me to Colonel Gregorski."

"That won't be necessary," a voice said behind him.

Mikhail wheeled to look at an officer who had just stepped into their circle.

"I am Captain Prokov, the colonel's aide," the officer said.

Bissa was in trouble.

The uniform fit fairly well, but the commanders had forgotten to provide a belt for it. He'd tied a length of rope around his bulging midriff to hold up the trousers, but they kept slipping down. He was too delighted to be playacting to be bothered by such a small irritation. He hadn't mentioned it to Raysta. He'd watched Mikhail and Raysta drive off and then had gone to his hiding place in a thicket near the non-officer entrance to the military compound. From his concealment he saw troops entering and leaving, some on foot, some on motorcycles, others in personnel carriers. When the blast from the port roared over the city, he picked up a small stone and dropped it and picked it up three hundred times. At the last count he stood up. He had no watch, but counting was better to fill the time waiting, anyway. He walked toward the entrance, trying very hard to remember everything Mikhail had told him to do. He had difficulty, after counting so laboriously for so long. The numbers kept getting in the way of his thoughts. Raysta had taken his watch because a soldier of a lowly rank simply couldn't own one, and he missed it sorely.

He was stopped by a tall guard who looked down at him curiously. Bissa saluted, and his trousers slipped halfway down. Still saluting, he managed to pull them up and hold them in place.

"What're you saluting me for?" the guard asked. Three other armed soldiers joined him. "Are you drunk?"

Bissa let his arm drop, disappointed. It was the first time he'd worn a uniform and saluted, and he'd wanted the guard to salute back.

"Me you're supposed to salute," he said in atrocious Russian.

"For Lenin's sake privates don't salute privates. Where the hell's your *propusk?*"

"*Propusk?*" Bissa scratched his head, and his limp cloth cap almost fell off. Behind them, toward the sea, the rolling thunder warned of the speeding storm.

"Your pass, soldier. How'd you get out of here?"

"Walked out," Bissa said.

"Well, you can't walk in without a pass." The guard turned to the others. "Better call the security officer. I think we got a pumpkin head here."

Bissa was affronted. "Who's a pumpkin head?"

The tall guard bent and sniffed Bissa's face. "If you've been drinking, you're in for it, pumpkin head."

Bissa curled his fat fingers into fists. "In they told me to go and in I'm going."

"Who told you?"

"*They* did," he said mysteriously.

A staff car pulled up and an officer got out. "What's the problem here?" he said to the guards.

"This one's been drinking. He hasn't got his *propusk*."

"Search him."

Two of the guards went through Bissa's pockets, and in the process, his trousers slipped again. They laughed as he tugged frantically to get them back up around his belly.

"He lost his belt," one of the guards said. "There's nothing on him."

The officer stood in front of Bissa, his hands on his hips. He spoke crossly. "Out with it, soldier! What's your name and unit?"

Bissa tried hard to recall what Mikhail had said to do at this point. "Two hundred three," he said, "two hundred four, two hundred five."

The officer's face reddened. "Soldier!" he growled, "watch your tongue!"

Bissa remembered. He pointed to the top of his head and pounded on it with his fist. He rolled his eyes. Then, taken up with his playacting, he jumped up and down in short bursts holding on to his trousers.

"What do you suppose he means by that, Comrade Lieutenant?" the tall guard said.

"I make of it that he got soused and someone beat him up and took his money and papers," the officer said. He glanced at the guards. "I've never seen anything as disgraceful as this!"

"Does he go into the dryout cell?"

The officer was thoughtful. "No. There's something strange about this. If someone stole his papers, there had to be a reason for it. Privates never have any money on them worth a robbery." He made the decision. "Take him to the interrogation rooms. Colonel Gregorski will want to see this one."

Bissa heard the name Gregorski and jumped up and down in happiness. Mikhail had been right! He flipped his head to the left and right, and his thick neck muscles bulged and unbulged with the movement. This was fun!

"Take the idiot away," the officer said digustedly. "We've orders from GRU to report anything unusual." He licked his lips. *"This* is unusual."

When they led him down the stairway into the basement section of the big building and down the long hall to the interrogation rooms, Bissa suddenly stiffened. A door was partially open.

A woman was shouting and the sound echoed.

And he knew who it was.

He stopped suddenly and grabbed the arm of the tall guard. "Now I remember!" he shouted. "It about a girl was!"

"What about a girl?"

"Me a message they gave for the colonel!"

"Colonel Gregorski?"

Bissa nodded vigorously and looked pleadingly at the guard. "His daughter a prisoner is!"

The guard looked at Bissa in amazement. "Fat one, you'd better know what you're talking about."

"Me on the head they hit," Bissa said defiantly. "Me they told to bring the message to the colonel." The building reverberated as the rain struck it full force.

The guard motioned to his companions. "Take him into

the interrogation room. I'll go find Captain Prokov and report to him." He turned to Bissa. "Even before you've sobered up, pumpkin head, you're going to regret you're alive."

Bissa sat erectly on the stool, his moist brown eyes taking in the severity of the room. He heard the boots of the guards going down the long hallway outside. Shirn had shouted cruelly, and he wanted to go to her. But Mikhail had warned him to stay put, and he fidgeted against the turbulent emotions he felt.

He thought of the day he and Raysta had met Shirn, looking lost, hungry, and lonely in the little village. They hadn't known what to do with the fifteen-year-old girl. Caught by the magic of her green eyes, the long black hair, and her youth, he'd offered her his *khootir;* he'd inherited it from his distant relative, the leather maker, the *kozh-zoomiaka*. With Raysta's help he'd fixed up the old stable behind it, and he was happy because he was near her. As she grew older he hoped someday to be her brother. In his fantasies he dreamed of her and was her brother, playing children's games together. Often he hated to wake up and greet the day. Fantasy was better than reality.

Now she was in another room, and he knew she was suffering. How could he save her!

Mikhail, the big man from the sea, was in command. He thought of the way Shirn looked at Mikhail, and he slumped heavily. Shirn paid so much attention to Mikhail. He sniffed in deep despair. Mikhail was the one Shirn had been waiting for. The few other men she'd met had come and gone, and she'd given them scant attention. But Mikhail was different. Would Mikhail save his Shirn? The sound of her pain-soaked voice came to his ears again, and he lifted his head. He'd heard nothing. It had been a memory of what he'd heard as he was led in. Shirn had been in terrible pain.

He began to cry. The tears ran down his plump face and into the blubbery creases of his neck, wetting his uniform shirt. He began to weave on his stool, his hands in his lap, and the guards looked at him in amazement.

"Moia zironka!" he said between sobs. *"Moia zironka!"*

* * *

"I insist there be security in the room with the microminiatures," Mikhail said heatedly. "I'll hold you responsible for it, Captain Prokov."

The captain remained calm. "The room is well guarded, Major Kulish. You saw that yourself." He stared at the ugly-looking burn mark on Mikhail's hand. He looked again into the brown eyes, noting the brown hair, trying to recall what he knew of Kulish.

"I must talk to you in private," Mikhail said, moving down the corridor, away from the entrance security post. The captain followed him, and Mikhail leaned close to his ear. "Don't be a fool!" he hissed. "Don't you see what's happening? All that nonsense in the city is a decoy to take our attention away from the microminiatures!" He looked around carefully. "We have intense development programs under way in seven technical centers, Comrade Captain. This is only one of the seven, but the most progress has been made here!" He looked into the man's eyes. "You're aware the Americans put a saboteur ashore not far from here? You're aware that Colonel Gregorski had just reported to duty in this district? You're aware of what happened this morning at the satellite command station at Nikolayev?" He said it all in flat statements without heavy inflections. "Don't fall into a trap. You must listen to me. Put more guards on the microminiatures!"

The captain's face whitened as Mikhail talked in low tones to him. "But any change in the security must be approved, by the colonel!" he protested.

"Then go get the colonel and be quick about it!"

"I can't interrupt him. He's interrogating a prisoner."

Mikhail put his hand on the captain's shoulder. "You and I both know who your superior is," he said evenly, keeping his eyes locked on Prokov's. "If anything happens to the microminiatures after I've warned you, you know how it will go for you. Is a prisoner worth that to you?"

The captain shrugged. "It's only a girl, anyway. She hasn't talked. She can wait." He moved away. "I'll get him." He hesitated. "Do you want to come?"

"I'll wait for you in the room with the microminiatures."

The captain turned, went down the long corridor, and disappeared down the stairway leading to the basement.

Mikhail waited, counting the seconds, and followed. Moving with deliberate strides, he went along the corridor, holding his briefcase easily. He walked down the stairway and paused at the last step. He heard excited voices echoing loudly.

"The soldier said your daughter is being held prisoner!"

"Where is he?"

"In number two interrogation room."

There was the sound of running boots, and Mikhail waited until a thick door slammed far down the corridor. He went down the final step and tried each door as he came to them. Two rooms were empty. The third contained Shirn and a guard.

Without a sound Mikhail placed the briefcase on the floor, and as he straightened, he sent his fist smashing against the startled guard's face. The man went down on one knee, dropping his rifle. Mikhail brought his boot up into the man's face, and the guard crashed backward and fell against the wall.

Mikhail closed the door and went to Shirn. She was huddled on the floor near the wooden table. Blood oozed through the back of her white blouse. Her hair was tangled. The ribbons had been torn from her head and lay tattered on the floor around her. Her legs and arms were bruised where she'd been punched and kicked. Her face was pasty. One ear was bleeding, a tiny, thin trickle of blood running down her neck. He lifted her to a sitting position.

She looked up at him in dazed recognition, her eyes blinking. There were no tear stains on her face. She had not cried. He put his hands under her shoulders. "Can you stand up?"

She shook her head bewilderedly.

"Get on your feet! We must get out of here. You have to walk." He pulled her up and held her until her legs straightened. He tied the scarf around her head. She held on to him tightly for support. He half dragged, half carried her to the door. He picked up the briefcase with one hand, holding her with the other. He managed to get the door open and to look around its edge. No one was in the corridor.

They made it to the stairway and up it to the main floor. "Lieutenant!" Mikhail called to the provost at the main entrance. "I need your help." The young officer came running. "Colonel Gregorski has ordered me to take this woman to the hospital. She's badly hurt. My car is outside."

The lieutenant called two guards who helped Mikhail carry Shirn out of the building. Raysta stood in the rain with the door open. Huge puddles had formed everywhere. The complex was slowly being flooded.

"Keep an eye on her," Mikhail ordered Raysta brusquely, putting the briefcase in the back with Shirn. "I'll be right back." He turned to the lieutenant. "I must tell Captain Prokov something, a very important instruction. Bring your men and come with me." He raced back into the building, running past officers who stopped to look at him. The lieutenant and the two guards followed in his wake. Mikhail ran up the stairway to the second floor. "Where is Captain Prokov?" he shouted to the security officers at the Computer Center entrance.

"He left with you," the senior officer said, confused.

"Lieutenant, wait here," Mikhail commanded. "He's down in the interrogation room instead of being here. I'll get him." He raced down the corridor and took the stairways two steps at a time, brushing by a group of soldiers coming up the steps. Going down the corridor, he heard voices from room number two, and he quickly went into one of the empty interrogation rooms, leaving the door open a crack. It had been close, very close.

"Why wasn't I told of this!" a sharp voice said from the corridor.

"They didn't know what happened to her, Comrade Colonel," Captain Prokov explained. "She was at the beach, and they lost her on the way back to your apartment. They've been looking all over Odessa for her."

"Get those women here at once!"

The sound of heavy boots filled the corridor. "Where is Major Kulish?" the sharp-pitched voice said.

"He's waiting in the room with the microminiatures," Captain Prokov answered. He sounded out of breath.

The voices went past him, and Mikhail waited until they disappeared up the stairway. He pulled his pistol from its holster, went out into the corridor, and ran to room number two. He pushed inside and saw Bissa sitting on a wooden chair, rubbing the side of his head. Two guards, rifles slung over their shoulders by straps, stood near him.

Bissa saw Mikhail first.

"Mikhail!" he cried. "Me the colonel hit! Me him hit!"

The guards swung their rifles in practiced moves and nearly had them pointed at him when Mikhail's pistol fired twice. The sounds were terrifyingly loud in the thick-walled room. Mikhail holstered the pistol and grabbed Bissa. "Come on!" He shoved the fat little villager to the door and, holding on to the back of Bissa's tunic, guided him up the stairway to the main entrance. He pushed by the wide-eyed guards without a word. Halfway to the car, bending against the rain, he heard a series of shouts from the entranceway. He pushed Bissa harder, and as he did, he felt a sharp pain in his left leg. The force spun him around, and he twirled in midstride. The ground tumbled up to strike him. He bounced twice and lay facedown in the inch of water on the wet sidewalk.

I'm hit! his brain shrieked. *I'm hit! I'm hit!*

He heard boots running near him and felt his pistol being ripped from his holster. He heard its sounds. Raysta was firing at the entranceway. It took him an eternity to move. He heard Shirn's voice in his ear, strident, clear, shocked. His fingers touched her arms, holding him.

"Mikhail, get up!"

He felt her hands tugging at him and rolled on one side, rain running from his face. He held on to her and made it to his knees. The pistol fired again, and he heard more shots from the administration building.

"The car!" she screamed. "We've got to make it to the car!"

He tried to move and failed. A giant numbness nearly immobilized him. "Run!" he said through teeth that were clamped shut. Something slapped against the pavement near them, and the pistol returned the fire. "Leave me here! Go!"

Her face came close to his, and her eyes were a blazing blackness in the rain. "Hold on to me," she cried, holding him in an upright position and propelling him toward the car. He forced his legs to move, crookedly, painfully. He'd seen the fear in her eyes and he responded to it. She wouldn't leave him there.

Something brushed against his right wrist, slapping it against his body. Then he was in the car, pulled by Bissa, tumbling into the backseat. He felt Shirn fall in on top of him and heard Raysta clambering into the front seat. The sedan lunged away from the curb, and metal slapped loudly against it. One of the windows shattered.

He groped for the briefcase. "Help me," he said to Shirn, who was fighting to regain an upright position. The sedan careened around corners, tires screeching on the sodden pavements. She found the latches and opened the case. He felt inside it. He was half on the floor, half on the seat. He found the flares and smoke grenades. He forced himself upright. His watch read eight thirty-six.

"Go right through the son of a bitch," he ordered Raysta as his long-range vision focused and he saw the checkpoint gate ahead. He moved to the window and pulled the pins to one of the smoke grenades and a flare. As they raced through the checkpoint, past the startled guards, he tossed the grenade and the flare through the window. They exploded, engulfing the complex entrance in a mass of hellish, dense red smoke. Looking through the rear window, he saw flashes of machine-gun fire through the smoke and rain.

"Do you remember where to turn?" he shouted at Raysta.

"I damned better remember!" Raysta yelled. Mikhail shifted on the seat, a spasm of pain shooting through his left leg. He felt the leg. The bullet had torn into the meaty section just below his pocket. Blood poured from the wound. His right wrist felt strange. A long red welt ran across it. Raysta hunched over the steering wheel. Bissa, next to him on the front seat, held his stubby arms braced against the dashboard. The sedan lurched and bucked as Raysta twisted the wheel. "The turnoff!" he yelled. "Here it comes!"

Through the whipping windshield wipers Mikhail dimly saw the curve ahead, but it was marked by a high retaining wall to the left. A second road turned off abruptly to the right, halfway around the curve. It was the road they had to take to get to the truck. As they neared the turnoff Raysta braked the sedan and Mikhail hurled two more smoke grenades through the window. They popped loudly behind the sedan, and the wet blackness was filled with a dense cloud of grayish smoke. He put his head to the open window as

Raysta carefully negotiated the nasty turn and then jammed the gas pedal to the floor to pick up speed. Concentrating, he could hear them. The security motorcycles and cars were closing the distance rapidly.

"Mikhail!" Bissa cried, looking over the front seat.

Mikhail whipped around. "What's the matter?"

Bissa's eyes were alarmed. "Shirn! Not breathing!"

Mikhail reached over and took Shirn in his arms.

Her head rolled loosely.

Colonel Gregorski was outraged.

"Where is he!" he demanded. "Where is Major Kulish!"

Captain Prokov swallowed. "He said he would wait here with the microminiatures." There were strange noises outside.

"This soldier said he did not return. He was in this room once, not twice."

"I don't know where he is." The captain was stricken. Where was Kulish? What were those noises outside?

The colonel walked around the room, looking carefully at the equipment. "It's all here?"

"Nothing's been removed. How could it be, with this soldier at the door?" The captain said it automatically.

The colonel was lost to his thoughts. His eyes were stark with concentration. He raised his head and looked at the captain.

"My daughter has been taken prisoner. The fat soldier was sent to tell me that. Your Major Kulish arrives and is worried about the security for the microminiature computers. He's not here, but he must be in the building. We will check every room." He paused as another thought hit him. "We have the girl and the soldier." He looked at the computers. "We have the microminiatures." He shook his head worriedly. "What does it add up to?"

"We must find the major."

There were loud shouts at the security desk, and the colonel began running toward the sounds. Security officers were racing toward him! He saw the fear in their eyes.

"What happened?" he demanded in a choked voice.

"Major Kulish killed the guards and took the prisoners with him!" one of the officers said excitedly. "We tried to stop him, and his driver shot three men at the entrance!"

"After them, you fool!"

They broke through the main gate! They exploded a red flare and a smoke grenade! The entrance guards are chasing them!"

"Full alert!" the colonel screamed. They were running down the corridor to the stairway when the black packages hidden under the microminiature computers exploded in unison behind them.

In seconds the shattered building was in flames.

CHAPTER ELEVEN

"She's out cold," Mikhail said.

He held Shirn in her arms, protecting her from the bouncing thrusts the sedan was making down the winding back road. The headlights picked up very little of the hard-packed clay road, and the rain obscured most of what lay beyond. He pressed his fingers to her cool temple. Her pulse was steady but faint.

Bissa sobbed. "Shut up," Mikhail commanded. "Take this flare and have it ready to throw out the window." He shouted to Raysta. "Have you seen the sign yet?"

"No, but it can't be much farther."

"She's going to die?" Bissa said, turning in his seat. He wiped tears from his flabby cheeks.

"Damn it! I said she's alive. That bastard beat the hell out of her. She's in shock." He returned his hand to his left leg where he pressed against the femoral artery to stem the flow of blood. From the holes in his bloody pant leg he knew the bullet had entered the outer length of the quadriceps femoris muscle. It had traveled on a straight line, back to front, with a slight trajectory downward. The man firing at him had been at the top of the entranceway of the administration building. Inches to the right and the femur would have been shattered. He'd lucked out. Two holes in the leg muscles near the side. He could thank the human element that made even good marksmen wild in the first moments of action. The guards at the gate could have riddled the sedan, but most of their bullets, fired in panic, tore up the road behind the racing sedan. His hand was sticky with blood, and he moved the handkerchief he'd slipped down the pant leg to press against the wounds. They had to get to the truck before he lost more blood.

The sedan rattled crazily for a moment as Raysta steered

over a wet roadbed that seemed to be made of logs. He saw
Raysta look quickly in the rearview mirror. Water splashed
in through the shattered window. "I don't see lights back
there."

Mikhail twisted to look. "The smokescreen and that curve
gave us the edge we needed." He turned back in time to
see faint blobs of white through the arcs made on the windshield by the struggling wipers. "There's the sign!" he
shouted. The headlights picked them up, three long sticks
stuck in the ground alongside the road, each with a soggy
strip of white cloth tied to the top. The UPA sign! The truck
was just ahead in the blackness. "Bissa, toss the flare." He
watched the cylinder go tumbling out the front window and
heard its popping sound. The night behind them burst into
a crimson glare. The UPA had to know it was them, not a
security car. Their spotters would have seen the rod flare at
the complex gate when they raced through it. Now they
were waiting with the truck. With Vera Gregorski.

Immediately ahead a small red light flashed on three
times. Raysta braked the sedan in the pelting rain and pulled
in alongside the old truck. Three shadowy figures in black
raincoats and rain hats ran from the truck into the forest.
With great difficulty Mikhail helped Bissa carry Shirn and
lift her limp form into the van. Raysta brought the suitcase,
sliding it in quickly.

Mikhail, in the sedan's headlights, had seen the new label
on the truck. Gone was the electric service insignia. In its
place was the name of the fanciest sanitorium in the Odessa
area, The Heights.

Vera, her hands tied behind her, a strip of cloth binding
her ankles together, sat huddled in a corner illuminated by
the glow from the sedan's headlights. Mikhail heard Raysta
slam the van door shut and then the cab door. The truck
roared to life and moved away. He pulled himself up to the
tiny window at the rear of the van in time to see the UPA
men run from the forest and pile into the sedan. It followed
a short distance, turned at the next intersection road, and
disappeared.

Bissa found the squat flashlight and turned it on. In its
light Mikhail opened the medical kit. He took the scissors

and cut his pant leg to expose the wound area. He removed the brilliant red handkerchief and threw it in a far corner. In the bobbing light he and Bissa wiped the leg muscle and emptied a packet of disinfectant powder over the neat holes. They fashioned a bandage and taped it on tightly. Then they attended to the raw scrape wound on his wrist.

Vera watched them silently. "I could help if you'd cut me loose," she said. Her teeth chattered from the hard bouncing of the truck.

Mikhail crawled to her and cut her bonds with the scissors. She rubbed her wrists. "You'll need a doctor for that. It looks awful. Are the bullets still in there?"

"Only one bullet. It went right through. Luck for me." He looked at her closely. Her eyes seemed dulled, and her long blond hair was disheveled, her dress disarrayed. "Are you all right?"

"I'm frightened and I'm hungry. What's the matter with her?" She nodded toward Shirn. Shirn lay on her back on the van floor, one arm outstretched, the other limply over her stomach. Her mouth was slightly open.

Mikhail crawled to Shirn. "Your father whipped her with a strap. He beat and kicked her."

Vera shook her head as if she hadn't heard correctly. "My father?" She seemed stunned for a moment and then she recovered. "Yes, of course. He's famous for that." She blinked in the rays of the light. "Here, let me help. Is that blood on her blouse?" She went to Shirn, feeling her pulse and pressing a hand to her forehead.

"Let's get it off," Mikhail said. "Help me roll her over. Her back's like raw meat." He motioned for Bissa to bring the light closer. He held Shirn while Vera cut away the blouse and brassiere. The raw flesh was awesome. Shirn's back and shoulders were striped with long ugly welts, criss-crossing in a senseless pattern. The edges of some were caked with dried blood. Fresh blood oozed from three curving cuts. Mikhail, sitting up, held Shirn against him, her head lying loosely on his shoulder, so that Vera could clean the bloody area. He watched as Vera expertly applied a medical cleanser, dabbing it on with cotton swabs. His leg burned terribly.

"Why did he do this?" Vera asked quietly.

"The GRU arrested her. He wanted her to tell him where we were." He couldn't keep the disgust out of his voice. "It's one of the ways he has of interrogating prisoners. If not a whip or a belt, then a blackjack."

Vera taped cotton compresses to the raw areas. She worked quickly and competently despite the necessity of kneeling on the hard wooden floor of a rattling old van. "She's the reason you kidnapped me? You did that so he would release her?"

Mikhail felt a sharp bitterness well up within him. "He wouldn't have released her for all the daughters in the Soviet. Taking you gave us a chance to unsettle him for a few minutes."

"He didn't trade her for me?"

Mikhail laughed caustically. "When he found you had disappeared, he left Shirn alone long enough for us to get her out." A sudden pity overtook him, and he looked away from her. "You bought us a few minutes of time, that's all."

"Can you get her to a doctor? Your leg should be looked at too. You've lost blood and you're risking a terrible infection."

He fell silent, thinking of the options. The pile of clothing was in a corner. They had to change soon from their military uniforms to Ukrainian clothes. The UPA would have useless red flares burning in dozens of places in and around Odessa to confuse the men who hunted them. But they knew he'd been hit. They knew Shirn had been beaten. They'd have every doctor and medical clinic under surveillance. There'd be no doctor. There was only escape.

"Vera," he said at last, "you're not responsible for what the colonel did, but you are a problem."

Fear was in her eyes. "You're not going to kill me?"

"You kill?" Bissa said in his blunt way. "Angry with you we're not." He squatted near them, holding the flashlight in both hands, his potato-shaped face still rain-wetted, his eyes concerned, his jowls shaking spasmodically.

Mikhail forced a smile on his face and saw the fear leave hers. "I didn't mean that. I mean, what will we do with you?"

"I could stay and look after her. What's her name?"

"We can't tell you any of our names, Vera."

"She's very pretty."

"Help me get some clothes on her," he said. It was difficult, but they managed. They wrapped clean gauze all around Shirn's torso and threaded her arms through a clean blouse and jacket. They made a pad of Mikhail's tunic and laid her facedown on the floor with the pad under her right cheek.

He motioned to Bissa, and they stripped their uniforms, jamming them into one of the cloth bags. They dressed in their Ukrainian clothes. Mikhail had tremendous difficulty in propping himself against the van wall and pulling on the clean trousers. The thick bandage made it nearly impossible. He finished, breathing hard, feeling weak and depressed. He stood, leaning against the vibrating wall, deeply tired. He ached everywhere. His mind was a jumble of incomplete thoughts. It was difficult for him to sort out his thoughts in an orderly procession. The plan! They must stick to the plan without any variations. Too many others were involved. They were not connected by radio. They worked only on a time sequence, and the timing had to be met.

Or they would die.

The thought of the radio reminded him of the security radio, and he hobbled to the corner where the pile of clothes had been. It was there, wrapped in its newspaper, and he switched it on. The security network was supercharged. He held it, listening to the stream of instructions coming from the Odessa military complex. The description of the sedan came at intervals, and he grunted. They'd never find that sedan. There was no mention of the destruction of the complex.

He turned to Vera. She sat cross-legged on the floor near Shirn, her hands in her lap, looking lost and confused.

"If you stay with us, will you do what we tell you to do?"

"I want to help."

"If you don't, we'll have to tie you up and leave you somewhere."

"I won't be any trouble."

"If you are, if you raise an alarm, you might be shot with the rest of us."

"I don't even know what you've done. I recognized your voice. You've changed your appearance. Now you have brown eyes and brown hair. What are you up to?" Her face in the inadequate light was incredibly beautiful. Her blue eyes were serious, and she began fixing her braids again. The long hair framed her face in a soft yellow haze. "When you were at the apartment, I thought you were KGB checking on my father."

"I'm not. None of us are. Not KGB or GRU or even militia. We're Ukrainians." He returned Bissa's sudden look. "Ukrainians."

"You're nationalists?"

"We're not even that."

She was puzzled. "Then why are you in trouble?"

"Your father. We learned that he was coming to this district. We didn't like that. We have reasons to make his life more difficult." He saw she was about to speak, and he hurried on. "We can't tell you any more than that. It would be dangerous for you to know more." He bent his head to listen to the radio.

"I won't pry. I know it's dangerous. You've kidnapped me. That's bad enough."

"See. You are a problem."

"I don't want to be one." She turned to look at Shirn. "I know you told the truth about him beating her. Mother left him because of that, did you know?"

Mikhail shook his head. "You're mother's been dead for eight years."

"You know so much about me. Did you know that's why she died? She was in terror of him. She knew what he did to other women. The terror made her old long before her time." Her eyes saddened. "He never hit me, never treated me badly. Not physically, anyway. But I could see the way his face was at times. I had people tell me things about him. I heard rumors. They called him sadistic. He was away for long periods of time, and we were always grateful for that. When he came back to Moscow, the last time, almost a year ago, he made me live with him. I was afraid not to." Her voice trailed off.

Mikhail's watch warned him of the time. They'd soon be off the country roads on the long roundabout trail back to the edge of Odessa, back to their hiding point near the Dal'nik airport. He put the radio down and went to the window that connected to the cab where Raysta was. He passed a nylon raincoat and rain-hat through the window to Raysta, hoping the coat would be long enough to cover his uniform. He watched as the tall villager drove with one hand at a time, getting out of his tunic and putting on the raincoat. He passed the tunic and army cap back to Mikhail, who shoved them into the cloth bag with the other uniforms. "We have only five minutes more," he said to Raysta.

"We'll be there sooner," Raysta said, not taking his eyes from the road. "We're comin' into the resort area."

Mikhail visualized the route they'd taken, expertly plotted by the UPA. From the military complex it had used back roads, skirting the more heavily populated areas, staying always within the security roadblocks, never leaving the checkpointed area. Now they were within a few kilometers of the huge sanitorium where the lords and ladies of Moscow came to rest.

The Heights.

It sat on the crest of a large hill overlooking the seaport. It had an electric stairway that ferried the vacationers from the top to the beach at the bottom, as a ski lift does. It had a dozen private villas and three dozen smaller family *dachas* surrounding the six-story hotellike building for the less affluent and less powerful Communist leaders. Khrushchev had stayed in its largest villa. Leaders from around the world had enjoyed its mud baths.

Mikhail tried to think of what else he'd learned from the Americans about The Heights. His leg was numb, and he reasoned that the holes were clotting and the germicidal powder was working. Still, he couldn't put his weight on the leg without it reacting sharply against the pressure. He went back to Bissa and Vera. "In a few minutes we're going to pull into the service parking lot of a sanitorium," he said. "When Raysta opens the door, we must get out quickly. Put your raincoats and caps on. It's dark in the lot and it's still raining." He tapped Bissa on the head. "Keep the light shielded until we're out, then snap it off. You and I will carry Shirn with our arms under her shoulders. We'll try to make it look as if she's walking. Someone may be watching." He shoved the briefcase and the army cloth bag toward Vera. "Can you carry these?"

"If they're not too heavy."

Mikhail looked around the van interior. Raysta would have to bring the bag with the military uniforms, the AK-47, and the shotgun wrapped in another cloth bag, the security radio, and the medicine kit.

The truck came to a halt, bouncing them a bit. They heard Raysta's boots hurrying alongside the van, and the door opened. A splatter of rain hit them, and they went down the little wooden steps into the darkness. Mikhail, with Bissa on the other side, half carried, half dragged Shirn. Raysta led the way, and Vera, laden with the briefcase and army bag, struggled along behind them.

Raysta went to the door of the darkened villa. "In here," he said softly in his high voice. When they were all in, Mikhail took the flashlight from Bissa's hands. He played it around. The entranceway and the first room resembled the set for a Hollywood movie. A crystal chandelier hung in the high dome-shaped ceiling. A winding white staircase lead to the upperfloor. The furniture appeared nearly new, a Moscow version of French Provincial.

"Sweet Cryil," Raysta said in wonderment.

"Change your trousers and get back to the truck," Mikhail said. "Bring everything we left, the long bundle and the radio and kit first. Move the truck to the other end of the lot, as far from here as you can get."

Raysta changed quickly, buttoned his raincoat, and pulled the nylon rain cap down low over his face. He grimaced but left, hunching forward against the driving rain.

"The bedrooms are upstairs," Mikhail said to Bissa. "Help me get Shirn up those stairs." He handed the light to Vera. "We won't turn on the lights until we make sure the windows are draped. Lead the way." It took them a long time, and the sweat of pain bathed Mikhail's face by the time they were able to lay Shirn on a bed, remove her raincoat, and examine her bandages. She had bled through them.

"I'll look after her," Vera said. "Get the medicine kit for me. I'll wash off the blood and we'll start fresh again." She sat on the edge of the bed in her wet raincoat holding Shirn's hand. Mikhail motioned for Bissa to remain in the bedroom.

He toured the villa, moving slowly, favoring his left leg. His wrist was burning, and he tried to ignore it. He removed his raincoat and hat, leaving them near the door. The flashlight was upstairs, giving a small illumination to the bedroom for Vera to work by. He could hear the water running. Russian plumbing was always noisy. The downstairs section had a spacious kitchen, a dining room, a card and chess room, a room where films could be shown, and a library. There were no books on the shelves. Russian paintings were on all of the walls.

He rested at the bottom of the stairway, wondering how the UPA had known that this villa would be empty. He shook his head. It was enough that they knew. What better resting place could they have before they made the run for the airport? Dal'nik was five kilometers away. The last tunnel out. His head was clearing, and he went to the large front window, a bay-shaped affair that jutted out from the domed room. He pulled back the heavy curtain an inch. Raysta had moved the truck and was walking back, the two bulky cloth bags over his shoulder. He'd obviously tucked the newspaper-wrapped radio and kit in with the weapons.

A car turned into the lot and caught Raysta in its headlights. It moved quickly to intercept him, and two men emerged from it. The slanting rain obscured their faces under their rain hats. Mikhail pulled the pistol from his hip pocket with his free hand. Holding the curtain with an elbow as he peered out, he carefully reloaded the pistol, taking the cartridges from his jacket pocket.

Raysta dropped the bags and gestured wildly with his arms to the two men. Mikhail fought an impulse to burst out the door shooting. It was out of the range of accuracy, but he'd have the element of surprise. Then he thought of Shirn upstairs and Vera and Bissa. He hesitated, his fingers closing and unclosing on the heavy pistol.

Raysta walked back to the truck, stamping heavily in the puddles, and pointed to it. Whatever he was saying, he was saying it loudly. Mikhail couldn't let the curtain fall back into place. He held his eye to the crack, fascinated. What was Raysta doing?

For a terrible moment the security men looked as if they

were going to come toward the villa. Raysta was pointing in its direction, obviously offering to show them the place. Then they got back into their car and roared out of the lot. Raysta picked up the bags and came across the lot and into the villa. Rain dripped from him in puddles on the carpeting.

Mikhail closed and bolted the door. It had been left open for them, but there was a free bolt separate from the key lock. He leaned against the door, feeling weak, the pistol hanging at his side. "Close?"

Raysta's long, crooked teeth shone. "Like a razor."

"What'd you tell them?"

Raysta guffawed. "I'm the only laundry asshole around here who works! See? I'm puttin' in extra time because I'm conscientious. These sheets and towels must be delivered to this villa tonight because a political commissar is arriving tomorrow." He looked around. "Where are they?"

"Upstairs. Vera's doing Shirn's back again. Bissa's keeping an eye on her."

Raysta nodded. "Tell me, why'd we come here? Why didn't we go right to the airport?"

"That's what the security bastards would want us to do. They'll have the place completely closed down. The longer we wait, the less tight the security there'll be."

Raysta thought about it for a minute. "If nothing happens at Dal'nik right away, they'll think we've gone somewhere else?"

"That's the size of it."

"How do you feel? How're your wounds?"

"Russian bullets have a way of hurting."

The villager eyed him soberly, respectfully. *"Kozak v lizhloo ne vmryaei."*

"The cossack doesn't die in bed?"

Raysta nodded and opened the long bag with the rifle and shotgun. "I'll clean these off. They got wet." He handed the radio and medicine kit to Mikhail. He stripped off his rain gear and pulled off his wet boots, tossing them in the corner. He walked around in his bare feet, looking again at the magnificence of the room. "Makes you want to become a Communist," he said thoughtfully.

Mikhail negotiated the stairway painfully, carrying the

radio and the kit. Vera had found a bottle of ammonia in the bathroom. She opened the kit, took out a cotton ball, and soaked it in the ammonia. She held the ball near Shirn's nose. Shirn moved slightly and turned her head from side to side to avoid the smell. Her entire back was cleaned and ready for a new dressing.

"Easy," Mikhail warned. "That's enough."

"Where am I?" Shirn said groggily, struggling weakly to sit up. Raysta padded into the room carrying the weapons. He looked cautiously at Shirn and sat down cross-legged to wipe the rifle and shotgun dry with a towel from the bathroom.

"Please," Vera said. "We've washed your back and we're going to put a fresh dressing on it. Can you sit up for a while?" She darted a glance at Mikhail. "Better hold her. She's very weak." She worked quickly, taking things from the medicine kit, dabbing Shirn's back, and wrapping the cotton pads on tightly with a thick winding of gauze. She taped the gauze in place to keep it from unraveling.

"Who are you?" Shirn said in wonderment. She looked at Mikhail. "Who is she?"

"Vera Gregorski. We took her hostage when you were arrested."

"Why? I don't understand."

"Her father had you in his interrogation room. We had to improvise. We needed time to get to you. We sent Bissa in with a message that Vera was a prisoner. It upset him long enough for me to get into the room where you were."

Raysta finished with the shotgun, reloaded it, and leaned it against the wall. He turned back to the rifle, pulling the clip from it and wiping it carefully.

"Mikhail," Shirn said, "you were hit. You fell. What happened to you?" She brushed her long black hair from her face. Her eyes were filled with confusion.

He sat holding her, feeling the warmth of her naked shoulders under his hands. Her complexion was turning more healthy. She was losing that ghastly grayness.

"In and out. Luck for me. It's bandaged and the bleeding's stopped." He bent and kissed her cheek. "You didn't leave me there."

"Oh, Mikhail," she said against his shoulder. "I could

never leave you." She trembled. "You know I could never leave you like that!"

Vera's voice struck them and they turned toward her.

"Don't move!" she warned. "If my father is looking for you, there must be a reason!"

She was holding the shotgun and it was aimed at them.

General Zagorsky received emergency treatment while lying on a stretcher in an undamaged room of the headquarters building. He half raised his bulk to look at the staff officers around him. His head was heavily bandaged where bits of flying brick and wood had pelted. "How bad is it?" he said to Captain Prokov.

"The Computer Center was destroyed, and the command headquarters two-thirds burned and unusable." The captain swallowed hard. "About half of the GRU area is gone—records, communications equipment, everything."

The general sank back to the canvas. "How did they do it?" A faint flush of pink wetness oozed through the bandage at the forehead.

The captain closed his eyes briefly and wiped dirt and soot away from them. He was in a mild state of shock from the tremendous explosion and the intense fire, which was still being fought by the complex's fire department and volunteer soldiers. "We don't know. There was a man who posed as Major Kulish. We now know it wasn't the real Kulish. He is still in Moscow. There was the fat soldier who brought the news that the colonel's daughter was kidnapped. There was a tall, thin driver, and there was the girl I arrested and the colonel interrogated." He wiped his face with a soiled handkerchief and stuck the cloth into his pocket. "If there were more, we haven't uncovered them yet."

"And they got away? They went right out the main entrance?"

"Yes."

"Our own men couldn't capture them?" The words were delivered in a wrapping of sheer disbelief.

"It was remarkably organized. They had smoke bombs, which they used just before a curve and a turnoff in the road. Two cyclists smashed against the wall and were killed. The lead car skidded and overturned. It caught fire. Two other chase cars crashed into it." The captain rubbed his hands together nervously. "Eleven men killed and four seriously injured."

"The casualties here? How many?"

"The closest estimate is at least ninety dead and one hundred and fifteen injured."

The general bit his lower lip and groaned. "The greatest military installation in the Ukraine, the best scientific development headquarters, the finest reputation." He intoned the words in the way of a priest. "And four people get through our security and do this!" He tried to rise, and his weakness forced him back to the stretcher.

"Get Gregorski!" he said savagely through his teeth.

"But Comrade General, he's leading the search. Every available man is out looking for these saboteurs. There isn't a way in or out of Odessa that isn't being triple-checked. Every military facility within a hundred kilometers is on full alert. Nothing is moving within this circle. We've pulled in hundreds of suspects, but none have been the ones we're after. The navy has sent its units in to seal off the port and coast. The air force has a squadron of its all-weather night units up." He paused and cursed. "This stinking rain! It's making it extremely difficult. There are so few paved roads, and the others are like quagmires."

"Get Gregorski!" There was no mistaking the general's order. The captain picked up the transistor radio near his boots and transmitted the command to the makeshift GRU headquarters in a building nearby. The headquarters basement was unusable. It was filled with water from the fire hoses and the rain.

The colonel arrived with a squad of security men. The staff officers around the general made way for him to kneel next to the stretcher.

"Have you captured them?" the general asked.

"No, we have—"

"Do you even know where they are?"

"No, Comrade General, we have—"

"Then you are as much in the dark as we are?" The general's eyes glittered wickedly.

"We will have them. They can't escape from our security around Odessa."

The general closed his eyes. He appeared to be going to sleep. "We will have them, Comrade Colonel, or we will have you." He said nothing more, and his eyes remained closed.

Colonel Gregorski was dismissed again. He knew it and he rose, pushing through the circle of staff officers. His guard fell in behind him, and they trotted from the place as a doctor and his attendants approached to take the general to the base hospital.

Captain Prokov helped load the general into the army ambulance, and when it pulled away, he stood in the rain, letting it cool his head. He turned to look at the fire fighters struggling to put out the last of the stubborn flames. Medical corpsmen and soldiers were carrying the injured and the dead. The area around the headquarters building was a maze of fire hoses, fire trucks, ambulances, military cars, and trucks. It was the nearest thing to bedlam he'd ever seen. This and Nikolayev! He shook his head and it hurt with the movement. How could this possibly have happened? One man from a submarine couldn't possibly have carried it out.

Unless he had inside help.

From the first he'd had the oldest suspicion. Inside help. How else could these people have moved with almost uncanny certainty? With uniforms? With explosives? With expert knowledge of where things were? The timing of getting the girl and the fat one out of the interrogation rooms had been a masterpiece. Even he'd been duped. He headed toward his own temporary office where the men who served him were pledged to the same branch of service and could be trusted.

Inside the room he removed his tunic and wiped the rain from his face and hair. There was no time to use his go-between. With his code book at hand he sat down at a cluttered desk to write a message to be sent by secret radio to his KGB Commander in Moscow. He would have to get the message to the KGB operator in a building in Odessa's center.

The GRU and Colonel Gregorski were in serious trouble. The KGB could take excellent advantage of this situation. As he wrote, a thought crowded into his mind. Gregorski had served for a long time in the United States. Time enough to make many acquaintances. Time enough to do many things that would not be healthy for the Soviet Republics. His hand stopped. There had to be a reason *why* the colonel, with such a great reputation for counterrevolutionary work and espionage, had permitted these disasters to occur.

"Why, indeed?" he said aloud.

Then he busied himself with finishing the urgent message and getting it to the hidden KGB communications specialist.

Shirn slid slowly from the bed and moved between Vera and the men.

"Don't!" Vera warned. "I'll pull the trigger."

Shirn, barefooted and bent with pain, moved within a meter of the muzzle. It pointed at her gauze-wrapped chest.

"You want to be like your father?" she said.

"I'm a Russian. If you've done something wrong, you should answer for it." Vera held the shotgun steadily. "If you're innocent, you'll have a proper trial and go free."

"You saw my back. Did your father give *me* a proper trial?"

"I know he beats women, but he might have had good cause for beating you."

Shirn swung her head and indicated Mikhail. "What was his reason for killing Mikhail's mother?"

Vera's face mirrored her surprise. "I don't believe you. It's one of your tricks."

"She died. That's no trick. She was a code clerk at the Russian embassy in Washington. Mikhail was nine years old. Fifteen years ago. Your father wanted to make her one of his conquests. She refused. She fell from a window."

"You're lying."

"Mikhail was raised by the Americans. He came back to kill your father."

"But he hasn't! My father's still alive."

"Mikhail had another reason to come. His own father has been in prison those fifteen years." Shirn waited, letting the words sink in. "In prison at the orders of your father." A sneer played on her face as she stared at Vera. "Your father didn't want him asking questions in Moscow about his wife's death. Do you know where Mikhail found his father?"

Vera's voice was softer. "No."

"He found him in Dombosky Prison. He found him without a mind, a shell of a man. He found him broken by fifteen years of being beaten and starved, in inhuman cruelty. Do you know what Mikhail did?"

Vera couldn't answer. She shook her head.

"Mikhail destroyed his own father rather than let him remain in prison, a vegetable."

Vera's eyes sought Mikhail's. He stood motionlessly with Bissa and Raysta a few meters behind Shirn. His dark eyes showed no emotion. He seemed poised for movement. The shotgun trembled as her grip on it became more difficult. Her palms were sweating uncontrollably.

"Look at me," Shirn ordered. "Mikhail never saw me before, until the day before yesterday. Why do you think I'm here?" She didn't wait for an answer. "Because your father had my parents arrested as parasites of the State! They were innocent, and this was proven at their trial." A bitter smile was on her face. "Oh, they had a trial because they also had friends. But to save your father's face the court sentenced them to deportation from the Ukraine."

"But they're alive!"

"They were sent to a New Lands camp. Six years ago. They died there."

Vera was unbelieving. "That's a crazy story. You made it up!"

"The friends of my parents hid me or I would have been sent with them. I was fifteen. When I heard of their deaths, I knew that someday I'd meet your father and kill him. Now you see why I'm in this."

Vera looked at the men. "The other two, why are they in it?"

"Because they're my family. They took me in six years ago and protected me." She breathed deeply. "Because they love me." She moved until she was a hand's length away from the muzzle of the shotgun. "Now go ahead, daughter of a sadistic maniac! Kill me!"

Vera began to shake.

"Kill me! Kill me!" Shirn shouted, and the room echoed with her voice.

Mikhail's arm moved around her and took the shotgun from Vera's trembling hands.

"She couldn't kill anyone," he said, placing the weapon against the wall where it had been. "She knows her father too well to kill in his name."

Vera began to cry, and Shirn took her in her arms.

Raysta's voice came to them. "We ought to have a party," he said casually in his high voice. "This is somethin' to celebrate."

"I know! I know!" Bissa said happily. "Shirn herself again is!" He began to bounce up and down in a little dance of joy.

The rain ended an hour after midnight, but a low fog remained. It swirled between the villa and the sanitorium lodge. Mikhail, standing guard near the window, could see only the dim lights of the lodge. Nothing moved. He felt someone near him and turned.

It was Vera.

"How long will you let them sleep?" she said in a whisper.

"Another quarter hour. Then we'll leave here."

"Why? Isn't it safe?"

"We never intended it to be. The truck will be checked again. It's just a matter of time before the security people return."

She leaned against the door, her shoulder touching him. "You've washed your hair, you're blond again. What were they, contact lenses to change your eyes? Now you look like yourself." She paused. "How do you know these things, Mikhail?"

"We have a plan. We worked it out and we're staying with it. We knew that once we got out of the military complex, the whole city would be looking for us. We couldn't move without being stopped. And we'd need rest." He waved his hand at the room. "So we borrowed a villa that wouldn't be used at night. A place out of the rain where we could sleep."

"You haven't slept."

"I'm too keyed up."

"What will you do with me? Have you decided?"

"You'll stay here. It would be dangerous for you to come."

"Then you're leaving Russia? You're going back to America?"

"Vera, I came to get my father. I found him dead. Dead because of what your father did to him."

"What about them?"

"At first they were to return to their village. But Shirn was arrested. They know who she is, and they've tied Bissa and Raysta to her. They know they were here with Shirn. It would be suicide for them to go back. They'll come with me."

"She said you were going to kill my father. Is that true?"

"I've already killed him, Vera."

She moved away from him with a start. Her blue eyes were shocked. "You killed him at the complex?"

He shook his head. "He's alive for the moment, but with what happened right under his own nose, he won't be alive for very long."

She put her hand on his arm to steady herself. "Then what you've done has been to turn the GRU against him?"

"Vera, it would have been easy to shoot him, to knife him, break his neck. Anything. But then he would have been a Hero of the Soviet Union. Younger officers might find his image appealing. What better way can you destroy a security officer than destroy the very things he'd pledged to protect?"

She leaned limply against him, her cheek on his shoulder, her hands tight on his arm.

"Then you must escape. If you're caught, he would still become a hero, wouldn't he?"

"You see it right. If we get away, and there are no prisoners, then he's failed in his job. The Kremlin will not accept that kind of failure, not from a man who's one of their most feared espionage and counterrevolutionary officers."

She put her lips close to his ear. "Mikhail, would there be room? Could I come with you?"

"You said you were a Russian. Can you leave Russia and come with us? Can you do it and not die a thousand times because you did it?"

"I've had so little, Mikhail. The way those two villagers love and look after Shirn. I've never had that. I've seen the way she looks at you. She's in love with you."

It was his turn to be surprised. "Shirn? We've only known each other two days. What do you see that I don't see?"

"Her eyes tell me. She's in love with you."

He fell silent and peeked out of the crack in the curtain again, to cover his discomfort. "Tell me about your mother."

"She was lovely. Very gentle. Her marriage with father was a terrible mistake and she regretted it deeply. He made her life a horrible thing. He was so important in the GRU. There was no one she could turn to. Life just became too much of a burden to her." Her voice faltered. "She was the only one who really loved me."

He moved and put his arm around her shoulder, pulling her to him. "That's not true. There must be others."

"When I saw you in the apartment, I thought it could be you, Mikhail. I thought I'd met the man I'd been looking for. Did you know I went to the beaches looking for you?"

"For me?"

"I went looking for you. Worse, if I'd seen you, I was going to invite you to take me to dinner." She pressed her face against his chest. "Dinner and everything."

His arm tightened around her. "For the first time since I was nine, I'm afraid."

"What do you mean?"

"I've hated for so many years, Vera. I've seen love in America. They have a great capacity for loving each other, but I never really felt part of it. Now . . ."

"Now you're losing your hate?"

"I'm beginning to sense what love is, the love I've heard so much about and only witnessed, never felt."

"I heard a lecture at Moscow University once. The professor said there's a fine line between hate and love."

He breathed deeply. "There's so much to learn about life."

She pulled herself around in front of him, and standing

on her toes, she kissed him. It was a long, warm, moist kiss, and his arms came around her, tightly, hurting her ribs.

"Take me with you," she whispered. "Please, Mikhail. Take me with you."

He kissed her again. He had never known anything as sweet as her mouth.

Vera's mouth or Shirn's mouth?

He relaxed his grip, and Vera moved back, trying to see his face in the darkness. A few rays of light came in the crack between the curtain and the window frame.

"If you come, you must do everything I tell you to do."

"I'll do anything."

He studied his watch. "Then wake them up. It's nearly three o'clock, time for us to go out the back."

"But the truck is in front, in the lot."

"We're not taking the truck. There'll be a car waiting for us at the end of the path, through the garden in the back."

"A car? Who'll bring it?"

"Some friends, Vera. Some remarkable friends." He kissed her again, taking time. "Now wake them. Raysta and I will fix some surprises for the men who'll come busting in here."

When she was gone, he took the American transistor radio from his pocket and switched it on. The "Voice of America" came through it strongly and the code sentence at one minute past three. "Washington enjoyed a peaceful day today without any further antinuclear demonstrations." The submarine and Captain Pell were waiting in the Black Sea for him and the out-tunnel airplane. He turned off the radio and returned it to his pocket. He felt immensely relieved. The plan hadn't been changed.

In twelve minutes they were ready, with their things packed in the cloth bags. The weapons were carefully wrapped. Only the briefcase and radio were left uncovered.

Mikhail, with Raysta's aid, hobbled around arranging the domed room in the form of a reception committee. They rigged the last smoke canister to the front door with a cord. The slightest move of the door would set it off.

When they were finished, Raysta turned to Mikhail. "I'd like to see the colonel's face!"

"You should never have that pleasure." Mikhail grinned as he looked around the room. "Let's get the hell out of here."

One after the other they left through the rear door, going along the narrow pathway through the shrubbed park to the private road that served the villa. They got into the gray car waiting for them unattended, its engine still warm. They piled the bags between them, and Mikhail got under the wheel, wincing at the quick pain in his leg. He moved the car down the drive to another road, which lead to the rear entrance of The Heights. He drove slowly and without lights.

The exhaust from their tail pipe barely had time to dissipate in the dark muggy air when four security cars pulled into the sanitorium's parking lot.

Colonel Gregorski climbed up into the van and peered at the spot on the floor where the excited officer pointed. Flashlights made everything visible.

"It is blood," he said. "Here, and on that cloth over there by the side." He was pleased. "We winged our animals." He dropped down to the rain-slicked pavement and summoned Captain Prokov. "They were in this truck. That is obvious. The report about this truck and the tall thin man with the bags of laundry was the only decent lead we had all night." He clapped his gloved hands together. The sight of the bloodied handkerchief in the corner had aroused him. "It's the one we waited for." He looked around the misty area.

So this was where the madman was! The report from the prison had unnerved him. Karlov! He'd almost forgotten the man. The mess at the embassy! The boy who was never found. Was this madman *that* boy? He looked around at the heavily armed officers with him and felt again that strong sense of power. Moscow must never learn if the quarry turned out to be that boy! He was in charge, and Moscow would *not* learn.

"The truck is here. They must be in that villa, the one the tall assassin with the laundry bags went into." His eyes glittered as he studied the imposing building. "Put a squad in the back and at the sides. No one must get out of that place!"

Captain Prokov barked the orders and the men, machine pistols ready, ran to their posts. He gathered the remaining men in two waves.

Colonel Gregorski removed his pistol from its flapped holster. He clicked off its safety. He motioned Captain Prokov to go through the door with the first wave. He checked his group, two of them carrying large portable floodlights, three of them armed with burp guns.

Captain Prokov hit the door with his shoulder, and the first wave of men was in the villa. The smoke canister exploded and the room was instantly obscured.

The colonel, right behind the first group, shouted, "Lights!" he blinked and coughed in the acrid stench. "Lights!"

"Fire!" he shouted. "Shoot the animals!" He emptied his pistol at the uniforms he could see in the swirling smoke in the room. "Shoot them all!"

Captain Prokov saw a moving figure and fired at it wildly. The men with him sprayed the entire room with their machine pistols.

"Enough! Enough!" the colonel screamed. "They haven't returned our fire. Something's wrong!" He stumbled outside, choking in the smoke. "Go in and bring them out," he ordered the second wave of men.

He was still gasping when the men came out of the villa. They carried the uniforms, riddled with holes, each tied together with cord and stuffed with sheets, pillows, and pillowcases. They'd been hung like puppets from the columns.

He looked through teary eyes at Captain Prokov and felt ill when Prokov sniffed delicately and turned away. He ran into the villa, waving his pistol, looking through every room. He came down the stairway slowly. The men had found the light switches, and the entire villa was bathed in light. He looked at the smashed chandelier, the broken windows, and the hundreds of bullet holes in the walls and floors.

He leaned against the railing and vomited.

CHAPTER TWELVE

Dal'nik airport was sealed off from the outer world. It spread into the distance, its lights hazy and indifferent under the low ground fog that hovered over it. The roads leading into it were heavily checkpointed. Additional lights set up by the security forces enabled them to carefully examine every vehicle and every person. At three thirty in the morning very little was moving, but what moved was checked often.

Mikhail, with the flashlight held under his raincoat, studied the map the UPA had tied to the steering wheel of the car. Crudely drawn, it showed the path to the fence near the hangar where the monoplane waited. He switched off the light and gave his eyes time to adjust to the blackness. The glow of the airport lights against the belly of the low-lying fog made ground identification easier.

"We don't go any farther on this road. We go overland until we reach that rise ahead. Then we walk." He looked over his shoulder at Vera, Shirn, and Raysta in the backseat. "For God's sake, when we get out, let's stay together. Hold on to each other's raincoats. Anything. We'll have minutes, no more, to get through the fence and into the hangar."

"How do we get through the fence?" Raysta asked, his teeth clicking with chill from the dampness.

"The UPA cut the wires and concealed the cut with bush branches. The hangar's easy to spot. It's the only one with a new tin roof." He waited until the pain in his left leg subsided. How was he going to make it through the darkness to the hangar? And when he got there, would he be able to fly the Russian airplane? What would Vera do? Would Shirn cry out if her back was inadvertently scraped? Raysta and his ulcer? The tranquilizers and the second bottle of antacid seemed to have helped. The lanky villager had made it through the villa episode without doubling over in pain.

"All right," he said with an air of finality, "let's make our run."

He edged the car from the muddy road and up a small grassy embankment. He followed a line of trees, not able to see the ground without headlights but able to see the trees silhouetted against the lighted fog ahead. Window down, he listened for helicopters. They had infrared spotter scopes that would enable them to zero in on the car. At the rise the car would be in range of the noise detectors stationed at the outer limits of the airport. Its engine would be heard clearly by the soldiers who manned the earphones.

For a perilous moment the car almost stuck in the boggy turf. He slowly reversed it and twisted the wheel to find firmer ground. It moved ahead lurchingly but it moved, and he breathed easier. They came to the rise and he cut the engine.

They slogged Indian file through the dense grass and wet underbrush, stumbling often in the darkness, until they came to the fence. He motioned them to gather close to him. "A patrol will be by here any minute. They don't vary by seconds. We stay flat behind these bushes. Not a sound! When the patrol goes by, Raysta, you're the first one up. Run along the fence to your right. Poke it until you find where they cut it. I'll be right behind you with the bags. Vera, you hold hands with Shirn so that if either of you stumbles, the other will pull you along. Bissa, come through the wire last and stick the branches back in it so it won't gape open. Brush our tracks. We don't want the next patrol to see them." They took their places, waiting.

He kneeled, studying the airport. The fog was thinning, but swirls of it still hung a hundred feet above the lights. The far buildings were obscured from view. At the main terminal building a cluster of passenger airplanes were tethered to the boarding ramps. No plane was warming up. Dal'nik was shut down, as much by the fog as by the intense security search going on in and around it. Jeeps with armed patrols circulated slowly and methodically in both circumference and crisscross patterns. Overhead a night-watch helicopter fluttered noisily, unseen through the mists. "Down!" he said, grunting.

The patrol went by, a jeep with a driver and two soldiers manning a machine gun mounted on it.

"Now!" he said, and Raysta was on his feet and running along the fence. In thirty meters he'd found the slit in the chain link and held it ajar as Mikhail, Vera, and Shirn crawled through it. He followed them and Bissa came last, sticking twigs between the wires to hold them together. He replaced the branches that hid the slit. With one of the branches he swept as he ran, beating their footprints out of the wet grass.

Mikhail grabbed the handle to the hangar's side door and was jolted to find it locked. He placed his heavy bags on the ground and lunged at the door with his left shoulder. The side frame at the lock splintered. He retrieved the bags and jumped through the door after the others. He reached for the oily wastes on the floor and smeared the grime over the place at the door frame where the wood had burst. He closed the door, nearly screaming with the pain in his leg.

The plane gleamed in the small amount of light that filtered through the dirty window facing the terminal. A single window. He was relieved. "Raysta, cover that damn window." He walked slowly around the craft, limping heavily. Painted on its sides was the identification UKRAINIAN GEOLOGICAL ADMINISTRATION, ODESSA. "Vera, take the flashlight and shield it with a cloth. We only want a glow to work by." When Raysta had the window covered and Vera had the light switched on, he said, "Shirn, you and Bissa hand the fuel cans up to Raysta on the wing. They're empty ordinarily, but our friends filled them last night."

"Isn't the plane full?" Vera asked.

"They never allow a plane like this to have more than half the fuel it can carry. We're going its full distance. We need every drop we can get into the tanks." He crawled painfully into the cockpit of the four-seat Volga craft. Built near Moscow, it was a standard single-engine monoplane with a low, long-spread wing, retractable landing gear, a fat fuselage, and a broad tail. He familiarized himself with the controls as Raysta clambered onto the wing and un-latched the fuel caps. Bissa and Shirn began the task of handing the fuel cans up to him.

Satisfied that the plane was ready, Mikhail helped him

fill the other wing tank. Then he took the sacks and emptied their contents on the floor.

"What are you doing?" Vera questioned.

"The KGB radio. I want to hear what's going on." He kept the volume low. A steady stream of orders and reports issued from it. Something had gone wrong at The Heights. Searching parties were fanning out from the sanitorium, and more men were being rushed to help with the tracking.

Mikhail handed Bissa the shotgun and gave Raysta the AK-47 and the clips. He took the manuals and the blueprints and began to wrap them carefully in thin waterproof cloth he took from the upper lining of his briefcase.

"I don't understand," Vera said, holding the light close to him. "What are those books and tapes?" She stooped to read the labels. "Mikhail! Those are for computers! For high-tech military devices! Where'd you get them?"

He finished wrapping them, tied a small flotation device to them, and put them in the cabin next to the pilot's seat. He removed the microminiature computer from the briefcase, and as she watched, he wrapped it in another water-sealed cloth and tied a flotation device on it. He placed it in the cabin next to the other. He turned to Vera and met her questioning eyes.

"Those are souvenirs, Vera. Souvenirs."

Indignation flashed on her face. "You took those from the computer center! Admit it!"

"Shirn, give me your head scarf."

"Why?"

"When we're in the plane, Vera's braids will be in the way. We'll have to wrap them."

Shirn's eyes blazed, but she handed him the crimson scarf and he put it on Vera, tying it below her chin. "Red looks good on you."

"You can't go!" she said, jerking away. "You stole those plans and part of a computer." She was furious. "You said you came to kill my father. I don't believe you. I don't believe a word you said. It was a sham to keep me quiet so that you could steal State secrets!" She clenched her hands into fists. "I've been a fool, listening to you!"

Shirn grabbed her and swung her around violently. "What kind of a fool are you now? Every word Mikhail told you was the truth. Now shut up and get into the plane!"

"I won't."

"You want Mikhail's love, don't you?"

Vera wavered. "He's stealing State secrets." She glared at Shirn. "And you're his accomplice."

"What does that matter? If you love him, you've got to get into this plane. We can't waste time. We've got to get out of here."

Vera turned to Mikhail. "Please, leave those things here," she implored. "Don't take them with you."

He motioned to the airplane. "Get in."

Vera jabbed her fists up and down in sheer agitation. "You're running from my father because you're spies, thieves!"

Shirn slapped her, sending her rolling against the fuselage. "We're *not* spies. Get in!"

Vera struck back, lashing out with her fists. Shirn was unable to get out of the way. She reeled against the plane and gasped with shock as her back slapped against it. "You idiot! What are you doing?" She grabbed the struggling Vera as Bissa and Raysta came toward her to help. "If you love Mikhail, think of what you're doing!"

"Let me go!"

"Listen to me. I'll stay. I won't go. You go with Mikhail." Shirn was nearly shouting. "You go with him. I'll stay here."

Vera broke loose from her before Raysta could reach her. She ran, bending low, and grabbed the radio. Her finger found the transmitter switch. She held the radio to her face. "Help! Help! I'm Vera Gregorski! The south hangar!" She burst through the entrance door at the side and disappeared into the night. Shirn started after her.

"Come back, you idiot," she screamed. "He loves you!"

Mikhail's big arm encircled her, and she was lifted into the cabin. "Get down on the floor," he ordered.

"But she's got the radio! She's giving the alarm!"

"Get down and shut up!" He turned to the men. "Open the hangar doors and get in as soon as I've got this bird out." He was in the cockpit throwing switches. The hangar doors rolled open, and the engine roared to life. The plane rolled slowly, wobbly like a drunken duck, from the hangar.

The sound of the engine was deafening.

Bissa stepped around the corner of the building and saw Vera running toward the lights of the terminal building in the distance.

"What are you doing?" a voice called from the darkness, and Bissa whirled to meet two guards approaching on foot. They held Sudarev submachine guns in front of them. He fired both barrels of the shotgun from his hip and the men went backward, skidding on their heels.

"Get in!" Raysta shouted, pushing Bissa to the plane. They clambered in as it began to roll faster. Raysta, last up, hung half in and half out, his rifle caught in the door. Bissa and Shirn tugged to free him. Mikhail piloted the awkward machine between the hangars, pushing forward on the throttle as far as he dared. They were out of the area and moving quickly to the runway when the headlights of a jeep struck them.

"They're gainin' on us!" Raysta shouted. He pushed the door open and thrust the AK-47 out of it. Hurry!"

"I can't go any faster or the engine will conk out," Mikhail said grittily.

Raysta, half out of the door, yelled, "The jeep's goin' to catch us! They've got a machine gun!" He struggled to aim his rifle from the door and found he couldn't fire it effectively at the pursuing jeep. "Get the hell out of here!" he shouted, and he was out of the door, falling and rolling on the ground.

"Raysta!" Shirn screamed. "Come back!"

Bissa started to go out of the door, and Mikhail's flailing arm knocked him back against the seat. "We can't stop!" Mikhail yelled over the sound of the straining engine. "We can't go back!" He kept the throttle at the danger point. "I can't see that side. Is he running after us?"

Shirn and Bissa pressed their faces to the cabin glass. In the airport light they saw Raysta kneeling in the classic marksman position, the AK-47 at his shoulder. The rifle fired methodically and evenly. The jeep skidded sideways and turned over. Its uniformed occupants flew through the air. Another pair of headlights swerved around the jeep and raced directly toward Raysta.

"Run!" Bissa shouted through the glass. "Run!"

"Raysta! For God's sake, *don't do it!*" Shirn's voice was a screaming siren.

A spray of tracers went by a wing, and Mikhail jammed the throttle full forward. The plane bucked to the command. It rolled quickly down the unlighted, fog-streaked runway. Its wheels lifted as the machine gun on the weapons carrier bearing down on Raysta opened up again. Bullets slammed against the belly and tail of the plane.

There were two more stabs of light from Raysta's rifle, and the machine gun turned from the soaring aircraft to Raysta.

Then Mikhail banked sharply and pulled the undercarriage lever. The wheels came up and locked into the wings. A giant searchlight went on, its beam pointed straight up in the mists. It was leveled rapidly in their direction. Mikhail began a series of skimming maneuvers to stay out of the beam. The perforated belly of the craft brushed the treetops at the end of the runway.

"Oh, *Raysta!*" Shirn was stunned. She looked back at the disappearing airport, then twisted and held out her arms for Bissa.

Bissa sat in the seat near the door, holding his shotgun as if it were a baby. Tears streamed down his cheeks. His eyes were closed. His lips moved in a childhood prayer.

"Bissa, Bissa, Bissa!" she said.

Mikhail's hand reached back to her, and she took it, bending down against the pain of her back and the terrible ache in her heart.

Her soul dissolved and flooded from her eyes in a boiling, torrential stream.

"Shirn," Mikhail said quietly. "Get my knife and cut my pant leg. I'll need a tourniquet."

"What?" she asked in a quivering voice.

"I've been hit again," he said.

The MiG-23 pilot rolled out of the formation and went seaward, keeping an eye on the falling altimeter. In the sheer blackness of the skies over the Black Sea, there were many military and naval aircraft, and ground control radar was acting peevish.

"Blue Three," he said into his helmet microphone, "lock me in." He took the reading from the ground and punched it into his cockpit computer. He pressed a button and the plane flew itself, homing in on the unseen smaller, slower craft skimming low over the water below. He watched the indicators carefully, refusing to touch anything while his fighter was closing in on its victim. A tiny amber light went on and his outboard rockets fired. A second light went on and his inboard set of heat-seeking rockets fired.

Below him and far in front there was a massive burst of light. He saw his rockets curve in their downward course and disappear. He took command, mystified, and pulled the fighter from its dive. He rose swiftly to join his squadron.

"Blue Three," he said again, "what happened?"

"Your bandit has eyes," ground radar control answered. "As you fired he dumped some sort of explosive overboard. Your volley went for the explosion."

"I didn't hit him?"

"If you hit anything, it was a fish, comrade."

"Blue Three," the squadron commander said, "set us up again."

"Sorry," control radar said flatly, "he's off our screen. It goes now to the navy."

Vera lay in a heap, her arms limply over her head.

Colonel Gregorski knelt beside her, snarling at the armed soldiers crowded around. "You damned fools!" he snapped. "You didn't have to shoot her!"

"But Comrade Colonel," one of the guards said, "we didn't shoot her! She was running from that hangar, screaming into the radio. She didn't hear us tell her to stop."

The colonel lifted one of the limp hands. "Then why is she like this?"

"We fired over her head to warn her. After all, she's wearing a red scarf like the woman who got away. We thought it was the woman, not your daughter."

"You mean she *fainted*?"

The guard tugged at his ear in discomfort. "When we fired, she threw the radio in the air and fell like this. That was just before you arrived."

"Call an ambulance. She must be taken to a doctor."

The colonel stood, brushing the dirt from his gloves. Not far away, dozens of soldiers surrounded the man who lay sprawled like a limp scarecrow with an empty AK-47 tightly held in his lifeless hands. The jeep was burning, and the weapons carrier was on its side, totally disabled. The airport was in a frenzy. Despite the swirling ground mists, search planes were taking off. He heard the familiar whines of the jet fighters from the military complex passing by. Helicopters labored overhead, and he wondered why now, when the saboteurs had gone.

The ambulance came, and Vera opened her eyes as she was being placed on a stretcher. "Father!" she said weakly, "I tried to warn you they were here."

His voice was cold. "Warn me! Why didn't you delay them? Why didn't you do something to prevent their escape? Why did you run like a stupid schoolgirl across the airport? You could have been shot!"

"But, Father—"

"You had them in your hands and you let them get away!" There was no mistaking the brutal disappointment in his voice. "You allowed them to kidnap you, make a fool of me, and escape."

"There were four of them, Father! How could I capture them?"

He turned away from her as a long black Zim pulled up alongside the ambulance.

Captain Prokov emerged with three other officers. He came around to bend down and look at Vera. "Are your hurt?" he asked. "Why are you on the stretcher?"

"She *fainted*," Colonel Gregorski said acidly. "We search the city from end to end while she's with the assassins! She runs away from them and allows them to escape!" The sourness in his voice grew thicker.

"Vera," Captain Prokov said. "Where are these assassins going?"

Vera looked at her father and saw only his back. "I don't know."

"What did they take with them?"

"They had something in a bag, but I didn't see what it was."

"Was one of them an American? Did one of the men talk like an American?"

"No. They were Ukrainians. All of them."

Vera saw her father turn and stare at her. She returned the stare coolly.

"What did they look like? Can you give us a description of them? The man who flew the plane. What did he look like?"

Vera locked her eyes into her father's. "I'm sorry, Comrade Captain, they never allowed me to see them. They kept a blindfold on me the entire time." She smiled weakly. "The red scarf was my blindfold."

Captain Prokov stood up and motioned for Vera to be put in the ambulance. He walked toward the colonel and said in an official voice, "Comrade Colonel, you are under arrest."

Colonel Gregorski stood frozen. "Is this your idea of a joke?"

"It is General Zagorsky's idea of placing the blame where it belongs."

"I warn you, I have friends."

"Will these friends understand how you allowed the four Ukrainians to run loose in this district? Will they understand why it was your daughter who was kidnapped and who allowed them to escape without even seeing their faces?" The captain was enjoying the game. "And what did the Ukrainians take with them? The most secret microminiature computer in the Soviet Union! Blueprints and instruction manuals for other top-secret computers. Computer tapes of our new space devices. Two military installations seriously crippled. More than two hundred Russian soldiers dead. The city of Odessa in a state of panic. Red flares and small bombs have been going off all night. We're having a hell of a time convincing the people that war has *not* been declared." He played the game a bit longer. "Will your friends understand that? Will they understand what we found hidden in the wall switch of your apartment?"

Colonel Gregorski remained motionless. Only his lips moved. "We shall see," he said. "We shall see."

"Surrender your pistol, Comrade Colonel. You will no

longer need it. You will come with me. General Zagorsky has some important visitors, and they don't feel that they can wait until morning. They want to ask you some questions now."

The colonel remained stiffly erect, his eyes searching the murky sky into which the monoplane had fled.

"Fantastic," he said in a numbed voice. "I never *saw* the man. He did all this in my district and I never saw him." He stared at Vera. "Tell me the truth. Did you see him?"

She shook her head. Her eyes were unreadable, protected.

He looked back at the sky. "It's unbelievable." He slowly removed the pistol from its holster and handed it to Captain Prokov. "There had to be a reason." He was thinking of a boy named Karlov.

Captain Prokov propelled him toward the black limousine. He felt an immense pleasure, a deep gratification, and it showed on his face. He was unable to hide a smile, a twisted smile that showed he knew what was in store for his prisoner.

"Are you certain you don't know what the reason was, Comrade Colonel?" he said smoothly.

The colonel walked woodenly to the car. At its door he turned to look once more at Vera as she was being carried to the ambulance. Then he looked at the captain. A veil seemed to cloud his face, and he appeared to wilt within himself. The captain got in beside him and ordered the driver to return to the military complex. The pistol was in his hand and lay cautiously in his lap.

He twisted the knife once more. "I hope you have answers for the questions they'll ask." He looked at the colonel and saw an incredibly old and exhausted man huddled in the corner, removing his thin leather gloves. The gloves were wadded and thrown on the floor.

Was the colonel actually crying?

"The bleeding's stopped," Shirn said. "Can you keep on flying? Does it hurt?" She sat in the copilot's seat, holding strips of bandage from the medicine kit and looking worriedly at Mikhail.

"I damn well better." He had a tourniquet on his right leg.

"How much farther is it?"

He looked at the gas gauges. "Plenty of fuel. Another hour or so, but we won't try to make land. We're going to ditch."

"Ditch?"

"Land in the water."

She folded her arms and looked at the blackness ahead of the airplane. The waves of the Black Sea were only a few meters below. "There'll be someone there to take us out?"

"That's the last tunnel of the plan. This has been a carefully plotted mission. It had to be. We left almost at four o'clock. It couldn't have been any sooner. If it'd been later, we'd have been captured or killed."

"You and your stupid plan. Did you plan on Raysta?"

"Raysta knew what he was doing. Why do you deny him his right to be a man?" He looked at her from the corner of his eyes. To the east the first faint glow of the new morning was showing. "Could anyone have stopped him?"

"You could have stopped this damned plane and gone back."

"We'd all be dead, stretched out on the cement at the airport."

She had to acknowledge the truth. "I don't like it. Bissa killed men this night for the first time in his life. Raysta believed he was back in the army again. We steal a plan and escape. It's unbelievable! I don't think I am alive."

"What do you think you are?"

She was sullen, thinking. "I don't know."

"Hear me out." His right calf burned with the bullet that was still in it. From time to time he'd loosened the tourniquet and blood would run down his leg. He felt dried, old, a husk. He was amazed that the monoplane, hit as it was, still flew so well. "Point one. You know that in order to get their help, we had to promise the commanders that we'd give Colonel Rakoski a great deal of trouble. Without that arrangement I'd never have gotten ashore. It was essential that I agree to their demands."

"I know how they hated Rakoski."

"You know your UPA. They're professionals. Without them we'd have been dead in a matter of hours. We knew that the Russians would spot one man going ashore. The problem was to diffuse the picture and confuse them. The second point was my father. I had to have help getting into the prison. It was the UPA who tracked him down for me. The Americans thought he was in another prison, but by the time I came to Odessa, the commanders had pinpointed him."

"You and your stinking Americans!"

"Everyone has their price, Shirn. They brought me here. They trained me. They had the contact with your people. They wanted to look at the microminiature computer. They wanted to see anything the Russians had in computer development. The manuals and tapes were extras I lucked onto."

"So everyone had to be paid off?" She was disgusted.

"Gregorski is as good as dead. I've seen my father, and he's dead. I came back because of my hate. Now I can go home."

"Home?"

"To the United States."

"What about me? Bissa?"

"You're coming with me."

"Why? Why would you want me? You wanted Vera!"

He grunted. "When I first saw Vera, I thought she was something terrific."

"What do you mean?"

"Vera never could have come with us."

"That's a lie! I heard you talking to her. I saw you kissing her. She's in love with you. If she hadn't seen the computer things, she'd be here with us."

He put his hand over and touched hers. "You've a lot to learn, you damned peasant. You think everyone acts the way you do. You forget what the colonel's done to Vera."

"You mean, her mother's death?"

He nodded. Shirn *had* heard every word in the villa. "With a sadistic father and a fearful mother, how could a girl grow up to have courage? I knew she'd run when she came to the choice between me and her father."

"Would she have killed us with the shotgun?"

"I told Raysta to put it there deliberately to find out. It unmasked her as far as I was concerned. If she hadn't grabbed it, she'd be with us now."

Shirn looked anxiously at his blood-soaked leg. "Why did you let her run away at the airport? We could have tied her up."

"It had to be that way. I wanted her to know what we were taking. I wanted her to have it in mind when she came to the point where she had to bargain with the colonel."

"You're not making sense. Do you feel dizzy?"

"I deliberately put the radio where she could grab it. I wanted her to yell for help. The last stone on his grave was to have him at the airport right after we'd gotten away with this State plane."

"What good did that do? Why do you say 'stone on his grave?' That's not Ukrainian."

"American. They used to bury them under stones in the West. It means the final touch, the last small irony of life. We escape. They lose a plane, the computer, and the manuals and tapes. At the airport is the colonel and his daughter. You know how a Russian mind works, from black to more shades of black." He turned to look over his shoulder. "How's Bissa?"

"He's with Raysta." She didn't bother to look around.

Mikhail blinked. "I see. Imagining."

"He's living again the good days. They had a lot of crazy fun, those two. They stole everything that someone wasn't holding on to. They drank twice their share of the vodka and beer. Raysta was once the best *hopak* dancer in the village." She bit her lower lip. "The war ruined so many things for him. It turned him away from reality." She trembled. *"Shcho boolo bachly, shcho boode pobachymo."*

He jerked as a wave of fresh pain ran through his legs. "Whatever is behind, only memory has eyes for it."

"What did you mean when you said that Vera would bargain for her father?" She asked suddenly.

"He'll blame her for not killing us. He'll never see it any differently. If she ever has a chance to free herself from him, it will be in the next few days." He was surprised at the change in her thoughts.

"You talk in riddles."

"It's simple. She knows what we look like, how our voices sound. She heard us say things. She saw what we took. She'll bargain by not giving him this evidence."

"By *not?*"

"It's the only bargaining position she has. If she tells everything she knows, there's nothing left. If she holds it back, she can live with herself on the high position and not the low."

Shirn thought it over for a while. "Even though the Russians will kill him?"

"If he lives, her bargaining power will dilute. He'll go out and capture someone and be a hero again. But if they try him and execute him, then she can gain power over him, in her mind, where it counts most, by refusing to reveal anything about us that might have helped him."

"I think the Americans operated on your brain!"

He loosened the tourniquet and a fresh trickle of blood ran down his leg and into his boot. "Help me get these boots off. Can you wipe off the blood so I don't slip when we get out?"

She looked out the window. There was nothing but blackness to the west and the faint glow in the east. "We're not getting out here?" she asked carefully. She struggled to pull off the boots and dropped them behind his seat. She took rags and wiped his leg and torn pants as best as she could.

He pointed ahead of them and to the left, to his side of the plane. "The Russians aren't about to let us get to Turkey, which is where they think we're going. If we keep flying, even though we've got the fuel to make it there, the chances are that they'll get us."

"What'll they do, Mikhail?" She stared moodily at the rolling waves just below the nose of the plane.

"The navy has us on its radar. We'll start with that. We're flying low and they'll have trouble keeping us on their screens. But we've been flying in a straight line for the last quarter hour. That's given them plenty of time to organize and get their hunters up. They'll be coming to intersect our course. What they'll try to do is blow up the water in front of us with air-to-sea rockets. They want us to crash and sink. Their divers can retrieve the computer, the manuals, and the tapes."

"Can they do that? Intersect us?"

"They sure as hell can. If we let them."

She folded her arms in despair. "You'd better not let them."

"Take the knife and unscrew the handle on the briefcase."

"Do what?"

"Take it off. There's a tiny IFF device built into it."

She removed the small screws, and the handle came loose. She gave it to him. "IFF?"

"Identification of friend or foe. Our friends waiting for us want to make sure it is us and not a Russian coming to them. Hold the stick steady." With Shirn piloting he removed the tapered cylinder from the handle. He unwrapped the long, high tensile wires from it. He attached the wires to the flashlight contacts. He rolled down the window at his left and pushed the cylinder out, letting it trail alongside the plane as he played out the wire as far as he could. He switched on the flashlight. Its light remained out. "Ingenious. Not much power, but it's giving off a signal they can read. It's the last part of the plan." He rolled up the window and took the controls. "Now hold on and make sure Bissa holds on. We're going to start our *hopak!*" He made a sharp bank to the right and straightened out on a southwesterly line. "I'm tacking. It will give them something to do besides home in on us directly."

"How do you know they're out there? We can't see them."

"They're coming." It was a simple flat statement.

"Are you going to throw out more of your explosives?"

"None left. That last one was luck. I didn't think it would go off soon enough to draw their rockets. Luck for us."

"If we're not going to Turkey, where are we going?"

"I told you. Into the sea."

"Mikhail, don't joke! I'm frightened enough as it is."

"There'll be a submarine waiting for us. It should be up ahead, just below the surface." He pointed past the nose of the craft. "They're reading our IFF and changing course to pick us up. If they're not there, we'll have to keep this bird in the air all the way to Turkey."

"Oh, Mikhail! How soon?"

The sea to their right erupted in a shattering explosion of red light, and the little plane bucked and whipped dangerously as Mikhail fought the controls. Overhead there was a tremendous earsplitting whining roar of jets. He righted the plane and resumed his tacking.

"What was that?" Bissa said numbly.

Mikhail looked at him over his shoulder. "How do you feel?"

"Going back for Raysta are we?" Bissa said, each word a blunt little hope.

Shirn turned in her seat, straining against the belt, and put her hands on his. "We have Raysta with us. We'll always have him with us."

Tears flooded down Bissa's fat cheeks. His watery eyes held the world's supply of pain.

Mikhail banked the plane left, and as he did so, the sea burst to their right. A cascade of water pounced on them, and the plane roared its anger as Mikhail jammed the throttle forward for more power. He leveled, flew a short distance, then banked again. Leveled and banked, leveled and banked. "They're over there!" he shouted, pointing to the east. The squadron of jets was silhouetted for a moment against the growing light in the east. "They'll come around. They've locked us in their radar."

"Mikhail! They're going to kill us!"

He took the plane down as close to the water as he dared. Far ahead a light blinked with startling brightness. He aimed the plane as it took the compass heading. The light went off. "Hold on!" he shouted. He jammed the throttle full forward and pulled the plane up into a steep climb. The craft vibrated horribly with the strain. Loud, protesting metallic noises came from its engine. He held the plane in the climb attitude until it was obvious that it was almost at a stall. He pushed the nose down to level flight and cut the engine.

"What are you doing!" Shirn cried in alarm.

"They'll switch to heat-seeking rockets. We can't give them any more heat from our exhausts. We'll have to glide in as close as we can." He trimmed the craft carefully for dead-stick gliding.

The light ahead came on again, a short rapid burst of incredibly bright light. He corrected his glide slightly and bent over the stick to stare out of the water-stained window. "Come on! Come on!" he coaxed. "Don't quit now!"

The water ahead of them seemed to be hit by heavy rainfall, and Mikhail swore. "Those bastards! They've got propeller jobs with machine guns!"

Something slapped the tail and left wing, and the plane rolled sharply with the blows. Mikhail nursed the wheel and brought it back into its glide. "Bend forward and put your arms around your head!" he ordered. "We're going to ditch. We can't keep her up any longer."

He took it into the sea nose-up, with its tail plowing a furrow and then with its wings scooping up giant sprays on either side. It bounced and hit hard, nose-down. Then it was under the water and rising.

"Bissa! Get out on the wing! Help Shirn! Hold on to the wing!" He pushed and shoved them both out of the door as the cabin filled with water. He grabbed the water-sealed packages and activated the floats. The noise grew from the distance, and they turned to look. The squadron of Russian planes was dipping down, and the swift, red blinking of their guns burst in an uneven line across the blackness to the north.

"Hold on!" Mikhail shouted, then dived as fast as he could with the inflated packages. For a terrible moment the sea and plane endured the deadly spray. Mikhail bobbed to the surface, blinking the cold water from his eyes.

Shirn and Bissa lay sprawled on the wing. Gaping holes showed in the other wing and the fuselage.

"Are you all right?" he shouted. Shirn loosened one hand to wave weakly. Bissa sat up on the wing and aimed his shotgun at the retreating fighters. The hammers clicked on the dead shells in the two chambers.

Then a huge black shape bore down on them, and a metallic voice said, "Easy does it. Stay where you are. We'll send swimmers to bring you home." A bright light bathed the sea between them.

The submarine was close, very close, and Mikhail, head held barely out of the water by the small floats, saw the rubber-clad divers go over the side and come toward them.

"Take the girl and the fat one first!" he yelled. Then he realized that he'd said it in Ukrainian. He repeated it in English.

A masked face came through the water, and a strong arm reached for him. "There's plenty for everybody," a Midwestern voice said. "Just relax and I'll tow you in."

Shirn and Bissa were hauled aboard, and Mikhail, being pulled up by a line, heard a familiar voice.

"How was your holiday?" Captain Pell, said, leaning over the edge of the conning tower.

"Interesting," Mikhail replied. A great weariness seized him. "I came back a married man."

"I just realized it. Is that a shotgun your friend is carrying?"

Mikhail wiped the water from his eyes again. "Don't try to take it away from him," he warned in a voice that cracked.

He was being carried down into the submarine when the blackness closed over him.

"We followed a lot of it on the radio," Captain Pell said. "It was amazing how much they put on the air without coding. It sounded as if they'd blown their top."

Mikhail moved himself an inch on the bunk, and Shirn was at his side instantly to help. She wore navy pajamas and a large robe. Her feet were protected by thick socks. Her hair was neatly braided and decorated with slips of bright-colored silk a crewman had donated.

The captain looked at Mikhail's heavily bandaged legs. "You lucked out. The second one was a sliver of the aluminum floor panel instead of a Russian slug like you took in your left leg." He grinned. "Do you know how many of those bastards were out there looking for you?"

Mikhail looked at Shirn. "I know how many found us."

"One hundred and six aircraft. Eighteen surface ships. Five submarines."

Mikhail accepted the honor. He leaned back and closed his eyes.

"I'm sorry about your father," the captain said.

Shirn sat down on the edge of the bunk and took Mikhail's hand in hers.

"The colonel is being flown to Moscow," the captain

went on. "His daughter is in an Odessa hospital suffering from exhaustion."

Mikhail opened his eyes. "Don't you believe that," he said. "She's tough. But it means she's found the way."

"Found the way?"

"To get the monkey off her back."

The captain shrugged. "Too cryptic for me." He moved to the door. "Your friend is sleeping well. We spiked his drink with sleeping tablets. We wanted to get that shotgun away from him and clean it before the seawater ruined it." He looked at Shirn. "Is there anything we can get you?"

"The commanders?" she asked. "Do they know about me? About Raysta and Bissa?"

"They know the story." The captain was sober. "What do you think of your cossacks, Mikhail? They came through rather well, didn't they?"

"Can you give them our thanks?"

"They know. They're going to take your tall one back and bury him near the village."

Shirn was astonished. "But how can they do that? The Russians have him."

"They did everything else, they can handle that too," the captain said. "He's their man. They'll take care of him. He's a number-one hero to the Underground."

Shirn's eyes began to mist.

"The Underground has something it hasn't had in a long time," the captain said quietly. "Can you imagine how the Ukraine is talking about what three villagers and a nutty Ukrainian from the States did to the Russians?"

"But Mikhail's a Russian!"

"Not anymore, not as far as the commanders are concerned. He's their boy, a real legend and all Ukrainian." The captain looked at Mikhail. "The electronics nuts on board have been whooping with joy over the space junk you brought back. Now we'll know where the Russians are stealing our high-tech developments from, who's giving it to them, and how they've come along with using them, along with their own creations." He opened the door and was smiling. "See why I didn't worry about you?"

"Thanks," Mikhail said, and the door shut behind the officer.

Shirn put a hand on his forehead. "How do you feel?"

"Like a fat sack of chicken dung," he said softly.

Shirn's face started to tighten. She was near tears again, and then suddenly she smiled. It was a warm, radiant thing. "We *are* proud of him, aren't we? That's love, isn't it?"

"That's all he ever asked."

"And Bissa. What he did."

She let go of his hand and stretched out alongside him on the bunk, careful not to touch the bandaged legs, careful of her back. Her head was on his shoulder, and his arm came around to hold her.

"Your name. What is it, really?"

"Volia," she said softly. "Volia Stepanova Lashchenko."

He grinned. Volia meant peace. "Why'd you use Shirn as a code name? It has no meaning in Ukrainian."

"That's why. I wanted a name that meant nothing, nothing at all. Now I think you can call me Volia. Now I think I have a meaning after all."

"It's going to be some wedding," he said, "with our thirty-five-year-old son standing there holding his shotgun."

She began to giggle uncontrollably and stopped only when he pulled her close to him so that his lips could meet hers.